JACOB'S LADDER

CHARLIE PIKE started his writing career when he lived in Turkey, teaching English to adults and children. When he returned to Ireland he worked as an advertising copywriter and freelance journalist, writing feature articles for Irish newspapers, until an opportunity came along to work for an Internet start-up. In 2003 he formed his own web company, Usable Design.

He met his wife, Birgit, in Turkey and they now live in County Wicklow. They have two children. Charlie is a graduate of Trinity College.

JACOB'S LADDER

CHARLIE PIKE

THE O'BRIEN PRESS
DUBLIN

First published 2019 by
The O'Brien Press Ltd,
12 Terenure Road East, Rathgar,
Dublin 6, D06 HD27 Ireland.

Tel: +353 1 4923333; Fax: +353 1 4922777
E-mail: books@obrien.ie.
Website: www.obrien.ie

The O'Brien Press is a member of Publishing Ireland.

ISBN: 978-1-78849-040-5

Printed Printed and bound by Norhaven Paperback A/S, Denmark.
The paper in this book is produced using pulp from managed forests.

Published in

DUBLIN
UNESCO
City of Literature

For Birgit

Our efforts are the efforts of the Trojans.

We imagine that with resolve and daring

We will reverse the animosity of fortune,

and so we take our stand outside, to fight.

Cavafy, 'Trojans', trans. Daniel Mendelsohn

1

It's nearly over now. There have been changes in the sun: dark spots on its surface; a sinister, unnatural heat in the air. I've seen men come back from the valley with burns they say they never felt until their skin started to blister. For months on end the aurora swirls in the North, day and night.

These are all the first signs of what our sun has in store for us. We watch the horizon anxiously for what we know will come. For the birds to start falling out of the sky. For the last day we can safely go outside.

When they first discovered that this would happen – long ago, when the planet was still teeming with people – they were clever and they believed their cleverness could save them. Plans were drawn up to build cities in space, far away from the heat; to colonise other planets; to fortify the atmosphere, even to live underground and grow their crops and raise their animals under man made lights. The distress call was the most desperate of all the schemes and the most hopeless: A message sent into deep space in the hope that someone would hear their plea for rescue. Someone in a position to help.

They didn't expect an answer. How could they? And yet, thirty years after the signal was sent, the first message arrived. Nobody can say anymore who received it originally, or how, since civilization was already coming loose at the seams and little wars were turning into bigger wars, but everyone remembers exactly what it said. We have to repeat it every day on the training ground.

We have heard your call

You no longer need to fear.

You will receive five messages, of which this is the first.

The last message will inform you of the time and place of your salvation.

2

5 MARCH 2203

There's not even a grey light coming through the window when I get the kick. The pain squirms into my mind and then the second kick bangs my eyes open.

'Leon, it's time,' hisses Axel.

I swallow down what I want to say; it would be a waste of valuable rage. Axel is a Citizen, he should know better than to kick an Initiate, but that's maybe why he did it.

I rise as quietly as I can. The room is full of sleeping forms under their blankets. Eran, two bodies over from me, is in the thick of one of his fighting dreams: muttering threats, striking out at invisible enemies. I do a pretty good impression of Eran asleep. On harvest nights, when jokes are permitted, I get a lot of mileage out of Eran's noisy dreams and my impersonation of Theo, trying to get over the wall into the women's barracks all those years ago.

The thought of it makes me smile now and I know it shouldn't. Humour shows an untamed mind. Undisciplined. Dishonest. I have been trying to rid myself of it all this year. It's been my special project.

'You nervous?' asks Axel as I pull my tunic on.

I don't even look at him. I'm trying to get my thoughts in order.

'I'd be nervous.'

'Shut it,' I say.

'Just saying, that's all.'

'Shut it.'

I step over Eran's restless body and make my way down the narrow aisle between the sleepers to the door, not caring if Axel follows or not. The cold comes right up through the cement into my feet. It brings a sudden, shuddering awakening. *This is real.* How is it possible that a lifetime of preparation has suddenly narrowed to this moment?

It is here, now, the most choreographed day in my life but I'm not firm and composed like I always imagined. I'm raw and brittle, blood tingling, a hot sensation in my stomach.

It's a little traitor inside me. A worm of doubt. Always has been. A coward that lives down deep in my blood. I will stamp it out. It will not survive the day.

Axel waits by the barracks door while I cross the courtyard to the mesh fence. The guard salutes me and stands. He's also a Citizen, but he's got more discipline than Axel and keeps his mouth shut. The thing is though, long after I have gone past him, I get the impression he is still at attention and still saluting. I pull open the corrugated metal door of the Divvy House and clap my hands once, sharply, into the darkness and then wait. A head rises between the slumbering bodies.

I clap again, harder this time. The pale skin on her bald head gleams with reflected moonlight from the one tiny window in the roof. She rises from under the blanket that she shares with two others. She is thin, with long wiry legs like a wading bird, and yet the lithe way she slips between the bodies, even the stripes of her tattoos, make me think of a wild cat in long grass. She stops only a couple of inches from me, silent, waiting. I can almost feel the cold radiating from her skin.

'Your time is nearly here, Martha,' I say, pointing towards the v of her neck. 'You can wear the Five Stars. A divvy to a raised man.'

A corner of red crescent moon is just visible at the edge of her tunic. The symbol of the initiate she served until this winter, now Risen and gone into the Soldier's Yard. She chose to take his sign but was too young to follow him beyond the gate. That honour will come soon.

Her lips don't move while I study her ink. She keeps her eyes on the doorway and the gathering light outside.

'Get everything ready,' I tell her. 'The supplies and my armour. I want them in the yard in time for my prep. Oh, and my blade and a bowl of water, I need that right now. If you're late your house master will hear about it. Do you understand?'

She nods. I search her face for any sign of defiance. There is no reading her. At least my gelding puts his ears back when he's angry.

'You're not going to let me down, are you? Out there?' I say, jerking my chin towards the mountains. 'Your world. If you can remember it.'

She blinks. Her eyes rest motionless on the distant rooftops. How many seasons now since they found that soldier up at Fallon's Point, his throat open and his divvy fled into the wilderness with his knife and his horse?

'Can you remember it Martha? What kind of hell did you spring from?'

Nothing. Not even a twitch. There never is. Not that it matters, in the end, who her people were or whether some war drove her here to our valley, or a hungry belly led her through the forests to our farms and food stores. This is where she lives now and where she will die. No divvy will ever go to Thule.

I wave her away. If she is relieved she doesn't show it. In a second she is across the yard on bare feet and dissolves between the buildings as if she and the shadows were made from the same substance.

I head over to the exercise yard, passing between the latrine and the women's barracks, which is quiet. They are not yet up. The cold air smells faintly of damp, promising rain by mid-morning. The aurora is green and dim in the near dawn. Her ropes of light wind and unwind over the sand and the roofs of the dorms.

I try to read her colours as she claws at the sky, eager to burn us silently where we stand. Theo says red is a bad sign, but that's Theo. The scents on the air hold no hidden threats: pine resin, wet soil, a soft rain off the mountains. No telling stillness or change in the quality of the light or darkness. Not today, and not tomorrow. Please not tomorrow. We will be a long time out in the open.

Martha comes running with a bowl in her hands, the water sloshing over the sides. She takes it to a ledge, jutting out from the wall of the latrine, and she places a sharpened razor beside it. There is a mirror mounted on the wall there and one of the few electric light bulbs in the Colony, which now casts a feeble light to help me shave. She disappears again to fetch the other things and I am left alone to prepare.

The water is only lukewarm. It was heated in the kitchen, but clearly they didn't get up in time to get it nice and hot. In the dark of the mirror my eyes look sunken, the skin on my cheeks craggy and loose, like an old man. I know it's just the cheerless electric light from above, but I can't help feeling how pathetic I look on my big day.

I press the blade against my scalp, and let it slide slowly, hesitantly, across the wet, raw skin. First the head in long strokes. The blade slips over Orion and the Dog Star and then Thule and her moons, tattooed neatly in blue ink on the crown of my skull and then along the edge of my ears, the figures on my sideburns, our Saviours, tall and pale, reaching for the sky.

After that, the neck, the sensitive part. I pull the blunt back of the razor horizontally across my adam's apple and imagine the real stroke I will make soon. The neat red line silently peeling open. Arterial blood welling at the lip of the slash. It is so sudden. I've done it to pigs and sheep a dozen times. There is only a moment to register the shock, widen the eyes, catch a breath, then the life spills out with the blood.

In the mirror I watch the tiny cuts bead all across my neck and under my chin while I recite my favourite part of the Third Message:

We have learned to live on what surrounds us;
To rule those who will be ruled;
To eliminate all sources of weakness.

The pain helps. The next few hours come right to me, all red and sharp. This is who I am. A blade in the dark.

It's at that moment that I hear it, faint but unmistakable: sobs, caught breaths, shudders. No surprise, at this time of the day. There is always some boy being punished around the barracks and the small ones will often cry in their first weeks. But now that I've noticed it, it's impossible to get it out of my head. I scratch with the razor at the last bits of stubble under my chin, quickly drop it in the bowl and go in search of this menace.

He's in the Four Walls, on the far side of the sand training yard. I go inside the palisade and find a small boy, a *cub*, at the bottom of the concrete ramp leading up to the fighting platform. He's no more than a month or two in the barracks, but already the nursery must seem like a lifetime away. He has a sack full of dirt and he is trying to drag it up the ramp. It is still too dark to see him clearly, but it seems he has given up.

At the sound of my feet crunching on the sand, he stops crying and looks up. I hear him catch his breath.

'What is it for?' I say, looming over him.

The boy says nothing.

'Answer me.'

After a moment, he coughs.

'Sir,' is all he manages.

'What is the bag for?'

'Falling behind sir.' The words choke in his mouth.

'Falling behind when you run?'

He nods. The ground at the foot of the ramp is still darkly speckled with the blood of the Initiate killed here in a standoff ceremony three months ago. I wonder is it the sight of those spots that has set him crying.

'No matter what you think, you can do it,' I say. 'Every one of us has been at the bottom of this slope. You are born weak, but you will find strength.'

I'm close enough to make out the boy's eyes: they are wet opals, staring at me. His arm has been raised all this time, expecting to be hit. Now it drops slowly to his side. I'd like to tell him about my first weeks in my family and how I used to come out to the exercise yard at night and speak to the wall of the nursery, as if they could hear me, all those chattering women that fed me, teased me and beat me into shape. And I would tell them all that I couldn't do it, I wasn't strong enough. Boy, did I cry then. I cried until I puked and then I cried some more. But of course you don't say that to an Initiate, or to anyone. You shouldn't even think about things like that.

'You understand me, don't you?' I say to the boy.

'Yes, sir.' He has steadied himself. The sobbing and choking have stopped, but his voice is still trembling. 'Sir?'

'What?'

'You are Leon. Today is -'

'So?'

'Will you go up there? To Thule.' He tilts his head towards the sky.

'That is not a proper question. You should not ask me that.'

'It's just somebody said it in my family.'

'Enough,' I've been caught off guard by how quickly this boy has gone from despair to insolence. 'I Rise today, to become an Elect. That is all I can possibly wish for.'

'But everyone says the last message is coming. It's got to happen soon.'

'I don't care what everyone says.'

'But...' he looks at me, his face changed, his eyes bright and eager. 'What will they look like? The Saviours. Will they be really tall and strong?'

'It doesn't matter what they look like. We can't choose them; they choose from us. So we have to be the best we can.'

'Someone in my family says you can't breathe up there in the sky. You have to take air with you.'

'The Saviours will have thought of that.'

17

'Will they let you take the air with you?'

'I don't know.'

'Maybe you can keep some, in a bottle or something. Maybe they let you suck it from a bottle.'

'Maybe you should listen to your teachers in Right Thinking and stop asking these questions,' I say. 'We all have families, and we do our best not to shame them.'

His head drops.

'Do you understand?' I say.

He nods.

'Can you imagine if you were dropped from training and they made you a Citizen? What would your family think about that? Could you face them?'

He sinks further down. I know he's just wishing I would leave him alone and, after a few moments of intimidating him with my stern silence, I do.

On my way back to the exercise yard I hear his grunt of effort as he starts his task again. He doesn't know it, but the sack is specially weighted and the gradient of the slope carefully measured, so that if he really pushes himself he will manage to get close, but he has no chance of success. His spirit must first be crushed, before it can rise.

Back in the yard, Martha is laying my bundled uniform on the sand. She nods in the direction of the mountains where the peaks are emerging from the darkness, pale and threatening. I'm late. I should already by dressed and at the council chamber. Worse still, there is someone coming from the direction of the courtyard and I quickly recognise who it is: my mentor, Joel. He has come to take me to my Rising.

I stop dead, snap my legs together and salute. He salutes back. My heart clenches. I fear what he's going to say until he comes close enough for me to see that he is actually smiling.

'Initiate Leon,' he says. I have never seen Joel smile. He's half a head taller than me. Stronger too, though only two years older – two years that may as well be an infinity. What must it be like, those monthly visits to the breeding shed? Coupling in the dark. The touch of a woman. He bears the knowledge easily, as if it was nothing to him.

'Hadn't you better get dressed?'

Flustered, not just because of my lateness but because of Joel's calm, amused expression, I grab the pile of clothes that Martha has left for me on the sand and dress hurriedly in my boots and my soldier's tunic, my leather arm and leg greaves, my belt, my cloak. Then I straighten myself and salute again.

Joel touches the row of teeth stitched into his shoulder guard, the teeth of his quarry, his Bind. A big man, they say, a hunter. Six foot five. No one can remember a bigger kill. Just the thought of it makes me shrink.

He is still smiling. In fact, it's not just him. There is a frozen expression on Martha's face, a stretch to the mouth, that could easily be a grin. I shoot her an angry look and she draws her lips tight. Joel tugs my cloak up higher on my shoulders and adjusts my lapels. He dusts down my cloak, lifts my chin and examines me.

'God help you,' he says. 'The Council is going to make mincemeat of you.'

I wonder if I'm allowed to grin as well. I want to, but Joel likes to keep me on my toes.

'Do I look okay?' I say, trying to sound only mildly interested in his answer.

'Leon,' he says. 'You're always worried about the things that don't matter, that's why I'm smiling. No one cares how you look. It's how you behave. But listen now,' he says, the smile gone. 'The council has something special lined up for you today. Be on your guard. This is going to be different.'

3

MESSAGE NUMBER TWO

Not everyone can be saved.

We will select only a few that can survive among us.

First, the strong must separate themselves from the others.

Live in small communities.

Adopt simple rules and follow them.

Keep your eyes on the horizon.

Once you have done these things, we will tell you how to prepare.

We're on our way to the council chamber and it's only when Joel tells me to slow down that I realise I'm practically running.

'You need to be calm,' he says. 'They can smell panic.'

So I'm calm. I try to walk at a steady pace, hold my back straight and strangle any thoughts about being unworthy or weak.

I'm calm, calm, calm, calm, calm.

Martha stops at the gate to the inner courtyard. I wish I could take her with me just this once, but it is not allowed. I jog across the sand to the steps. The doors of the chamber stand open. Joel claps me on the back.

'Good luck,' he says. 'You'll be fine.' He hangs back while I go inside.

The thirty-six members of the council are arranged in tiers on the wooden benches. Above them, in tiny, arched crevices, are the skulls of our ancestors, many of them now yellow and jawless. Their eyeless sockets are a more welcoming sight than the grim benches of old men, set in their rows waiting, like the teeth of a snare, for one false step.

My eye strays to the wooden door on the far side of the benches. There is a corridor beyond it, and at the end of the corridor, a room, with a fire kept permanently lit. I have not stood there since I was a child but I know what waits there still. The Palladium. The bringer of the messages.

The awful, long stretch of silence that follows is finally broken by General Hilles, his small eyes hooded under steep brows. His collar is low enough to reveal his unusual scar, neat and round and tightly knotted. They say it was made by a bullet.

'We will begin,' he says.

This is my cue. I have to recite the Messages.

We have heard your call.

You no longer need to fear ...

At first I speak slowly and my voice is so unsteady, so dry and hoarse, that I start to imagine seizing up completely. It's the soothing rhythm of the words, as familiar to me as breathing, that help me gradually relax and by the middle of the second message I feel a steadiness returning.

I finish and it's silent again. Through the open chamber doors come the gentle sounds of my family, the Five Stars, gathering in the exercise yard. Soft voices. Feet thumping on sand. Even on this day, my day, ordinary things go on as they always have.

General Hilles rises in his seat and begins the ritual reminders of our history. The first prediction of the solar event that will destroy life on our planet. The plea for help, sent out into the stars. The arrival of the first message and the hope that it brought to a despairing world.

He talks about Vice President Grove and the founding of the first colony and how he, of all men, truly listened to the messages from the heavens. Then comes the well worn description of the first hard years when the old world, with its shining cities, its teeming millions, faltered and then fell. The wars. The coming of the Satz. The terrible devastation in Asia. How the bio bombs emptied those cities.

His voice is monotone and dreary as he delivers this old, well worn story. It warms a little when he starts to recount the spread of the Grove Colonies. The arrival of the second, third and fourth messages, telling us how to ready ourselves for selection and for life on Thule.

'This was the task appointed to us,' he says. 'To prepare the way. And only now can we gaze around us and see that it is almost complete. From now on every Initiate has a new and graver responsibility, since they, or their children, or their children's children might yet be the ones to stand before our Saviours and face the test. We cannot be content with what we have done in the past, we must strive for better, work harder.'

He turns his eyes to me, the other councillors murmuring their agreement.

'Initiate Leon,' he says. 'Are you prepared for what is to come?'

I have to speak clearly. No thinking. Everything must be a reflex. 'I am,' I say. 'I will do what it takes. No matter what that is.'

'No matter what task we set you?'

'Yes sir,' I say, though this throws me a little. There is doubt in his eyes. A flicker of distrust.

'You are one of our brightest Initiates, Leon, and the time is drawing near. But you are not yet a man.'

'I understand.'

The General seems satisfied with my answer. His eyes rove the benches and the men sitting there. Their faces are like knuckles with eyes painted on them. Each one marked by a cut, or a burn, a lost eye, smashed teeth, half an ear, scars like growths on the skin. Not one among them will ever stand on Thule soil. They will finish their hard lives in this world as a skull in a niche, the rest of their old bones under the planked floor of the Four Walls.

One of these men, a younger one surely, could well be my father. Someone with my squat body, thick nose. In the small hours of the night, in the dorm, we have often speculated, looking for likenesses in a face, some striking feature. It is our forbidden game.

'We are all born manacled to the earth,' says the General. 'Weak, dependent; a prey to our emotions, our attachments to women, fathers, mothers, friends. All of these ties must be severed if we are to be raised up, into the heavens. It is for this reason we are conceived in the dark. There are no lovers in the True Path. No father claims his son. No mother comes running when the babies cry out in the night. We are raised with a firm hand by wet nurses. To our brothers in the dorms, we owe our loyalty, but only until the day of the test, the last day, when we will stand before our saviours and each man will be examined on his own merits, and taken or left behind. Will you be picked Initiate, should your time come?'

'Sir,' I say, pulling my feet together.

'When an Initiate Rises we must take a young life from the villages in our valley,' he goes on. 'So that we can prepare our men for the test to come. They are the sharpening stone, we are the blade. "Cut away your bonds," that is what our Saviours told us and each of us must learn to sever those ties with the earth, to be able to turn their backs, when the time comes, and leave it behind. We thank the villagers today for their sacrifice and we will carry the flame of humanity, theirs and ours, to our new home on Thule.'

The General steps forward and puts a book in my left hand and my knife in my right and then he steps back and looks me hard in the eye.

'Initiate Leon, you have in your left hand the learning of your people that has come down to us from the very dawn of history, and in your right, the future of our race in the form of a strong and true blade. I now ask you to swear your loyalty to that future.'

I repeat the words I know so well, like each one was a fist thump. That worm of doubt is all gone. The home straight.

I swear to let nothing hold me to the Earth. To go to Thule when I am called.

I will uphold our laws where they do not conflict with the laws of our Saviours.

I will be the best of humanity. An example to all.

'As I thought,' says the General when I finish. 'Spoken like a man. I have watched you all these years, Initiate Leon, and have been mostly impressed by what I've seen, but I have wondered about your cleverness. There's a danger in having a subtle, questioning mind. Our survival is in the hands of others far more sophisticated than us. We can't reason for ourselves how best to prepare; we must do what we're told, follow the rules. But I believe you have made great strides in Right Thinking this year. I, for one, am happy that you may Rise.'

A positive murmur travels through the benches.

'It is decided then,' he says. 'Leon will Rise, on the cutting of his Bind.'

With that, the General nods towards an orderly, who brings me a plain, bronze necklace with a pattern of five steps between two twisting rails: the Winding Stair. If I fail they will rip it from me and I'll go to the Four Walls. Only a killer can wear The Winding Stair.

The councillors file out past me, each one shaking my hand. General Hilles is the last. He takes my right hand in both of his and grips it tightly.

He has other scars on his arms: ridged, clumped lines in his skin, like plough furloughs and patches of mottled flesh. Wounds received from Old Sally, the scorching rain that comes through the valley now and again. Sally the Stripper.

He leans forward and whispers in my ear, 'You have to know I never doubted you for a second,' he says. 'I had to make sure there were no doubters in the council.' He slaps me gently on the shoulder and then nods towards the door, where I must now go and meet my Bind.

'You will think that we dishonour you, but that couldn't be further from the truth,' he says.

There is a brief, awkward moment. He still has my hand; his eyes look into mine. I sense some desire to speak, to share something, an intimacy or secret, but it is quickly over. He releases me. I can hear the crowd and commotion starting outside. The General takes the necklace from my hand and puts it around my neck.

I go out to the courtyard. My family and two others are drawn up in salute along the opposite wall. The councillors lined up on either side of the council chamber steps.

In the centre of the courtyard is a lone, kneeling figure, his head covered with a sackcloth hood, tied loosely at the neck, and the rest of his body hidden inside a cotton sheet. It's hard to tell how big, or strong he is. From the angle of his elbows I can see his hands are tied behind him. His head is bent towards the ground. He's exhausted. Broken already. He's my Bind.

At last I feel that sensation come into my body and mind that should have been there all morning. It's like I've grown, my muscles filled out, my blood thrumming in my veins. Talking was not for me. This is. The fear I can sense in this boy tells me everything I need to know about myself.

I walk slowly down the steps to the courtyard. Every eye is on me. The red dawn light is spattered on the sky, just above the mountain peaks, like a cough of blood. I draw my knife from my belt and approach him. When I'm close enough I can hear him taking shallow breaths in his hood. I rest my hand on his head and close my eyes.

'I thank you today for the gift of your life, given to me so that I will Rise. I promise that you will not suffer at my hands and that your cutting will be swift. You will have a day and a night to try and get away from me before I come seeking you. If you escape me, I will never search for you or try to harm you again.'

I run the blade gently along the hood and down to his shoulder where I press it against his flesh.

'The name of the blade is Stella,' I say. 'It means star. But I chose it because it also sounds like steel. Her sure steel is like a promise. Death will be instant.'

There's something about him. I can't quite place it. The air around him is wrong. His whole posture and presence is wrong.

'Are you afraid?' I say, loudly enough now for everyone to hear. The kneeling figure says nothing but the rapid breathing continues. 'Do not be. Your sacrifice is essential for humanity.'

I bring the blade up in front of his face and through his sackcloth mask he must have seen a glint of the metal because he lets out a strangled cry, high pitched and feminine, jerks up onto his feet, wobbles slightly before he gets his balance, and then runs. The assembled crowd starts to laugh. This does not usually happen. The release of a Bind is supposed to be a solemn occasion, but we're all thinking the same thing, all the Initiates and the Elect: he's like the pigs we kill in training, in the Four Walls. How he darts blindly around, bleating his heart out.

I almost think I should kill him now. He's not going to last long enough in the wild for me to actually catch him. They've given me *this* to Rise with. Our ancestors fought wars and had a chance to die for their colony. They stood on the conquered walls of Esperanza, the last city.

I move around him, deliberately crunching my feet in the dirt so he can hear. There's another spurt of awkward laughter as he stops and listens. Okay then. We'll have fun with him. We'll make a show. A glance at the councillors tells me they do not disapprove. This is strange, but I'll take it.

I come around his other side and crunch on the dirt again. He charges in the opposite direction. With his hands bound behind him he can hardly keep his balance and he's constantly stumbling. The crowd can see what I'm up to. Circling him, directing him with my feet and some well timed coughs until he is going exactly the way I want him.

'Over here,' I say, in a quiet voice.

He bolts forwards, straight into the flagpole in the centre of the yard. The impact on his shoulder sends him spinning to the ground, where he hangs, limp, at the bottom of the flagpole. He must know now how beaten he is. He seems small and light on his feet. Just how old is he?

You will think that we dishonour you, but that couldn't be further from the truth.

I must get my mind back to where it should be. No more games. He goes stiff and quiet as I draw near to him. Maybe he doesn't believe that I'll let him run at all. He thinks I'm going to do it here, now, with my knife. Maybe he even wants that.

I crouch down in front of him and gently undo the knot on his hood, making soothing noises. 'Shush now,' I say. 'Enough.'

He's not breathing. The westerly breeze tugs at his hood.

I take a fistful of the cloth, clutch it tightly and then yank it off his head. A collective gasp escapes from the crowd. Now I understand my special test completely.

I touch the cheek of my Bind and marvel at the softness of her skin and her long delicate fingers. They want me to slit a woman's throat.

4

MESSAGE NUMBER THREE

Our home is not like yours.
Every day is a struggle.
We have learned to live on what surrounds us.
To rule those who will be ruled.
To eliminate all sources of weakness.
Do these things and you will be ready.

The courtyard has shrunk to this foot of space. For a moment, everything else has vanished. My Bind glares up at me, not hopeless and trembling at all but defiant, savage. Jaw set. Taut muscles standing out on her neck. Beads of sweat on her dark skin.

I look across at Joel, standing with a group of his fellow soldiers at the council gate. He doesn't have his mouth open like some of the others but his eyes are narrowed and there is outrage there. His man, his apprentice, given a woman for his Rising.

If she was out of the women's barracks, a trained Elect, then she might be a worthy adversary for me. But that's not possible and never would be. She is a woman from the villages. A person. Nobody.

She bares her teeth at me and darts glances past my head at the crowd. There is almost a full circle of men and boys around the yard, with few gaps between them, and since the pulling of the hood there has been a change in them. They have darkened and merged together, like one solid mass of threat.

Instinctively, I stand up tall and step between my Bind and them. She accepts the shelter, slipping behind my back. It must be dawning on her now that something worse could happen to her than a straightforward slitting of her throat.

The General separates himself from the other councillors and approaches me.

'Not what you were expecting, Initiate?' he says.

I open my mouth. That's all I can do.

'You would have liked a warrior. A real challenge. Even to go to war, like the soldiers of the past. Well, the times have changed. That kind of glory is not available to us anymore. For your generation the tasks will be harder and require greater strength. You think we dishonour you with this Bind, don't you?'

I do. I can't help it. I do. I think of Joel's hunter. I was sure they would honour me with a man like that, someone who's strength and ferocity would reflect well on me. There's no glory in this Bind. When I find her and kill her no one is going to cheer or tell that story in the Colony.

'When you pictured your Rising,' says the general, 'as I'm sure you did a thousand times in the Four Walls, or in front of the mirror this morning with your razor blade, you had a man at your mercy. You cut a man's throat.'

'I did, sir.'

'You did. And now you wonder if you can do the same thing at all, to a woman. You've spent all your young life here, since you were a cub, in the men's barracks. Only the divvies to look at. Your instincts are confusing you, Initiate Leon. They are telling you not to harm or kill. How to even touch that flesh with a cruel knife.'

My Bind does not look at the general. She has dropped her head, but not in defeat. She is twisting herself down, tightening. A clenching fist.

'Beauty is the world's trick, Initiate. You must now reach deep into your training. No retreating now. Harden your spirit. To spare a life, even if it's crying out to us, is to cheat our future. The real future, Initiate. The one shining down on us from the stars.'

'Yes sir.'

'You will do this, kill this woman, not so that she will die, but that we all might live.'

He nods to me.

I will. I can.

Forcing confidence into my movements, I cut the rope away from the woman's hands and grab her shoulders and yank the rest of the sheet away from her. A current runs through every boy and man in the yard. She is wearing a simple tunic of some rough cloth, not unlike what we wear in the training ground. It reveals the shape of her body, though she instantly shrinks down behind me, wrapping her arms tightly around her chest. Still snarling with her teeth and eyes but mortally afraid in everything else.

'Open the gate,' I say. I intended to shout it but it comes out of my mouth strangled, like I didn't really mean it to be heard at all.

Even so, after a long pause, someone scampers off to the gate and pulls it open. Beyond is the ring of farmland outside the camp: the Citizens village, the horse and cattle paddocks and finally the old ditch that once served as a first line of defence when there was something to defend against. It is only a few paces from the ditch to the tree line that marks the start of the endless timbered hills and the wide empty world.

A bear is going to get her before I ever do, or a Sat Worm, or just the weather. Or worse still, she may just lie down somewhere and wait for us to come. They do that sometimes.

She cowers behind me still, until restlessness and hostility spread through the assembled men. Elect stamp their feet and clap sharply. Time now, woman. Enough is enough. When she finally rises up and faces them, her whole appearance changes. Her defiance ripples into her muscles. Her back straightens. She walks direct and firm, without any hurry, towards the gate, causing the men standing there to back up uncertainly, the line to buckle and then break, opening a gap. She senses the powerful effect she has on them, attraction and repulsion. She directs her stride towards a boy at the edge of the group, an Initiate from Ceres, who retreats so quickly he stumbles and nearly ends up on his face.

It makes me think of a day out by the mess hall, long ago, when a rat found itself in the open. Its back legs had been crushed by a cook, and a mob of Initiates closed in around it. These were killers, each one, and he was hobbled, a blood trail following him all the way from the peelings behind the kitchen, and yet the rat had them scared and enthralled. For the longest time they performed a kind of ritual dance: tightening the circle, the rat taking a lunge, the Initiates flying back, screaming and laughing. You could almost touch their fear with your hands.

What was the comfort of numbers to the one Initiate who gets bitten, with the diseases and poisons the rat's mouth might be harbouring? This woman exerts the same kind of magnetic force. She passes them without looking them in the eye. Keeping the same slow, resolute pace through the gate, out into the farmland where Citizens stop at their spades and hoes to watch. At no point does she break into a run before she enters the tree shadows and disappears.

I silently will her on. She must run. Flee. Go up into the mountains where we might lose her scent in a swift stream or she might get beyond the reach of the horses. A test for me. A challenge.

As the crowd disperses, all of them avoiding my gaze, and the yard emp-ties, the General remains at my side.

'They are not ashamed of you,' he says. 'Ashamed *for* you, maybe,' he says. 'None of them would like to be in your shoes.'

I nod. The last of the Elect, Initiates and Councillors have left the courtyard. The gate has been pulled shut once again. General Hilles runs his hand gently over his bald pate. He seems vague and distracted, until he raises his eyes and fixes me with that frank stare of his that goes barrelling right into my soul.

'There is something else I wanted to discuss with you,' he says. 'A more disappointing story. I want you to take Theo with you, on your hunt. I'm afraid he will not Rise this year. Despite showing some progress recently. He has returned to his old ways again. He will never find his path to certainty. So it falls upon you, the one he looks to as a brother, to take him out there with you and when you are at the furthest distance from the Colony, give him the choice he deserves, for coming this far.'

I nod. This is a hard thing and it throws yet more darkness over my Rising, only I'm not in the mental state to absorb it.

'Cut away your bonds,' he says.

I nod.

'There's no dishonour in the task you've been given,' he says. 'This is serious work. The woman is not from the villages; she comes from further away, from the South. Do you understand?'

Really I don't. Can't think beyond what I just witnessed. I know this is somehow important news. People from the South. How is it possible?

'We have questioned her and learned a few things, which I will share with you later,' says the General, 'but the important thing is that you don't underestimate her. She came this far over some wild and hostile territory. She's a survivor.'

He puts his hand on my shoulder. Once again, that question in his eyes, as though he is trying to figure me out after all these years. He nods, with a sly grin towards the murky weather front crawling over Rutger's Dome, ditch water grey, the rising sun nestled in its throat.

'Just ordinary rain,' he says. 'Don't worry. Do you know that song the divvies sing?'

'Sir?'

'Old Sally,' he says. 'The little rhyme –'

He runs a finger over the scars on his arm where Old Sally, with its scorching drops, made a landscape of his skin, churned and clumped, the ridges and gulleys. Did he ever have fear in his gut? Was he ever a frightened boy looking out of the colony gate at the world beyond?

I watch the weather and remember the rhyme. Something about Old Sally that came to the Colony from outside, maybe on the lips of divvies. I haven't heard it since I was a child.

One kiss for your lovely limbs,
The second for your skin,
Three to touch the gates of hell,
Four to go in.

5

MESSAGE NUMBER FOUR

You will be tested before you are taken.
If you fail the test, you will not be chosen.
You can take nothing with you,
So learn to live without attachments.
The life ahead of you will be different from everything you know.
Cut away your bonds,
Put aside your history.
Those things will die in the fire.
Prepare to be born anew.

We ride out the next morning. This time there is no audience. No Elect or Initiate has risen to watch the hunting party cross the ditch: five hooded men on horseback, their mounts damp and steaming in the morning frost, angered at the savage bits that hold them. Their withers and heads daubed in white war paint: skulls, teeth, bones. The bloodhounds out in front, scampering in all directions with their snouts scouring the ground.

Martha sits behind me with her arms around my waist. The others, on their horses, fall in on either side of me. My little army. I would rather be out in the wilderness alone, maybe even on foot, but that is no longer allowed with the sunbursts.

Theo has his hood pulled all the way over his head. All I can see is the tip of his nose. If he has any idea why he is riding out with us today he doesn't show it. But he's no fool. He knows he's not here because we need him.

We ride in silence, listening to the first of the morning rain in the treetops, the thump of the horses hooves and the steel clanking of their bits. Several miles into the forest we stumble upon muddy tracks that run along the bank of a stream for a distance and then trail in amongst the beech trees, headed north, towards the mountains. The dogs don't want to go that way, but we take a look regardless. It is not long before we find hoof prints, and more footprints and then a boulder stained with blood and more blood on the leaf litter around it.

'The Rising last week,' says Theo. 'I saw them go out.'

'There's a new Elect in the women's barracks,' I say. 'Congratulations to them.' I am heartened a little to see that this Rising only lasted half a day, at most. The Bind did not really run, or ran too late. There is no sign the True Path woman had any real difficulty, no evidence of any struggle. She cornered her Bind at this boulder, and bent down and did the deed and returned to the Colony with the body. Was she disappointed? Did she ride through the gate quietly, a little ashamed to be back so soon, or was she simply relieved it was done and she had managed it without fuss?

My Bind has made it further, at least. When we return to the scent trail it becomes clear she has not headed north, for the mountains, but straight through the forest. The quickest route to put distance between us, but not the safest.

There is no place to hide from the bloodhounds here. The streams are too placid. She needs fast flowing water, and then only if she forces her way up against the current. In the forest, with the twigs and under-growth taking swipes at her she is constantly shedding clues: sweat, scraps of skin, maybe tears. I'm half expecting to spot her this afternoon and it will all be over.

It's the weather that saves her. In the late afternoon we are forced to stop at a break in the forest as the heavens open. Going around this unsheltered spot would cost us too much time, with the bogs and streams in this part of the country, so instead we sit on our mounts for an hour at least watching the thickening rain pass through the meadow grass in waves. By the time we get moving again, we are already losing the light. The dogs may be able to find their way through the gloom, but we can't, so we make camp in a clearing and build a fire and try to get dry around it.

In the way they always will on a first night in the giant silence of the wilderness, the Initiates sit wordlessly in a huddle. Theo pulls his blanket tightly around him and stares into the snapping flames. Martha gets busy constructing a tripod over the fire for her stew pot. Eventually Theo breaks the silence that has been with us all day.

'Those sheds,' he says. 'Out near the ditch. Does anybody know what's in them?'

'No idea,' I say. 'Why?'

'I heard; that's all.'

'Heard what?'

'That there's something in them. Big machines, with wheels.'

'Who told you that?'

'There was one of them nearly fell down, about a year ago. Some Citizens were sent out to clear it away. Axel said he saw these things, they were metal and they had seats. He said they were nearly rusted away but you could see enough to know what they did.'

'What did they do then?' I'm only half interested, but I'm happy that Theo is talking. 'People went around in them in the lost times. Even the True Path used them.'

'Maybe,' I say. 'There were a lot of things they had in the lost times that are gone now. We don't need them.'

'Still,' says Theo. 'Imagine.'

'I try not to. You should as well. It doesn't do anyone any good to think about the old days. They're gone and that's that.'

Theo goes quiet for a long time. He pulls his hood around his head and shivers. After a while he mutters something about needing more firewood and gets up and walks out of the clearing.

Martha makes to go and get him, but I raise my hand to stop her. 'Leave him,' I say. I can only imagine what he's thinking about now.

The clouds have parted a little, allowing the full moon to cast some stark light over our clearing. It helps Martha get a pot hung and the soup started with the vegetables from the saddlebags. In a couple of days we will need to start finding live food for ourselves but it's good, in this weather, to have something we don't need to catch.

I like watching Martha work. A sliver of moonlight on her skull and the small bones of her face, her quick hands peeling and cutting. The best divvy in the Colony. A few people have said it. If they had recognised her potential earlier she might have been admitted into the women's barracks. She might be rising now, like me.

When she has completed her service and they make her a citizen, what mark will she treasure most? The crescent moon of her previous Initiate, or my Five Stars, when she takes it? Will she touch that fondly and remember how she was honoured?

As I watch her make the soup, Theo emerges into the clearing again. 'You've got to see this,' he says.

'What?'

'Come on,' he says.

The other Initiates all look at me in shock. The biggest of the three, Con, jumps up from his blanket. He's going to put Theo in his place, which is the last thing I want, so I wave to him to sit down.

The other Initiates look on as I follow Theo. There's just about enough moonlight now to see our way. We walk for a minute or two and arrive at another, smaller clearing, where the humped forms of exposed roots litter the ground. Only, as my eyes adjust, I realise they're not tree roots at all, but bones and skulls, all partially buried and covering every inch of space. I walk into the clearing and look at them. The ground itself crackles and snaps under my feet.

'Who are they?' says Theo.

'How the hell should I know?'

'There might have been a battle here,' he says.

'There just might.'

I carefully work a skull out of the ground and examine it. There is a jagged hole in the back, about an inch wide. A quick inspection of some of the other skulls reveals the same story. The bones, on the other hand, are either strewn around or snapped into bits.

'It's an execution,' I say.

'What do you mean?'

'I mean whoever killed these people, whacked them in the back of the head with something very sharp, one by one, and then they just dumped the bodies here. Smashed them up too, it looks like.'

'Why would they do that?'

'Because – '

'Because what?'

'Theo, I don't know. I wasn't here when it happened. Again, this is old stuff that went on before you or I were born.'

Theo's eyes are hooded. I have only his voice to gauge how serious he is.

'Theo,' I say. 'Let's go back.'

'You heard the story, didn't you? The Five Elects.'

'Dorm talk,' I say, with a sigh.

'Dorm talk in every dorm, not just Five Stars, Ceres too, and Orion. Those five men tried to leave the Colony. You must have heard this stuff, how could you not? All the talk about the messages and how we weren't told the whole truth. Those men said they were going south, to find out when the last message is coming. If it's coming.'

'There were four of them, not five. The General explained it to me. It isn't the first time something like this has happened. Sometimes you get weak people who can just about manage the training but when they kill for the first time it damages them. A crack opens. You know, they kind of go crazy. Those men were like that. They couldn't be helped. They asked to leave and the council let them go. If they talked about the messages or the Palladium or anything it was because they weren't thinking straight and you, of course, being Theo, listened to that stuff. You had your ears wide open.'

He blinks. Looks around at the scattered bones. 'It was Damian who heard it, and he told me,' he says, in a quiet voice.

'There you go.'

I remember as if it was yesterday, when they brought Initiate Damian out from his beating in the Four Walls. How his left eye wouldn't close and he would just sit on his blanket for hours star-ing at the floor. It went on for about a week until one morning they took him away and we never saw him again. I reckon they buried him outside the Colony. A boy like that doesn't go under the boards.

'He saw them leave and he saw the party they sent after them the same day. At least twenty men, armed to the teeth.'

'And you think this is their grave, do you?'

It's impossible to tell, from the wreckage in the clearing, how many complete skeletons are here. It looks a lot more than four or five.

There is nothing in the rules of a Grove colony that says you cannot leave. Only that once you do, you can never come crawling back.

'We should talk,' he says. 'I wanted to get you alone.' His voice is trembling. I'm waiting for him to ask about the Choice. I will tell him about my orders from the General if he asks me straight. 'There are things going on. Strange things.'

'Can't you learn to shut it? You will get into trouble.'

'Nobody can hear us out here.'

'I can.'

Slowly Theo slides his hood away from his shaved head. Thule and its moons are black etchings, like craters, in his scalp. He composes himself. Let's out a slowly, heavy breath.

'People are worried,' he says.

'Who's worried, the divvies?' I shouldn't let Theo talk like this at all, but he is a boy on the verge of a terrible choice and such boys should be given something.

'We still haven't got the Last Message. Sunbursts are getting worse. Nobody ever told us how the messages come to the Palladium. What if there are others out there? What if they have it already? What if the Saviours are here, on earth, gathering up the survivors right now? You said yourself that woman comes from the south. How many people are really out there?'

'Did you never listen to anything you were taught?'

'What if they lied to us?'

'Who?'

'The Elect. The Council. Everybody. There are things they're not telling us.'

I give this the short, loud, cynical laugh it deserves. 'You know Damian screamed like a Citizen when they took him to the Four Walls,' I say. 'Didn't you hear that? The way he mewled and begged for mercy. It made me sick.'

I turn to go. I had hoped he would get this off his chest and then he would feel better, but this is relentless.

'There are others, Leon,' says Theo. He takes a step towards me. I turn back to him. 'Initiates who asked questions and then didn't come back from a hunt or a Rising.'

'Theo, enough.'

'We're running out of time.'

I drop my hood too and glare at him. His eyes are bright and wet and childlike. I take a long gurgle at the back of my throat and then I hoike a lob of spit at his feet. 'You're a fool.'

I leave him like that, standing and muttering amongst the skulls and smashed femurs and ribs and go back to the fire and the warmth. When I get there, I nod at the men and sit down and pull my blanket around me. Nobody asks me about Theo. He follows a few minutes later and plonks himself down across the far side of the fire from me, his head bowed, his hood back up. It would be just like him to glare at me from his hiding place in the dark of the hood, too afraid to speak like he did in front of the other Initiates. Con or Sully would sort him out quickly enough.

Martha has the soup ready and I get the first bowl before each man-boy in the squad is served.

With our bowls in our laps, we sit in silence in the floating embers and the smoke. I can find nothing to say that might lift the weight, the gloom, of this strange, shaming woman hunt. The general had said many strong things outside the council chamber and he would say them again if he was here. But I'm not him. I don't have his gift for leadership. I have to trust in each boy to find in himself the conviction he needs for the coming days.

The smoke blows across the fire-lit faces and carries upwards to where the aurora swirls, coiling and uncoiling. No warmth in that light. Nothing but cold claws and teeth.

When we're finished our meal, I tell everyone to get some sleep while I take the first watch. Martha eats and then she sleeps too.

I spend several hours on my own with the dwindling fire and wake Con only when my eyes are getting too heavy to keep open. Theo wakes up too and offers to take Con's shift. All trace of his irrational mood seems to have passed. He's all 'yes sir,' and 'no sir' and I'm glad that I didn't do anything to shut him up. Whatever it was that was eating him it's out of his system now. Only, when I'm curled up in my blanket and just drifting off to sleep he says something else, in a soft, comforting voice.

'They'll choose you,' he says. 'When the day comes.'

'How so?' I mumble into my blanket.

'Because you're the best and because you love the messages and follow them,' he says.

When we are out at the furthest point from the Colony, I will do as the General asked. I will take Theo aside and give him his choice. Come back to the Colony with us and become a Citizen, or walk out into the wild and never return. I know what I would do. I could not possibly spend the rest of my life watching my family Rise and become men and each take their place in the ranks of The True Path.

If he makes the right choice, then there will always be this mark of respect against his name. Not risen maybe, but not a Citizen either. A boy with the courage of a man.

6

A corridor. Candlelight.

A councillor with a vice-like grip on my hand, yanking me along behind him.

A memory, or a dream maybe. I am small. Have to crane my head back to see his pitted, bald skull.

A room at the end of the corridor. A fire burning in a pit at its centre, the smoke drifting out through a round hole in the roof. On the far side of the fire is a slatted screen. Shapes shifting behind that screen. Clothes rustling.

The councillor takes me by the shoulders and turns me to the left, to face the alcove where the Palladium stands. A single plate of coloured glass on a stone plinth. At the bottom, three lights – two lit, one dark – that looked nothing like the electric bulbs I have seen: they are neat and perfect and glow with a light that comes from deep down inside the glass.

He tells me to stand on a white box, etched into the floor.

Are you ready, Initiate Leon?

I am, sir.

Are you frightened?

No, sir.

A little?

A little, sir.

You should be. We are all being watched and judged, every hour of every day. We must pass the test if we are to be saved. Do you understand, Initiate?

I do.

You do or you're just saying you do, to please me?

I do, sir.

Because if you don't measure up, Initiate, then the Palladium will know. It doesn't matter that you are a cub just out of the nursery. The Palladium can see right into you. There is nowhere in your mind that you can hide a lie. It will seek it out and find it.

Every word the councillor utters is like a coin dropped into an iron bucket.

When I give you the signal, you will approach the Palladium. You will not make a sound and you will not hesitate or deviate. With the index finger of your left hand, you will touch the glass. When you feel a pressure on your finger, do not remove it. Hold it there. When I say so, you can take your finger away, and only then. Am I clear?

Yes sir.

Good.

The councillor turns his eyes to the slatted screen. Who could be there? My soul is naked before them and I will be found out. They will see the *lie* inside me. *Cheat. Weakling. Doubter.*

What will it do sir?

It will put something into you.

He indicated with a nod that I was to step forward.

Left hand, said the councillor.

I can see my own reflection, dimly, in the glass. I press my finger against it. Hold my breath. The surface looks smooth but it is rough to touch.

A pulse begins, near the bottom of the Palladium, and it spreads like a deep current through the glass. A soundless force quivers in my skin, my muscles. As it passes my finger the rough surface bristles and cuts into the flesh.

I concentrate on keeping my finger there and not drawing back. The pulse rises a second time. I press down harder on the glass and brace myself. It hurts. Sweat breaks out on my forehead. I want to cry, or run, or scream out. An invisible thing has entered me. It travels up my finger into my arm and through my neck into my head. So quick, and yet I felt every millisecond of that journey. How it seemed to writhe. To burrow in.

Stand away now, Initiate.

I pull back slowly. The passage of the thing through my body had shocked me.

Stand away.

I stare at the small, globe of ruby blood at the end of my finger. My tiny, shivering reflection inside it.

Stay still and bend your head forward.

I do as he says.

Has it seen? Does it know me now? I didn't feel any anger or shock from the councillor or those watching me from behind the screen. It is just possible that I have passed. And yet I have a *lie* inside me. Surely there was no way of hiding it.

The councillor crouches low and examines the lights at the base of the Palladium. A new, different light has appeared above the row of three. Not a circle but a twisting Ladder, like the Winding Stair, but with only three steps.

When he finally breaks the silence his voice is shaky. 'Observe,' he said. 'Not a single failure in this batch.'

Mutters from the other side of the screen.

You can go now Initiate. Back to your dorm.

These thoughts keep me up, and even when sleep comes, it is filled with uncomfortable dreams.

In one of those dreams I'm in the nursery. Someone has pushed me through the gate and then the gate is slammed shut behind me. The other men are laughing. The women come out of the dorms to see what's happening. They laugh too. One of them grabs me by the ear. Perhaps it's one of the women who nursed me, or even my mother. She knows me, whoever she is. Calls me by my name. She throws me down onto the ground and presses her foot onto the back of my head.

The dirt tastes funny: like metal, like rust.

I wake up. The dawn is almost here. The stars are gone under cloud and the smell from my dream is not just in the dream, it is in the clearing. An intensity in the air.

I sit up and look at Theo, still awake and on watch. He looks at me. We're thinking the same thing: the wind's turned.

Old Sally.

7

How long have we got?

We listen hard. Out there, beyond the sound of the wind in the trees, to the east: there she is. Not a familiar noise for rain to make, even the hard rain of spring storms. This is heavier. It has the heft of something huge and solid. Like a colossal beast is pushing steadily through the forest and flattening the trees in front of it. She is coming on fast. We may only have minutes.

'Get them up,' I say to Theo, in a voice as slow and deliberate as I can make it. 'Now.'

I drag Martha up by the arm and she lets out a yell of protest before she's fully awake. She blinks her eyes open and stares around. She sniffs. Catches the burnt, sour smell on the air. Gives me a startled look.

I nod. 'She's nearly on us.'

The Initiates rise quickly, quietly and without fuss, as they do on any morning in the dorms. Sully is the only one who pauses to look. 'It can't be,' he says. He's about to say something else until the expression on my face stops him.

We passed a stone outcrop just before we found this clearing: a big piece of limestone at enough of an angle to provide an overhang. There's room under there for most, if not all of us. I order my squad to head towards it now.

Everyone grabs what he or she can. No time to roll up or pack away. Martha is dragging saddlebags and pots into the cover of the trees.

The horses are stamping and whinnying. Two of the Initiates have the dogs on a short leash and are trying desperately to settle them down as they snarl and leap at the darkening sky to the East and the rising clamour of the rain. Into this mayhem comes the first drop. It plonks with an audible whack onto the tripod that Martha constructed the night before. It fizzes for a moment and releases a pale smoke. One single drop has discoloured the wood.

Another drop falls. Then another. Anything we're not holding now is left. Anything we can't carry comfortably is abandoned.

I scream at Theo and Sully, 'Get the horses out of there.'

Sully is momentarily frozen in indecision. He's only inches from the trees. He hadn't even considered that the horses might be saved. He blinks. Theo is already running. Sully stumbles behind him.

I yell at the others to go on to the rock, while I help with the horses. Tendrils of smoke are rising out of the ground all over the clearing where the raindrops are striking. They're the outriders. The real rain is on its way and as I leap across the edge of the fire I hear it drumming through the trees to my right.

One of the horses – my gelding – is rearing. Theo is trying to take the reins and draw it down.

'Leave it,' I say. 'Take the others.'

Sully has untied a mare and yanks on the bridle but she resists him, dragging her head up until she nearly lifts him off the ground. She wants to stay with the herd, in the moment of danger. Her nostrils flared, her eyes huge and white. Theo helps her but she still won't budge. It takes the three of us, all pulling on the reins, to haul this one pony out of the clearing and into some cover.

'Nothing we can do,' I have to shout because the downpour is so loud now. 'Let's just take this one. She has the medical supplies.' I don't even know if we can save her since we can't bring her under the outcrop. We have to hope the trees provide enough protection.

Once she is fully separated from the others she comes more willingly. I leave her with Sully and Theo while I run ahead to see what's happening with the rest of the squad. I'm not far from the clearing when it becomes the centre of the deluge. The trapped ponies make a sound I wouldn't have thought possible. A terrible outraged howl, high pitched and mournful. The worst thing about it is that it lasts only a half a minute and then it stops. That's how long it takes then. A large body falls with a thump. The others follow in quick succession. Theo and Sully need to just drop the pony they have and run like hell. Which they do.

They're on my heels by the time I reach the others. They can sense how close Sally is and they must have heard the horses for sure and they're beginning to look a bit like them: eyes wide and wet and scared.

The dogs are pulling frantically on their leash, aching to find their way back to the scent trail. I grab the leash from the Initiates and wave to everyone to follow me.

All these lives are in my hands. Either I lead them to safety or we all get burned down to nothing by Old Sally who doesn't care how long you've trained or whether you were selected to lead your colony and receive the Fifth Message. To her you're just flesh that can be skinned. Bone that can be teased apart.

She's picking her teeth on the pines, taking her sweet time, before she looks up to see where we've gotten to. Then, with a swish of her skirts, she comes crashing in upon us.

The ground opens up ahead. This is the place.

Only it's not. There's rock here, but no outcrop. I hear the others stop behind me. Feel my blood freezing up. She has us. We took a wrong turn. Stupid dogs. They are pulling me ahead now and there's no option but to go with them. This is too open here, not enough trees. The worst place we could possibly choose, but all other options have melted away. The leash goes taut, then slack, then taut again as the dogs scour the ground, jolting my shoulder out of its socket.

'Come on,' I yell. Rain pops on the tin bowls that Martha is carrying. Greets the metal with a hiss. I can hear the pony Sully and Theo abandoned neighing wildly, but she has the sense then to bolt, crashing into the undergrowth. Good girl.

There's an old, moss strewn, fallen tree ahead, bridging a natural dip in the ground. It's the best hope on offer.

'Come on. Over here.'

I rein the dogs in tight and wave everybody past me down to the tree. Martha throws the kit on the ground and quickly squirms in. Theo is next. He takes the dogs from me and forces them down into shelter. There's not going to be room for us all. Why was I even thinking of saving the ponies? Old Sally thickens into dark clumps and pulls her shadow over Sully, who has somehow fallen behind the group. He stumbles. For a frozen moment I can hear his intake of breath. I scream out Sully's name. He stumbles again.

Old Sally has him for the briefest of seconds and his face almost vanishes under the pelting drops before he jolts forward and staggers towards us. I run. Take him under his shoulder. His body falls into mine and soon I'm carrying almost all his weight. They're calling out to us from the fallen tree. This is like nothing they have ever seen in all their young lives.

Sully's face is hanging at my shoulder, his cheek red and seething, his body hot. The rain is on the back of my own legs. It hasn't penetrated through to the skin, but even still it's burning.

The last yard is the hardest. I practically toss Sully at the tree. The others pull him down to safety like ants dragging a beetle or a moth into their nest. They're all in there; somehow they fit. When I squeeze myself in my arm and one foot are still exposed and my heart is hammering hard in my chest.

That's the way I have to stay, still as a lamb in the mouth of something large and mean. Praying.

Sally is here.

She walks her fingertips along the surface of the log. Snapping on the bark. A fizzing breath in the moss.

We push up against one another and listen. I haul my exposed limbs under cover as tightly as I can, but I just have to bear it when the drops fall on my leg and ease their way through the fabric to my skin. The evil liquid sizzles like it's on a hot pan.

Theo is muttering as the thickest part of the squall presses down on the wood. The log creaks and crunches like it's snapping in two, but just as quickly the pressure is released and those wandering fingers of rain move on.

Old Sally. Sally the Stripper.

The dark goes with her and the light returns, though the sound and the smell linger. Leaving us with the deafening quiet and the moans of poor Sully, crying like he never saw the Four Walls in his life. Like he's standing for the first time in the sand arena, his bowels loosening, and his mother's smell still on his skin.

8

'**S**ully, look at me. Sully –'

He won't pull his tunic down from off his face and let us see the damage. His whole body is shaking. He's a tough Initiate, but this is beyond him. While we waited until we were sure it was safe to come out again, he gradually got hold of himself and managed to stifle the sobs and moans, but the effort cost him. He can't keep his body still and can't seem to speak. I need to know how badly he's hurt.

'If that's what it did to him,' says Theo.

'Drop it, Theo.'

'What about her? Your Bind.'

I shove Theo away from Sully. We are all thinking it. What will Sally leave for me to hunt? If she catches my Bind in the open…

'Take a drink, Sully,' I say. 'You have to drink something.'

I call for Martha to bring some water. Martha doesn't appear. I look around the group and everyone just shrugs their shoulders. I remember how she darted into the hollow under the tree and vanished. I leave Sully for a moment and climb down into our hiding place. At the far end of the trunk I find a gap, a little 'v' of sunlight that leads up and out the other side. Footprints show where she scrambled up the bank, past the rocks.

That's the divvy mind for you. At the first sign of real danger, with everyone distracted, she bolts, abandoning everything she has worked for:

the good name she has earned in the Colony, the safety of our walls. We will have to keep watch over the next couple of nights, in case she comes back for some of the remaining supplies, which consist mostly of things that were close to hand by our beds or the fire just before the rain hit the clearing: A couple of water bags, enough for two days at the most; a single saddlebag with some food, the iron stew pot, a couple of bowls and cups and our knives.

This patch of forest is ruined after just a brief shower. Trees have lost clumps of themselves, their trunks bitten and pockmarked. Fallen branches and shorn leaves litter the ground.

'She ran.' says Theo.

'That's what divvies do,' I say. 'They're mindless.'

Still, I am disappointed. I thought Martha was stronger.

I'm trying to prise Sully's fingers from his face, but it's like they've been burned into it. 'Forget her. She'll either come running back for help or she'll starve.'

Martha might have been a real burden and slowed us down, now that we have no ponies, so in a way, this is a kind of blessing. I doubt if she is actually going to die in the wild, though. Not with her skills. She's in her element out here.

I finally tease the tunic away from Sully and his face to reveal the angry red glow on his cheeks and forehead, like a warning of the pain to come. Where the drops have run down his skin there are branching wounds like the scars on the General, only raw and new and open for infection.

It's a minor exposure and the burns are not immediately life threatening, but if they turn septic we have nothing to treat the exposed flesh.

I will go and hunt for some plants when I get the chance, but there may not be any remedy out here that will make a difference. Our medical supplies, what they were, are gone.

Theo puts the water to Sully's lips and Sully takes hesitant sips between long, shuddering breaths. Slowly, he's coming back to himself, little by little. His hands are burnt too, parts of his arms, his neck, but the face is the worst. If it comes to it, I will send the others away and offer him a choice. Go with us, and endure the pain, or I will end it with Stella.

Not that I need to think about that right now. If we can keep his wounds clean, and get him back to the Colony soon, then Sully will be fine. Scarred, sure, but out of danger.

'Sully, it's not so bad, really' says Theo.

I shoot Theo an angry look. Sully doesn't need false comfort. He would prefer to take this like a soldier. He just needs time to recover from the shock.

'You're doing good,' mutters Theo, looking anxiously at me.

Before I can say anything, Martha appears out of nowhere, a bunch of weeds in her arms. She doesn't acknowledge our looks of astonishment as she roots around in the saddlebag and comes up with a rusting tin jar. She pops the lid with her fingernail and scoops out a handful of thick white cream. With a grunt at myself and Theo she pushes between us, so she can get close to Sully. Once she has him to herself she goes quickly to work, testing the texture of the burns with her fingertips.

Sully winces, looking to me for some explanation. I shrug. Happy to accept it without question right now, while with quick, proficient hands, she applies the cream to the flaming skin on his cheeks and temple and along his neck and his arms. She tugs the leaves off the weeds she has and binds them around the wounds, using strips of cloth. I think the weeds are burdock, which she could not have found in the forest. She must have gone out into the open somewhere. And with Old Sally still close by.

'What is it?' I say.

She holds the jar up to me, as if that is enough clarification. I smell it. Don't recognise it. She has brought treatments of her own for just this kind of emergency. This could be some folk remedy she has brought from the Divvy House, in which case it might do nothing or it might even do more harm than good.

Without so much as looking for permission, she then yanks my own trouser leg up and examines what Old Sally has done there. All I can feel is a mild throbbing but now that I look at it, the skin is bleached white and swelling, already seeded with tiny blisters.

She tries to dab some of her cream on it. I pull my leg from her reach. 'Enough,' I say. 'Sully, can you move?'

Sully nods his head. He's still trembling.

'Right. Let's take what we have and get out of here.'

9

It's an easy thing to find our way back to the camp. The foul air left by Old Sally does not hide the raw stink of burnt horseflesh. Flies are already picking drowsily at the carcasses. Many of the trees are blackened and smoking, whole branches shorn off by the rain. The bags and bedrolls we left behind are full of holes.

We do manage to salvage some food and water, though our medical supplies are in the saddlebag our escaped pony took with her. Sully will have to make do with Martha's treatments. We poke about for as long as we can bear the smell, then we press on.

It amazes me, but even after this devastation, the dogs have the scent. It's not as clear or strong as it was the night before. They have to stop and dig around with their noses, but they find it just the same. The tiniest particle of skin is enough. A bare trace of an odour in the air. She can't wash it away.

It's always possible that after that downpour, she might think she's safe and stop running. That would be a big mistake. She should seize her advantage, now that she has it. We have no horses and we're carrying wounded. We have to move at less than half the swift pace we set yesterday. I'm no longer concerned about catching her too fast; I now have to worry about losing her altogether.

Sully is trying not to slow us down and he shrugs off Martha's attempts to tend to the wound. She's at him constantly, poking under the bandages. She tries to take his arm when he pauses or loses his footing and he pushes her away. He's the limping solider, like an old veteran. Scowls like an ancient warrior too. He's going to be ugly for the rest of his life, but that's no bad thing, I reckon, in a True Path colony. He shares his scars with the General now.

The pain, if there is still pain, he keeps under a tight lid, through gritted teeth. When Martha comes picking at the bandages again he yells at her, pushes her over and gives her a kick in the ribs, following that with another attempted kick she manages to skip away from.

'Sully,' I yell. 'Leave it.' He doesn't look back at me, but he stops his attacks. She has transgressed, she ran off without permission. But she is a divvy of the Colony and she has rights. Her motives were good.

She leaves him alone after that. Her lips are busy forming soundless words. Something about him rotting in his own bandages, I'll bet. Though Martha does not speak, since we left the Colony she's become a whole lot more expressive than she used to be.

Still, I'm quietly grateful that we took her. If the cream works, I will not be burying an Initiate corpse out here in the forest and we do not have to waste time hunting out healing plants.

Despite our painful progress, we are gaining on our quarry. The scent is thickening. The dogs are getting excited, panting hard, struggling at the leash. Letting out agitated yips when we won't let them run as fast as they want to go. This might well be a sign that the woman is injured or dead.

That would just be my luck now. I'm going to return to our Colony with a Bind that has been killed by the rain, a limping, ruined Initiate, half our equipment and no horses. This is the Rising of Initiate Leon.

What a return we will make. It will be a triumph: our ragged party stumbling back to the gate while the True Path watch from the parapet in astonished silence.

At least I don't have long for daydreams. We have come to the northern edge of the forest and the dogs have gone into a frenzy. She's here somewhere. I look up into the trees, in case she has climbed, but the foliage is so dense there is no way of spotting anything from the ground. The dogs are circling, circling. There's something about this point here, where the forest gives way to open, hilly ground.

We have a good view of at least a couple of miles north and northwest. This would not be a wise location to make a break for the mountains for that reason. There is little in the way of cover apart from occasional cluster of horse thistle and deer grass that stretches only a little way beyond the tree line. Unless of course, you thought you had time enough to make it to shelter before you were spotted.

The dogs have something.

'Let them go,' I say. The Initiates snap open the leash. The dogs bolt. They take only a couple of bounds through the grass before they've got whatever it is they were looking for.

She's dead. She's dead. It's all been pointless. A mess. I get Stella out of her sheath and run after them. Theo is nearly there already.

'Leave it,' I yell. 'Get back.'

He stops. Looks embarrassed. He should have thought.

The dogs are growling and scraping at the ground. Trying to scoop something up. I imagine melted flesh and a gloopy mess of bone and burned tissue but when I reach the place all I find is the woman's tunic, half buried in the ground.

The dogs don't want to leave the thing, despite my shoving and yelling. Con and Ash come to help and, after a fierce struggle, manage to haul the crazed animals back, saliva flying in all directions. I slowly draw our one piece of evidence out of the soil. Slowly because the ground is damp and acidic. It hisses nastily at my fingers.

It's in bad shape, but what's odd is that it's not full of holes. Instead, the top, around the neck is almost completely burned away while the bottom half is intact.

'Sweet mother,' says Theo, from behind me. 'It just...dissolved her.'

'Not possible,' I say. 'There'd be something left. The downpour isn't long enough to do that. You saw the ponies.'

Theo grimaces. 'Then what happened to her?' he says.

I raise my hand to shut him up. I need to concentrate. I look carefully at the ground around the tunic. The grass has been trampled, between the forest and here, with faint footprints leading in one direction – here. Nothing beyond. If she left this spot then she managed to destroy any trace of the route she took. It's as if she did, in fact, dissolve away completely. Or she simply vanished into the air.

The dogs have no interest in going beyond this point. It's where the scent trail ends. I follow the path of flattened grass back to the forest and look up into the first tree I come to, at the edge of the meadow. I hand my pack to Theo.

'What are you going to do?' he says.

'I'm going up,' I say.

It's the start of a fruitless search that drags on most of that afternoon. We take it in turns to climb trees. We bring the dogs to each one to see if there are any they favour. Nothing. Unbelievably, the scent trail has actually been lost. She has beaten the dogs. I don't know how that is even possible. I remember the General's warning:

She came this far over some pretty wild and hostile territory. She's a survivor.

The dogs give up on their hunt and slump down onto the forest floor for a rest. With their mouths open and their tongues slack and hanging over their jaws, they look like they're sharing a sly, ironic joke, and maybe they are. *She* might be mocking us right now, out there. A grin forming on her face as she strolls away.

The only thing that occurs to me is that the rain did get her after all and then some animals, forest dogs or wolves, found the body and hauled it away. But that too would leave evidence in the grass and there would be blood for sure.

In baffled silence, my bruised and beaten squad makes a fire and settles down to eat. I feel their expectation press on me once again. I should say something inspiring or hopeful, rouse them, and encourage them to be patient and resolute. The words are there, I can almost touch them, but they seem false to me when faced with the reality of our situation. It is too strange, how our luck has changed from one day to the next.

Theo's eyes are on me. He watches me steadily from behind his hood. He thinks, maybe, the lost scent is another proof of the paranoid fantasy he laid out for me last night. It takes all my strength not to walk over there right now, yank down that hood and drag him out into the trees and beat him. Instead, I take my frustration out on Sully, who is nodding his head back and forth and muttering as if he's losing his mind.

'Sully,' I say. He stops. Says nothing for a while. Then he looks at me. There is a thin, fiery scar over his left eye, a lucky miss.

'What if she's a witch?' he says. His voice is trembling and yet his pain and suffering have earned him a special place in our squad. It's like he's already wiser, wrapped up in his bandages.

Con darts a glance at him. I feel a twitch of fear around the fire.

'Sully, enough,' I say.

'Women in the villages are witches sometimes. It's true,' he says. 'They might be able to mess with the dog's scent. An Elect told me witches can excrete all kinds of smells and poisons. They can leak them out of their skin.'

'I'm not sure about that,' I say. Con is nodding like he's heard all of this before and it has the ring of hard truth.

'It's real,' says Sully, encouraged by Con's support. 'I saw one of the divvies once in Five Stars dorm. She was yelling and there was blood coming out her, you know...pouring out of her between her legs only she wasn't wounded or anything. It was just spilling out.'

To my surprise, Theo appears uninterested in the discussion. He has turned to look at the spot where we found the woman's tunic. After a few moments, he gets up and walks out to the deer grass. He takes a long time there, gazing across to the mountains. When he comes back he has a shocked look on his face.

'What? What is it?' I say.

'I know what she's done,' he says.

'What then?'

Everybody stops what they're doing to look at Theo. His eyes are alight. He's in awe of her.

'She went out into the rain,' he says, jerking his head in the direction he just came from. 'She took her clothes off and stood right in it. She let it wash her scent away.'

10

We stand in a circle on the grass where the dogs found the remains of the tunic. The scene of her burning. Her scalding. Con has a torch taken from the fire and holds it close to the ground.

'There's no way,' he says. 'How could she?'

'She could and she did,' I say. 'Theo's absolutely right. There is no other explanation.'

'But –'

'Con, this is good news. She's a worthy Bind. Here, look –' I point to the slight prints and signs of disturbance she made on her way from the trees. 'She was naked. Dumped her tunic and stamped it into the ground and then, even when her skin was melting off her bones, she took her time stepping backwards into her own footprints. There's no shame in hunting this woman.'

'Would an Elect even do that?' says Theo.

'I don't know,' I say. I quietly thank the General and the council for choosing her for me. For their act of faith. 'The question now is, where did she go?'

'She would have gone back on herself,' says Ash, one of the younger Initiates, who has said little since we set out the previous morning. 'That's what I would do. Come around us, and behind us, so there's no way we'd find her by accident. Then maybe she'd go north or south, depending.'

'Depending on what?' I say.

Ash shrugs his shoulders. 'Where she wants to get to, I guess.'

'But that's the thing,' says Theo. 'Where does she want to get to?'

Sully clears his throat and we all look at him. He hasn't spoken since his outburst about witches. 'South,' he says. 'She's gone south.' I wait for him to explain. It takes time before he speaks again. 'A couple of folks in the dorm met the Elect who found her. It all had to be a secret from you, sir, because of the Rising, and they didn't say she was a woman, just that they got someone from out of the valley and she was headed south. Something about Esperanza.'

'Esperanza?' Theo leans into the torch light and stares at Sully.

'Calm down, Theo,' I say. 'There is no Esperanza any more. She might be from that area, where the city used to be, that's all. If that is where she's headed, she's not going to make it in her state. If Theo is right, which I think he is, then she is badly burned and she has no clothes. To me, that means she has to get help and the only place she could possibly go is one of the villages. There is no way they are going to take her in, since they don't want a visit from us, but I just don't see any other options. On the one hand, she's got the dogs off her trail. On the other hand..well..we all know what the rain did to Sully.' I look across at Sully. 'Sorry Sully,' I say. 'But you know what I mean.'

He nods. He does.

'So that's the only thing we have to go on,' I say. 'In the morning we head for the villages. She can't go far without leaving some sign of herself and her wounds. We'll find her. Wherever she's going, she's not travelling any faster than we are now.

We're up and out before dawn. The villages are south east of here. I'm assuming an awful lot by heading in that direction. She might not even know about the villages, or where they are. And yet, something tells me she does and that there was a reason she came to this valley and that reason was not to meet with the True Path.

The dogs get a whiff of something familiar only a short way from our camp. My hunting party looks impressed. Leon the hunter. That scent comes and goes but the thing is, as long as we head southeast, we keep running across it. So my faith in my own decision is increasing with every step.

Which makes me feel all the more foolish when we discover the real source of the scent the dogs have been following: it's our lost pony. Under a stand of boxwood, by a stream, we find hoof prints. By the looks of it, the pony was not galloping anymore, so likely she had outpaced Old Sally or simply run out of breath. She was still in good enough condition to stand and walk, at least.

The confusion and disappointment descend on us once again. Martha is the only one unmoved by this latest defeat. She squats over the prints, her lips parted as though she was about to speak. Does she want her Initiate to Rise or does she want our prey to escape?

I decide to follow the prints, since the pony and its saddle bags of food, water and medicine are worth the loss of a little time to retrieve. The tracks skirt the stream and there the hoof prints head down the bank into the water, so she must have stopped regularly to drink. She was slowing down, probably burned and desperate. Maybe she even rolled in the water to cool her hide. I think of the scream my gelding made when Old Sally struck.

Further upstream we find a point where the pony has stopped and then actually crossed the water to the other side. The prints climb the opposite bank and disappear in amongst the leaves and pine needles. I listen out for the hollow thud of her hooves. Is she close? Why did she leave the stream? I look carefully at the prints. On this bank they go deeper into the soil. Is the ground softer here? I go back and look at the other side again. They are deep here too, much more so than even a few feet further back along the shore. I get down on my knees and examine the ground.

At the edge of one of the hoof prints I find the slight indentations of human toes. Here she is, my Bind: her skin still burning, she has stepped onto the muddy bank on her tiptoes to get a hold of the pony. She found the same prints we did and she followed the pony the same way up stream, until she found her drinking here. The pony stayed quiet for her. Maybe she was scared. Maybe the woman had no smell and she simply didn't notice her until she was right up close.

One way or another she got on the pony and she's riding her now. She could be miles away already, but at least she's leaving prints, and we have the scent trail of the pony.

I get up from the ground and look at the expectant faces that surround me; each one in turn.

'Either we can outrun that horse,' I say, 'or we lose her. And I'm never going to let that happen.'

11

'If she has the horse,' says Con. 'That's it. We're never going to catch her.'

She must be riddled with seeping wounds right now. Jostled around, naked on that skittish pony. Every movement brings pain.

I stand up and look each Initiate in the eye. They hang like defeated troops, abandoned on the bank of the stream. No longer warriors on a hunt, more like boys lost in the woods.

'Four legs against two now,' says Con.

'On a frightened pony,' I say. 'That might throw her.'

'She has supplies in the saddlebag. The medical kit. Bandages.'

'A lot of things weighing on both sides,' I say. 'We have a battle on our hands. A battle to relish.'

Sully has collapsed against a tree. Breathing hard and shaking again. I send Martha over to him and she changes his dressing rapidly, without fuss, remembering the boot she received last time. Still Sully tries to hit her when she makes him wince. She is not afraid of him. She has the gift of staying out of arm's reach. In a knife fight she could have your guts out before you could land a punch.

When she's done and he is steady on his feet again, I go around the squad stripping them of supplies: a pot, changes of clothes, two spare pairs of boots and a blanket. 'Everything we don't absolutely need stays here,' I say. 'We have to be light and quick. No more rests until sundown.'

We restart our chase at a jog. Really, she cannot be going much faster in her state. A slow trot at best. There is only one route wide and open enough for the pony, so there is no trouble finding our way. It winds into the foothills, west of the villages and by late afternoon we reach the end of the dense forest where the ground is rougher, rockier. Here we pause briefly to gather some firewood, and bundle it into our cloaks before striking out from the shelter of the trees.

The wind freshens and the rain comes, not the burning rain, the sweet, wet rain, bringing a welcome cool to our faces, but also misting the way ahead. We step gingerly and sometimes we stop altogether. The dogs are as sure of their path as ever, but I don't want us picking up any more injuries. There are traps out in the wild, set long ago. Snares, pits, and clickers. Ancient things, buried just below the ground. They can blow limbs into the air. Send heads rolling into the grass.

Theo yells through the rain that we need to find somewhere to camp and I nod in agreement. We have less than an hour of daylight left and there is no sign of any good place; we have to press on until we find shelter. Building a fire is impossible out here.

Our luck changes when we stumble across a ruined building, standing behind a shallow trench snarled with brambles. There were two storeys. The top storey is mostly gone but for a section of the back wall and a portion of the floor. This bit of floor will give us shelter. There's no one about and no sign that anyone has ever camped here. The doorway is doorless; four steps of a staircase lead up to a crumbled stretch of wall.

This was not a village house; it's from the lost times. It has stood alone here in this rocky meadow since then. It's possible we are the first people to step through this doorway in a hundred years or more.

74

The walls are riddled with ragged holes. Black fire-stains on the brickwork. Out here, in this remote place, they might have thought they were safe, but someone came for them in the end. Someone took the trouble.

I go and fetch my platoon. I'm not going to risk calling out to them, just in case the woman is within earshot. We have space, under the broken second floor, to build a fire and fit ourselves around it, in what must have been the biggest room in the house. Theo stares around.

'Who lived here?' he says.

'You're asking stupid questions again,' I say. 'There's no way of knowing. They're long gone.'

'Yeah, but look.'

In the centre of the room sits the mostly rotten frame of some piece of furniture too large and heavy to burn and it is surrounded by tiny fragments of card decorated with pictures that have long since faded to mere smudges of colour. I can see from their odd shapes that they're designed to fit together somehow.

Theo wanders around the shell of the house in the rain until I tell him to sit down. The firewood we gathered before we left the forest is enough for an hour maybe.

'Where did they go, do you think?' says Theo. Martha loads up the kindling. The wood is well seasoned, even though it is damp. It takes the flame like an old friend.

'Nowhere,' I say.

'I can't help thinking about it,' he said. 'They might still be out there somewhere, or their children.'

'They're not out there.'

75

'They might be. You don't know that for sure.'

'They're not out there.'

He nods slowly, like he's trying to take what I say to heart. Trying to believe it. 'I heard something once,' he says. 'Outside the gate. I was up early one morning because I couldn't sleep. I was on the training ground and there were voices coming from outside. Elect voices and someone else, with a strange accent. It was a long time ago, but I can't forget it, because nobody ever talked about it. It was like a secret.'

'Theo, give it a rest.' That was Sully. His head down. His face unreadable under all those bandages.

'Yes, Sully, sorry,' says Theo quickly. 'Are you okay?'

The look he gets from Sully silences him. That's the end of the talk.

Once we've eaten the rest of the dried rabbit, everyone settles down to sleep as best they can on the hard, lumpy ground. The rain slackens to a thin drizzle, transforming the night into something stark and lonesome. I wait until they're asleep and then I head out for a quick scout around our camp.

My clothes are drenched and heavy and I shiver and walk quickly to try and stay warm. There's nothing out here but dark, bare country in all directions. Eerily silent. The sky is still overcast and the aurora plays dimly behind the cloud like the shadow of some far away fire.

My Bind is out there somewhere, riding through the dark on the pony or making her own camp, if she dares risk it. Does she know we are still after her or does she think she's escaped now that she has shaken the bloodhounds? Either way, it can't feel like much of a relief or a victory, with what she's suffered.

There is something wrong that she should be hurt. An animal part of me doesn't like it at all. That is my test. Beauty is the world's trick, to make you love it, want it. It is my duty to see the true path when it seems wrong. To experience doubt and then to crush that doubt. Ground it up under my foot.

We are connected only in this instance, and for this one purpose: predator and prey. And that is how I picture her now, riding the pony through the rain, stretched out over her withers, her head lolling at the horse's neck.

Stay alive for me. Just a little bit longer.

I do a circuit of the house, using the walls to get my bearings because I can see little else. The breeze brings a heavy scent to me from the other side of this meadow. It's familiar and it doesn't take long to recognise it: Horse shit.

There is one likely source: the mare is out there in the dark. I can't see her, there's no movement, and yet horse shit doesn't stink that power-fully for long. It is fresh. She is close.

As quietly as I can, and careful not to lose the scent, I step across to the hole in the wall that used to be a window and hiss at the sleeping figures by the fire.

A head rises. It's Sully.

'Wake 'em up,' I say, low but sharp. 'Follow me.'

I can't do this alone. If I go for the pony, my prey will spot me and she could use the dark to give me the slip. Then we'd have to wait until morn-ing to look for prints and she could be long gone. We need to cast a net.

When the others assemble, they crouch in front of me, exchanging excited glances. I give them their orders: Theo and Con to sweep out wide and south to come out on the far side of the pony; the others to take the west and east. Martha is there too. I tell her to stay in the house. She just looks at me. Blinks. Doesn't move. I don't want to raise my voice now so I just leave it and hope she'll at least stay put. I'll deal with the insolence, or whatever it is, later.

I'm going to be the one to scare the prey out of her hiding place. As soon as she is up and moving, the others will spring the trap. When everyone has had time to get to their positions, I head out in search of the source of that smell. The pony knows my scent, so while there's a risk she might startle and bolt, I suspect she will let me approach her, if I am careful.

The breeze is shifting a lot and it's not easy to follow the smell. Shapes loom up all around me: bushes, boulders; a line of old fence posts. The stink thickens until I can see one or two little mounds of manure and then I hear the pony's rapid, shallow breathing nearby.

I find her lying on the ground surrounded by a reek of urine and shit. She lifts her head slightly when she notices me, but then drops it again. I'm thinking Old Sally must have caught her after all and she just about made it this far before her injuries took her down.

I go to her. Whisper soothing words into her ear while I run my hands down along her broad neck and withers to check for any damage done by burning rain. I feel no ridges or broken skin. The pony shivers under me.

Around the edges of her saddle her hair is sticky and dark. I take it in my fingers and taste it: blood. It's not her blood; I can find no cuts on her. There seems to be a lot of it, along her stomach and on the saddle itself. It's fresh.

My Bind is close. She's injured. I take out my knife. Listen. Only the patter of soft rain. The breeze in the grass.

I continue the examination of the pony. On one of her hind legs I find more blood and this time I think it's hers. I probe around the fetlock. There is a wound. It's a hole. I can fit my finger into it. She lets out a moan when I do.

'Easy,' I say, putting my hand on her neck. She is tight and sore there too. When I feel around the other side I find another tear in the skin. This is not the work of Old Sally and I don't think the woman would have stabbed her own mount.

I look around me again. In the distance I see the head of one of the Initiates, probably Con. It disappears quickly. I'm hoping, of course, that's she's going to make a run for it and I'll spot her, but that's a slim chance, given that she's injured.

I take a few careful steps away from the pony. I'm awake to everything, every sound and odour. There's little in the way of cover here, so she might just be lying flat on the ground, trying not to breathe.

Which way? There are places, here and there, where the grass seems flattened. Hard to tell in this darkness. I quicken my pace, stepping hard, noisily, when I hear the metallic boom under foot. It takes a moment to register.

I stop dead. My heart goes straight to my mouth. A clicker. I stood on a clicker. Stupid idiot. I should have looked. Let the excitement get to me.

Oh God, Oh God, Oh God.

I don't move. When you move they get you. It could be a broken one. They don't always detonate. Some of them are hundreds of years old, after all.

I can hear my own heart. Sweat on my face and arms already. This is it. This is how I go. The breeze rolls over my stiff body, frozen in mid-stride, the cold welling inside me. Don't let them see. Let me do this alone.

Only it wasn't really a click I heard. Clickers are supposed to click and that could not really be described as a click.

I am supposed to be fearless. A soon-to-be-Elect. With one deep breathe I step off the metal thing onto the grass. Nothing explodes. It was not a clicker, or it was a dead one. I get down on the ground and look at it. It's not really buried, so either the wind has uncovered it over the years or it never was buried in the first place. When I run my hand gently over it I find a handle on one side. I pull it and it lifts. It's a lid.

Under that lid is light.

12

From out of the hole, with its swaying light, comes the sound of her breathing. She tries to stifle it – there are brief silences – but she's not strong enough. The echo carries it up to me, so shallow and rapid and faint, like something waiting for the final blow to fall.

The light is sharp blue, not candlelight or a lightbulb. I feel around the rim where the lid was until my hand brushes over the first rung of a metal ladder.

I stand up and whistle into the dark. The others will be here in a minute or two and I'm going to have to wait for them, since they won't be able to find me otherwise.

Sully arrives first. He looks at the light and the hole.

'Is she – '

I nod.

'What is it?' he says.

'A room. Some kind of hideout.'

'She fell in?'

'No, it had to be opened. She knew it was here.'

The others appear in a group. Martha is there too. So much for my orders. She has lugged a saddlebag from the house, and she has a full water sack tied at her belt. Did she think I was striking camp? They all stare in mute wonder at the blue light.

'I go first,' I say. 'Sully is to follow. I want one of you to stay up here, just in case.'

'In case what?' says Theo.

'Just in case.'

With my knife still in my hand, I clamber on to the ladder and start to climb down. The bolts are loose and my arrival is announced with shrieks of metal against concrete. Not that it matters. She knows only too well that I'm here.

When I reach the floor I turn, but only an inch or two, because something flashes in the dark and hits me square on the head. I spin, crash into the ladder and lose my footing. She hits me again, this time driving her body right into my torso and knocking me to the ground. She's ferocious, snarling, but her voice is full of pain. She has me by the hair and with surprising strength she whacks my head off the side of the ladder.

'Leon sir,' I hear from above.

She drives a tiny, sharp object into the back of my neck. It makes a hissing sound. I try to turn, catching a glimpse of the thing – black and thumb sized with a spike at one end – before she grabs me and bangs my head again, the impact already weaker with this second blow. Still hard enough to send a flurry of colours and that eerie blue light flashing across my vision.

I can hear her frustration. Her energy sapped and draining away. She's wounded, exhausted. She can't prevent me from reaching up and snatching her wrist. My grip feels like iron compared with the lightness of her bones. I could snap her arm in two.

She drops the object she spiked me with and it clatters on the floor.

'What was that? Was it poison? Did you poison me?'

I scramble up against the ladder, her wrist still in my hand. Her eyes are all pain now and defeat. Her muscles slacken under my grip. Once I'm standing I take her neck in my other hand and hurl her across the room. She staggers, and when she puts her weight on to her right leg she lets out a yell and it gives beneath her, sending her tottering into the far corner. She collapses with a creak of iron springs and more metallic screeching.

'Sir,' from above.

'It's all right,' I say, steadying myself. If she jabbed me with poison it has not started to act yet. The pain in my neck is tiny, a pinprick. Any dizziness is down to the banging on the ladder.

'You can come down now,' I call to the others.

I spot a black line meandering along the floor. A trail of blood. The room is solid concrete. The light is coming from a glass lamp hanging from the ceiling. To my right and left are shelves stocked with all kinds of equipment and small, conical, metal objects. There are boxes on the floor and at the far end of the room is what looks like an iron cot. The woman is now leaning her head against it, still watching me.

There is another light, a tiny white one, blinking rhythmically, on the front of a rectangular device that sits on the shelf, to the right of the cot. It makes a faint crackling sound, with an electric fizz to it.

The ladder creaks behind me as the others climb down. It's time. All my questions – the strange light, the hole, the things on the shelves – they can be answered later or never at all.

I let her see Stella as I cross the room. She remembers it, I'm sure. The shape of it she saw through her hood when we first met. Her face is mostly veiled in bandage cloth from the saddlebag, and she has made herself a rough covering out of the rest of the supply. I'm glad I can't see much of her skin and what she has done to herself in that meadow, only the dark blotches around her eyes and mouth.

'I'll be gentle,' I say, in a low voice. 'I promise.'

She's bleeding and dying. It's a mercy.

'What the hell is this place?' says Theo, behind me.

'Shut it,' I say.

'Leon, what's that on your neck?' Theo blurts out before someone else – I can't tell who – hisses at him.

I touch the wound left by the spike. A little knot under the skin. Tender but not bleeding. I feel no poison.

'It's nothing,' I say. 'Leave it.'

'But there's -'

'Nothing.'

'Sir, you really should – ' says Sully.

'Leave it.'

When I lean over her she puts up her hand. Her lips are moving. Is she praying? We learned in Right Thinking that the outsiders pray to gods who protect them after death. Bring them to an afterlife. Whatever she believes, she mouths her prayers, or curses or ravings while her gaze traces the blade of my knife from tip to handle. There's still some fire in her eyes. They meet my own and hold them. Deep down in my gut that queasiness stirs once again. The worm of doubt.

To my right, on the shelf, the crackling machine starts to talk. At first I think it's just another electric noise, but gradually a distinct human voice wavers to the surface. The woman darts a glance at it.

'Esperanza,' she mutters.

I have to lean forward to hear her.

'What did you say?'

She glares at me. Her lips moving.

'Esperanza.' She means the box, or what is in the box.

The voice gets louder. I reach over the cot and touch the blinking light. It's hot. There are things on the surface of the box, controls of some kind. When I twist them, the noise changes. I twist one and the noise dies down. I twist it the other way and it goes up again. Now it's loud.

'Vanesa,' says the voice in the box. 'Vanesa?'

It babbles in a strange language. I think it's Satz.

I take a step back. Look at my platoon. All but one are down here with me now, including Martha. They will not approach the box, my hardened initiates. They press back towards the ladder. Mouths half open. Eyes huge and skittish.

'Vanesa?'

'Esperanza,' the woman says again. She barely has the breath for it. Blood is seeping through her bandages leaving a dark stain on her thigh.

'What is this?' I say. It's not right. None of this is right. I push down on this reeling dread that's just starting to take hold of me, as if a bird has found itself trapped in my head and started flapping and squawking and beating against my skull as it tries to find a way out. It could be the effects of spike she drove into my neck or it could just be that I'm in a concrete bunker with a talking box.

'What the hell is that thing?'

The woman doesn't answer. The box goes quiet. Then it speaks again.

'Who is this?' it says, in accented English. 'Quien es?'

'Leon,' I say. I can't hide the quiver in my voice.

'Leon,' says the box-man. 'Who are you? Are you NAA?'

I shake my head. My Bind grins at me through her cracked lips.

'Leon? Leon, whoever you are. This is important. This woman here is called Vanesa and she is on a special mission. You must not hurt her. Please listen to me. What she is doing is vital, for all of the people. For you too.'

There is no Esperanza any more. Our warriors killed the last of them and then came back from the South, the deed done. People don't talk out of boxes.

She moans when I take her by the neck and drag her out of the corner she's cowering in.

'You've got to listen,' says the voice.

The trapped bird in my head goes still.

'Venesa has news. Good news.'

I kneel down behind her and lift her chin, take her lips between my thumb and forefinger and pinch them closed. 'Shush now. There are some words I have to say.'

'Vanesa? Are you all right?' The man's voice is distressed; close to tears.

I look to my squad of initiates.

'There is news from Esperanza,' he says. 'They are coming from all corners of the West. Vanesa was sent to tell you all. The message has arrived. The Salvatores are coming. Listen, you have to listen. The Salvatores. They have communicated with us. They are on their way. Come to the West. The beacon at Esperanza. You'll find us. Vanesa will show you.'

I see Theo's startled look and I want to reach out and grab him and shake him.

My Bind stops breathing when the knife touches her skin.

'Please. She has a child. Vanesa has a child. She's a mother. Don't hurt her.'

Her skin is rough where it has been burned; silky smooth where Sally didn't touch her.

I look to my men once again, for that nod of agreement that what I do now is right and true. The thing that makes me a man. Only the face that I see first is not theirs, but Martha's. And what I find there isn't what I'm looking for.

She stares right through me. Like she has seen the bird in my head. Seen it. Known it for what it is. Her lips are parted. Slowly and deliberately, she shakes her head.

I've broken bones before on the training ground and you know instantly when you hear the crack or the way your leg twists at an angle it just shouldn't. I feel that right now, only it's not a bone, it's deeper. A part of me, not visible and yet firm as a whip, that shouldn't be touchable or breakable and yet it just snapped in two.

I discover that I have let go and the woman sinks down into my chest, breathing again. Even the voice has stopped.

The silence that follows is filled only with the crackle from the box. Somebody needs to say something. I want Martha to wipe that righteous look from her face.

Finally, the crackle changes and the voice speaks again.

'Vanesa?'

I'm up. I let the woman fall away to the side as I clamber onto the cot, scoop the box from the shelf and send it flying across the room. The thin metal splits with a crunch when it hits the wall. A single last spark illuminates its guts of coiled wire before they come spilling out through the tear in the case.

I let the rage take my body, my limbs, and do what it likes. I charge over and stamp on the ruined machine. Smashing down on it with my heel. The crackling has been silenced.

'Leon,' says Theo.

'Shut your mouth.'

'But –'

'Shut it.'

The voice is gone. I killed it. It's crushed and twisted. I shut the woman's breathing out of my head. I look at Martha. The expression on her face has not changed. I lean right into her and take a swing. It's loose and wild enough that she manages to duck out of it. She slides along the wall to the floor.

Even that is maddening, the crumpled, helpless, shaking form, turned from me like she's ashamed. I hear my own voice in the room, babbling. Something about being a divvy and nothing. Nothing to anybody.

All my weak, scared little initiates are pushing back to give me space. I shove my way through them. Up the ladder. Con is up there. He salutes. I'm already well beyond him when he yells, 'Congratulations on your Rising sir,' as he watches me go, nearly at a run, into the meadow.

So attractive now, all the empty lands and mountains. The distance I could put between myself and this hole in the ground. It is not Theo who will make the choice and go into the wilderness today, it's me. None of this matters if I never see anyone again. The animals are not going to know. What do the trees and rivers care about Saviours, or the True Path or Risings?

I kick through a patch of tall grass, feeling the damp rise up my legs. What are the others saying now? Down in that hole. Are they planning what they're going to do with me? They now have to get hold of me somehow and bring me back to the Colony. Good luck with that.

I spot movement up ahead. At first I think it's the pony, but this is smaller, quicker.

A squelch of mud only inches behind me. I stop and turn. That's a mistake. Strong arms grab me from behind and shove me down on my knees. The source of the squelch rises up in front of me, a tall figure with a mean face. I have a second to note the malice in his upturned mouth before something heavy cracks against my skull.

'Move now and you lose that pretty face of yours,' says a rough voice from behind me.

I double over, trying to stay on my knees and manage the pain.

The other man, in front of me, steps up. He's tall. I'm looking at his stomach, which droops right out over his waist. He gurgles a mouthful of spit at the back of his throat and then sends it in a volley over the top of my head.

'Look at this. Buyurun, Umut.' says the man behind me, pulling at my cloak. 'He's got the mark. Insanlar. He's a sechnik.'

'What are you talking about?'

'Right here on his neck. Clear as day. Jacob's fucking Ladder.'

13

The man with the belly stands in silence a while before replying. 'Something for all our trouble' he says.

'Hell of a thing, they just let him wander around outside their camp.'

'Hell of a thing, indeed.'

The men speak together for a few moments in some foreign tongue that is not Satz. The words are dense and soft, with rolls of the tongue as if they have to be peeled and teased apart.

The man behind me presses something cold and metal into my neck, hollow and cold. I know what it is. A gun barrel. It's been a while, years maybe, since the General last opened his old box full of rusted pistols and rifles, and let us carry them up to the palisade and take imaginary shots at the Citizens in their fields. A good game. I liked the heft of the rifle in my arms. The butt tucked firmly into my shoulder.

'We can get the others now, I guess, we're done here,' says the man who has me at gunpoint.

'You sure you can handle him on your own? He's valuable.'

The man in front of me doesn't get an answer to that question; at least not a spoken one. He spits into the grass and takes a long, hard look at me.

'Your friends over there are depending on you now,' he says to me, in a voice that sounds like he's grinding up dirt at the back of his throat. 'You try to cause trouble and the harm that's on its way is gonna come to them, not you. You hear me?'

I don't answer. It's been no more than a minute or two since I was in that hole with a knife at my Bind's throat.

'You little men might be fast, but I've got something a whole lot faster, and that's a bullet.'

He spends some more time examining me until he sees something in my eyes that satisfies him, and with one more volley of spit into the grass, he heads off in the direction of the hole.

'The True Path,' says the man with the gun, pressing it against my spine. 'Doghru Yol. Trained to kill.'

I know I ought to act now. I am still the leader of my squad, after all. The clouds part a fraction and a sliver of moon sharpens the scene all around me. The ground is rough, little clumped bushes and hillocks and rocks. The walls of the house are etched distinctly into the night like my Thule ink.

As his friend walks off, the man behind keeps chattering. 'Boy were we pissed when you freaks got hold of that bitch. We'd chased her must be fifty, sixty miles upriver. Thought that was it. We were on our way home when we spotted your smoke.

'A prize like that, a Pioneer, and what do you retards do? You play games with her. Set her running out in the middle of nowhere. What is that all about? You that bored?

'I had money on her not comin' out o' them trees. It was what? Two days? They told me about the shit you guys go through in trainin' and I thought well – that girl's gonna run hard but she ain't comin' out o' there alive. You got them dogs; you got horses. Seems like you don't leave too much to chance.'

I spot a clump of busy shadows close to the house. Five at least. Hands waving in the air. Guns.

'A bunch of you hotshit lunatics against one naked, unarmed woman,' he says. 'You really are the toughest of the tough. Then we see her ride out of there, with you nowhere in sight, and stone me if she hasn't taken your horse.' He follows that with a long spate of dry laughter. 'I got to tell ye, I nearly shat myself when I saw that.'

She was just a few feet from her hideout and safety when they caught her. So close. They shot the horse out from under her and then, perhaps by accident, they shot her. The wound on the pony and the wound on her thigh both make sense now.

'Hey,' he says. 'You're a little killer ain't ye? You gonna do a little spin in a minute? Catch me off my guard? Snatch the gun? Somethin' like that. Hadi, buyurun sechnik bey. Show me your killer skills.'

While he talks away, I get the feeling we're not alone anymore. I can detect a presence off to the right, coming around and behind him. He hasn't noticed it. It is whisper quiet. He gabbles on. How will I kill him? Will it be strangulation? Am I going to slit his throat, maybe? He stops talking when the ground crunches right behind him. He grunts before he's hit hard.

The man falls back and away from me. I spin. Leap. Go for the gun. There's a crazed figure on him already, like some tiny demon: arched shoulders, bandy, powerful legs wrapped around his hips, a bag jostling on her back. It's Martha.

She's fighting like the woman in the hole fought me, in a wild, thrashing frenzy with everything she has: slashing with her hands and nails, kicking wildly with her feet and when none of that quite does the job, digging her teeth deep into his wrist.

He yells out, more in confusion than in pain. He still has a hand on his gun and now he swings it at her head. I grab his wrist before he can get any energy into his thrust. I ram the palm of my hand into his nose and drive it up and back into his skull.

He takes one shuddering breath. His eyes go wide and frozen. In a second the blood starts to pump in black clots from his nostrils.

I take the gun from his hand easily and stand up. The blood is now all down his chin and his chest and still flooding out. His eyes are fixed on me, but not really seeing me, or anything. I bring the barrel of the gun down on the side of his head. It snaps to the right. His mouth hangs open. He's out cold.

I look at Martha. 'What have you done?' I say.

She squints, confused.

'If they come back here and find I'm gone they're going to take it out on the others. They're going to shoot them.'

Really, it's not that that angers me. They're going to shoot the others, and probably me and Martha anyway, regardless of what I do. What makes me furious is that after all that's happened, she's back here coming to my rescue. Does she not have the sense to abandon a lost cause? If she just returned to the Colony now she would be re-assigned to serve some new Initiate. A boy who will rise.

I drop the gun, since I have no idea how to actually use it, and I wave at her to follow. Before she does, she goes back into the dark and retrieves the water sack she must have dropped before she pounced. Together we head off towards the hole, keeping as far to the left of the house as we can without losing our bearings.

Out there in the distance, silhouetted against the wall of the house, are the figures I saw earlier. They're shifting about; busy at something. I think I can see Con. He's down on his knees.

'C'mon,' I say, and wave at Martha to follow.

We find cover on high ground behind a spiny shrub. The brief fight with the gun man has galvanised me at least. Not that I know what to do against a bunch of men armed with guns. I cannot get close enough for a surprise attack and running from here would make me an easy target.

Con turns my way and I see enough of his face to be sure it's him. There's no sign of the raised lid of the woman's hideout. They have closed it.

There's a heated discussion going on, some shouting. One man's voice booms out above the others. He's gesturing with his arm in the direction from which we just came. He must be the 'Boss'.

Another man arrives at a run. I can just about hear his voice, but not what he's saying. The boss listens to him with his hands on his hips and then, when he's finished, hits him in the face. The man falls down immediately. They just got the news about my escape, I'll bet. The boss paces, shouting. He shoves another of the men as he does a complete circle, roaring at each one, until he comes to a halt beside Con.

He directs two of the men to go down into the hole. When they come out a few moments later they are hauling something out, a body. Hard to see it. More men come to help them. They drag it over the rim of the hole and lay it behind their boss on the grass. I feel in my bones that the moment to act is now, but what do I do?

The boss says something to Con. Con looks out over the meadow, before one of the men strikes him on the head. His body tilts at an angle, flops back and then vanishes into the hole.

I half rise. Martha grabs a handful of my belt in her long fingers and yanks me down. The boss moves into the front, looking down at where they just pushed Con. He has an oval object in his hand that he tosses after him. I can't see what it is; too small.

They drop the lid again, just before a searing flash highlights the rim and lifts the lid several inches off the ground, quickly followed by a powerful crack, deep in the earth. I feel the shockwave under my knees and it nearly knocks me to the ground.

It passes swiftly through me, like the pulse in the Palladium. Tearing through my blood, stomach, muscles, ringing in my skull. My failure is complete and all the men I brought with me are dead.

14

The bang has killed everything, even the wind.

I get up out of my hiding place. Martha is clinging on to my belt, frantically trying to keep me down. My ears and my head are seared with a high pitched whine, the undertow of the bomb.

I open my mouth to yell at the men. They spot me. A moment of confusion, followed by recognition. A gun is raised. A flash. A bullet whips past me into a bush. A second bullet goes over my head.

It takes a few frozen seconds to register all of this: the bullets; the fact that I'm still standing here, that they missed me. The man who took the shots lowers his gun to look, before he raises it to his face again.

'Stop the shooting, asshole. We want him. He's a sechnik.'

Martha is at my shoulder. She tugs. I should fight. I would, but they have guns. So I let her take me by the arm and lead me away, walking quickly at first and then running. We get a little distance between us before the men follow, roaring and cursing.

We reach a hollow, a ditch, some kind of old defence work, spiked with fragments of razor wire, and stumble down into it, out of sight from the gunmen for a moment. The ground crunches under our feet. Sharp stones or glass. Another bullet hits a rock behind us and clatters in the undergrowth. Martha yelps in pain, but it is not the bullet, she has stood on something. She grabs her foot, limps, stumbles forward. Her breath catches. They're running up behind us.

In the distance I can see two of them looping around to cut us off.

I could leave her. This would end it. No witnesses to my failure with my Bind. If I dropped her here it would slow them down while they dealt with her and I would have enough time, just maybe, to get away. But despite having failed my men and abandoned my mission, I can't bring myself to do this one last cowardly thing – and for a divvy.

The thing is, the limp hardly slows her down and she navigates the dark landscape as if she had cat's eyes. In no time, we're leaving all our pursuers behind and though we have no idea where we're headed, it is at least away from them. They have to go carefully and make sure they don't miss us in the dark.

They yell for others to help. We're getting clear. We're going to make it.

Up ahead, there's a black smudge against the horizon. It could be trees. The edge of the forest. I make for it. Martha has found a rhythm with her wounded leg, skipping on every second stride.

The cloud is all the time threatening to betray us and let the moon out. More men are coming from the direction of the house. Another crack from a gun but I can't tell where the shot went. Nowhere near us. When I look back I spot a lone figure stumbling through the tall grass. He's the one they're shooting at. He stops. Sees me.

'Leon.'

The shout is clear, the wind is behind it and takes it right to me.

'Leon.'

It's Theo. I can't see his face but he looks, somehow, broken. Only one of his arms is moving. The other is hanging limp at his side. He's holding his head at a funny angle, his ear almost dropped to his shoulder.

Theo. His name comes out of me in a squeak. I'm not even sure if it sprang from my mouth or somewhere else. Theo can't hear it. The men are close to him. One of them stops and raises his gun.

'Leon.'

Martha is tugging on my arm. We'd all die if I went to Theo's aid now. It doesn't make sense to me, with all the good men I had in my squad – Sully, and Con and Ash – why it should be him.

That last thought is all I have time for. The flash briefly bathes the face of the shooter in a sharp orange light, his left eye closed and his right eye open at the barrel. When Theo hits the ground his legs go straight up in the air.

Again I let Martha drag me away, as if my cowardice was her fault. Theo has helped us. There's confusion behind and a lot of shouting.

'Who the hell was that?'

'Get over here. There's somebody here.'

More shouts in their strange language.

The smudge looms up until it becomes what I hoped it would become: a line of trees. The trees are safety. A lot of good hiding places in the trees.

Behind us, somebody yells: 'Fan out, fan out. Don't stop. They're still out there. Don't let them get to the forest.'

Moonlight leaks into the meadow. For a moment, just like the shooter, we are brightly illuminated. Another crack. My shoulder jerks with a fleshy thump. The fizz of a bullet. The world is suddenly spinning around me. The tops of the trees are like circling birds coming down and down in a narrowing arc. I can't hold my legs up. They are floundering as if I was kicking in deep water.

I feel Martha's weight, balancing me. Not now, just inches from safety.

'Where was he hit? Anyone see where he was hit?'

Through gritted teeth I roar at Martha, push her forward and we plunge into the forest. It's just one tree after another, striding up to us out of the dark. My shoulder is the epicentre for wave after wave of pain. Pain that's here now and pain that's coming.

Swift flowing water somewhere out ahead of us. Gurgling over rocks. It keeps me up and moving. Something to reach for. Martha has her arm through the crook of my elbow. She steadies me, holds me up.

After what seems like an age, bent double and stumbling along, we find ourselves on the bank of a river and the rush of the water smothers every other sound. We wade in, struggle to find our feet on the rocky bed and we push downstream and that's when the last of my fragile consciousness starts to give way, folding softly inwards as if it had gotten wet. I fall into Martha's arms and feel her body stagger under my weight. Feel the water on my shoulder, already dousing the fire there, soothing and cool.

Later, I come to my senses briefly and discover that we are in a reed bed, still in the water but hidden and out of the current and peaceful. A scattering of stars show through a hole in the forest canopy.

Our Saviours will come for us out of those stars, one day soon. Maybe it's the cool of the water or the tranquillity that has settled inside me, but I'm thinking that they might well smile on me after all, and take me with them, up into those endless points of light, to Thule.

15

There's no pain as long as I don't move. When we were still in the river, as close to the bank as we dared go, she dug my knife – it must have been my knife – deep into my shoulder and fished the bullet out. The blade rooted around in amongst the muscles for a long time, and when it connected with the metal embedded under the collar bone, it twisted and coaxed and twisted. I heard myself scream, but as if it wasn't me there, in the mud, but some animal instead, howling like the pigs we used to kill in the Four Walls. Martha's face was upside down over mine, whispering things I didn't understand but knew, by their softness, were words of comfort.

It's over now. My shoulder is a rigid, throbbing pulse. The crowns of the trees above me, unimaginably high, nod in the wind.

We have been in the sun all afternoon with the smell of damp things drying. I am aware of her presence nearby only through faint sounds: the scratch of the tinder box, the muted fizz of sparks on damp kindling.

I catch a smell in the limpid air of the clearing: roasting meat. Fat crackles in the wood smoke. Saliva rises in my mouth, making me aware of the bloated shape of my tongue, packed in behind my teeth like a fist. With my tongue like this, a bulging tumour, all I can do is grunt. Enough to get her to look up at me.

'You have a fever,' she says. 'Only water for you.'

When I crane my neck around – as far as it will go without hurting my shoulder – I can see her parcelling out meat from a duck carcass. She works quickly and neatly, spearing the chunks onto sticks and propping them over the fire.

I grunt again, or maybe it's a groan. She sighs, shakes her head and comes over to me with the water sack. I turn my head away.

'Drink,' she says.

She presses the sack to my lips, while I keep them tightly shut and after a few attempts to squeeze some water over closed teeth she gives up and goes back to the fire. I can turn my eyes away, but I have to listen while she tears up the meat and gulps it down.

Sometime in the night she brings a handful of maggots, squirming between her fingers and packs them like mud into my shoulder. I feel them dig and wriggle their way in. She says something about maggots being hard to find when you need them. They are busy all night eating the dead flesh.

Later my body shakes violently, like someone has taken a sack full of bones by the opening and just swung it around.

Her long fingered hand touches a wet cloth against my cheeks and my forehead. Sometimes the fingers run over my inked head and glide gently over my scalp, sending a tingle of warmth across my skull, down my spine.

By morning I can speak again, my throat has cleared, my tongue has returned to its natural size, and I call her by her name, Martha, only she tells me that is not her name. She is Ulya.

She talks a lot, this Ulya. She has an accent, which I'm sure is Rus. Ulya Moiseyev. That is her real name.

'Practice,' she says. 'It will help you.'

She tells me that in the time of the bio bombs, her people lived in the Ukraine. She doesn't remember the place, but she had a picture of it in a box that was lost when she was taken by the slavers. The town they came from was on a river called the 'N-e-e-p-e-r'. She makes me say it over and over, even when I tell her I've had enough and she should leave me alone.

N-e-e-p-e-r

The river is easy enough, but the name of the town is a mouthful.

N-e-e-p-r-o-d-z-e-r-j-i-n-s-k

I'm pretty pleased when I get the whole thing.

N-e-e-p-r-o-d-z-e-r-j-i-n-s-k

'You can sleep soon,' she says. 'You are doing better.'

Ulya had a little sister and an older brother – her name was Lara, and the brother, Alexei. Alexei is big, a brute, and he hits her, but also brings her presents: the best cuts from the things he has hunted; a toy he has fashioned from a plug of amber he has hardened in a kiln. It's a bird, apparently, though by the look of it Alexei has never seen one.

Lara is just small. A nothing. She totters around on unsteady legs.

Papa and Mama are quiet people. They scratch out lives in poor soil, keeping their heads down. This is hostile country. Their only defence is their isolation.

'I remember when we crossed the ice, out of Russia,' she says in that halting, accented voice. 'I thought everybody in the world was there. Everywhere you looked, people, families. Just walking and walking and walking in the white empty land, with no hills, nothing. So many lost in the hard walking and the cold. Every time we left a camp and a fire, there was somebody who didn't wake up. I saw a woman frozen and dead in the snow. She had a blanket in her arms and out of the top you could see a baby's head. It was bright blue. I remember thinking that if I hit it, just gently, with a spoon, would the head break open like an egg? Such a thing to think, but I couldn't help it. I was small then.'

'Valentina led us over the ice,' she says. 'Valentina Klamenko. Everyone followed her. We say her name in our prayers now. If it wasn't for her we would be dead long ago from the gas bombs or the bio bombs. We would be little lumps of ash in the ash cities.'

I imagine those cities when she describes them. Great mounds of ash, hundreds of feet high. The whites of the piled-up bones. I don't know if that is what they were really like, but that's how I see them.

Valentina is their saint, a special woman. She never wavered. So unlike me. She promised them a new land, with green meadows and cattle, and that is what she gave them, only she never stepped foot in it herself.

'They brought her body down,' she says, 'into the valley, on a bed of sticks. Ten men and women holding it up. Everyone in a line along the road with their hats in their hands. Her skin was white, and it had a shine or a glow like ice. I thought she looked happy,' she says, lost in the memory. 'She had finished her work. She had done it.

'And it was mostly good, up in the North, where I grew up. There was nothing to eat in winter, but it was quiet. We were far away from towns or cities, and they left us alone.'

She's dabbing at my wounded shoulder, and then she's removing the maggots with her fingertips and dropping them to the ground.

'There is new blood,' she says. 'That means they finished the bad flesh and they are starting to eat the good.'

I'd like her story to end in the fields where they built their mud and wooden homes and kept their animals. But Ulya presses on as though she cannot hold it back now.

'The night the slavers came,' she says, her voice quieter, more distant. She has turned her face away from me. 'It was black, dark, and there was no warning. I could hear shouting in the town and there were lights outside the windows. Torches. Fire. Sparks flying up over our roof.

'Papa got me up. Got everyone up. The strangers were in the streets making a lot of noise, banging sticks on the doors and the cart wheels to make panic, like we were rabbits and they wanted to scare us out of the grass. Papa pushed us out a back way, across a meadow. Only these men had the town in a net, and they came out of the forest all around us, with spears and guns. Mama fell on her knees. She screamed for help. She held Lara. They took her by the hair. They lifted her like that and dragged her while she screamed.

'Everyone was locked up into big carts with bars, or nearly everyone. Not the old ones. There weren't so many, you know, who got over the ice. After all that, after surviving the ice, that's what they got. The men killed them right there in the village. They didn't scream or call out. I saw it from the cart, and I couldn't even cry. I just sat and watched. After that, I prayed to Valentina to come and save us again, but Valentina was dead in the ground and she wouldn't come to us. Not until the Last Days, and then only beside the Lord, to help him pick out the good ones and take them to Heaven.'

Who is this Lord? Ulya doesn't say.

'We went a long time on that road. Mama held Lara tight, because Lara cried a lot. She had been sick before, and now she was worse.

Mama hid her under her coat, stroking her head and trying to keep her quiet until the crying stopped. For a long time after, Lara didn't make any sound. Then some time, some morning, in the middle of nowhere, the slavers came to our cart and took Lara from Mama and they carried her body out into the forest. When they came back, they just got on their horses. We went on. Nobody said anything. Mama didn't speak.'

Ulya stops again. I can hear her breathing. We stay quiet for a while, the clouds easing overhead, the fire sputtering and sighing. Finally, she finds whatever it is she needs to continue.

'I can't, won't believe she is still lying there on the forest ground, alone. All naked. I don't know, maybe an angel came and took her straight up to Heaven. Or maybe it was Valentina, come to see where everybody was gone, and just found her there. I like to think Valentina has her in her arms. That she just has her.

'At some dark and dirty town, they split us up. Mama and Papa and Alexei went east. I heard the name New Brazil. Alexei ran up to me and he put his necklace in my hand and held me. The slavers pulled him back. I beat at them as hard as I could with my fists. Tried to bite them. It was no good. Alexei's face was gone in the crowd and I never saw him again.

'Now I can't remember if he was blonde or dark; short or tall. When this is all over, and you are better, I will go and find him in New Brazil.'

She stops, maybe to see what effect her words have on me, but I really don't have the strength to do anything but listen. She goes on.

'The rest of us they took for many days into the mountains. An empty place. High and cold. And then one night men came out of the forest with mud on their faces and attacked us. I woke up in the cart and heard the screaming. The attackers were quiet though. Their knives made a soft noise in the dark, like a bird flying. It was the True Path. The slavers didn't last two minutes. They sliced them to bits. Dropped their bodies in a ditch.

'They didn't try to rob anything. They didn't search their pockets. They only wanted the slaves, like me. They made us stand up in a line at the side of the road. We were cold and shaking, and we knew that they would kill us like that, and we would go into the ditch with the others. We were just waiting for it. The True Path captain marched up and down in front of us. His face was black with the mud and he was all in black leather, so we could hardly see him, and he asked all of us (his Rus was not very good), if we would come and live in his Colony. I didn't understand what this was about. I could only think about the cold and if the knife would hurt when he stuck it into me. I just tried to be ready and not to be afraid. When he looked into my eyes, I nodded my head. Others said yes out loud. Only one said no. Koshkin, the son of the priest. So, they left Miroslav Koshkin there in that nowhere place and the rest of us went for a long walk to the Colony. Ten days. Maybe more.

'One night, I went to touch the necklace Alexie gave me and it was gone. I was so angry. I shouted at them. I think I punched one. I wanted it back. I asked them who stole it. The True Path soldiers laughed and told me to be quiet. "You don't need necklaces or shiny little things where you are going," they said.'

Ulya gives the True Path warriors this silly, heavy voice like they are talking with their chests stuck out. It makes me smile.

'"You must forget everything in the past, and you must take a new name, for this new life ahead of you." I shouted at them. I tried to kick them. All they did was grin, and they called me Martha. "Your life will bring you glory, in the service of great men," they said. "If you work hard and behave with honour you could be a Citizen: a safe life. Protected." I don't know what I thought about this. I spoke the words they told me to, the oath. I was still waiting for the knife in my neck.

'I watched these men, with the dark, muddy faces. The way they worked on their knives with leather straps around the fire. They hardly talked. Their faces were all the same. The ink. It was like they followed a God who hated them. The bread they made on the hot stones tasted like dirt or old skin. But the strangest thing was those Messages. I had never heard anything like them before.

Cut away your bonds,

Put aside your history.

Those things will die in the fire.

'They told me I had to forget Rus, that it was no use to me anymore. Part of the dead world. I had to learn English, like the Elect, but the best language of all was silence.' She laughs at that. A cheerless laugh that makes me think of the men she described, stropping their blades by the fire.

'So, I didn't talk anymore. I spoke Rus with the divvies in the dorm at night. Whispered it. Just to remember. Not to lose the words. I didn't really care though, if I forgot all my words – Elect and Rus – and never spoke again.'

This Ulya is doing a lot of talking for someone who doesn't want to speak.

Me, I feel like I don't know anything about the world at all. As if I've only just been born. Lying on the forest floor, naked, like little Lara, watching the clouds make their steady way across the sky.

16

That sweet numbness doesn't last long. Dawn seeps into the clearing and with the dim light come cold, sickening thoughts.

My men: Con. Sully, Ash, Theo. All dead.

My ears still ring with the blast that killed them. My chest is tight. My shoulder stinks. With my waking eyes I can see Theo calling out my name, his body skewered by the gunshot. As each memory returns I actually feel my cheeks getting hot. I remember who I am now and what I've done.

And she, this chattering divvy, could have left me to die in the forest and I'd be at peace. But she didn't. She nursed me with all her skill and because of that I have to face whatever the day brings. Maybe this is her plan all along. To raise the dead just enough to be her slave. Be nothing. Punishment for all her years in the Colony.

I pull myself up against the trunk of a tree. Just that simple effort causes a violent spasm. The pain yanks its wires through my shoulder all the way down to my groin. This is a shock. I thought I was closer to getting better.

When she returns, she has a pile of dry wood in her arms. She sees me and runs over to me and tries to take my arm. I swat her away.

'Get off me,' I say. She looks hurt. 'Get the hell away from me.' The skin at my shoulder is at tearing point. 'What did you do? Why didn't you leave me?'

She watches me as I come away from the tree, feeling queasy still but the anger is carrying me and soon I'm stomping around shouting I don't know what. It's the pain, as much as anything, that's doing the talking.

'They would have found me here and taken me back to the Colony. As far as they knew, I would have been a hero. I was killed in action. They would have laid my body out in the council chamber and made speeches about me.'

'Speeches?' she says, her head cocked to one side. Yes, it's true. My divvy is actually talking to me. It wasn't a dream. Martha can speak. Boy, can she speak. 'You must sit. Your shoulder -,' she says.

In my blind fury, my only plan of action is to stamp all over the fire she has just recently lit until the flames are gone. Then I kick the sticks and ash all around the clearing. I'm watching myself do all this from some distant place where I am no longer connected with my body. It's not the first time I've felt this way.

She gazes at me without any sign of shock or fright, her head still to one side, like she's trying to find an angle from where my behaviour makes sense.

'You want to be dead?'

'Better dead than alive like this.'

'You don't mean that.'

I stop kicking. What is the point in arguing this with her? What does she know? If I could talk to anyone right now, it would be Joel, but he's back there in the Colony, with all the respect of his people. Is he worried about me? Does he sit at his fire at night and wonder if I will rise? Or does he think I've already made it? His model Initiate. The General's man.

'Why don't you just shut the hell up and do like you're told,' I say and because she doesn't react or at least back away from me, I add, with as much acid in my voice as I can muster – 'Martha.'

She drops her head. I hit the bullseye. She mutters something under her breath. I think it's that name she called herself by when I was in no state to argue – *Ulya*.

I sneer. 'You were given a name. Is it not good enough for you?'

'Yes, sir,' she says.

'What's that? What did I hear you say?'

'Yes, sir.'

'What is your name then?'

She takes her time answering. There's a small movement of muscle under her left ear. Her lips squeeze together. When she says, 'Martha,' her voice is submissive, just like it should be, but the tiniest flicker crosses her eyes before she can turn them away, like a spark thrown from a horseshoe when it hits a stone. Her face is such a mask that the smallest change betrays her. It's not even a rebellious look she gave me, it's just the hint of a look. That there might be a look.

'I will go and find food,' she says. She wants to get away. I notice, for the first time, that she is not really bald anymore. Her head is padded in blonde stubble sticking out of the dark tattooed scalp like barley cut down to the soil at harvest time.

'I'll get the food,' I say.

At that moment, both of us turn our attention to the same thing: the ruined fire I'm standing on. There are broken sticks strewn all around me, the glowing embers peeping from under my feet. The energy that it took to act out my temper tantrum has left me drained and light-headed.

The smoke is getting in my eyes and I should move out of the way but I'm not moving; not while she's here. We both know I'm not going hunting anytime soon.

Ulya cuts a very different figure. She has Stella sheathed snugly at her belt and it looks like she belongs there. She's been using my knife for a while and probably doing quite well looking after both of us while I was in the full heat of the fever.

Now that I'm awake it's going to be more difficult for her, but she is patient. She is waiting for me to see sense, to sit down and let her tend to things, and she is probably trying to determine just how much trouble I will be.

I can't see Martha anymore, past this new girl, this Ulya. I try to remember the divvy that used to shadow me in the colony. An extra limb that moved to my every thought. This new girl has stepped between us. She won't get out of the way.

'How long have I been out?'

This stranger, Ulya, looks at the sun. 'Six days,' she says.

It's done then. My men are dead. There's no going back. Everything that I was and everything I was going to be are distant memories.

My legs start to tremble. They won't hold me anymore. She has to go. I don't want her to see me fall.

'Go find something to eat then,' I say.

She turns on her heel immediately, as if she had been waiting for the order. As she leaves, I notice a slight limp that she is trying to hide. I remember how she kept running when she was in pain and with a saddlebag and the water skin. She got me to the river. I even remember how she held tightly to me in the dark and cold of the water and spoke softly into my ear, for how long? For hours? For a day? She dragged my limp body up the bank. Either I really felt or just dreamed her hands hooked under my armpits and the staggered moans of her struggle. From there she somehow got me on my feet and she brought me here.

I touch my shoulder through the bandage, where the skin has folded in on itself and darkened like a rotten apple. It is still wet with puss. She didn't have the cream that she put on Sully's wound but she has found plants in the forest that have helped with the infection. The bandage was made from the sleeve of her own shirt.

17

It's hot. I sit up in the clearing or in some place like it and see the sun, a white squint above the trees, and I know instantly, I feel it, a wrongness, a change in the air.

I look down at my arm, where the hairs all the way from my wrist to my shoulder singe and curl, the skin reddens and swells and dissolves before my eyes. My finger bones emerge from under the streaming flesh.

I hear my own voice, disembodied, thin and whining. I stop, listen to it, and it wakes me. The moment I open my eyes I realise I have screamed out loud. A real scream that could be heard for quite a distance. Ulya would have heard it. If a party from the Colony has come looking for us yet, then they would have heard it too.

It was the infection. I'm not in my right mind. I scramble up. Bleary eyed. She's still not back and it's near dark. I'm hungry. The dream has done one good thing, it's reminded me of the danger we are in. We shouldn't have been out and open to the sky like that for so many days with the risk of a sunburst. It is just tempting fate. So I take matters into my own hands – about time – and gather up some of the firewood I've scattered all over the clearing and the backpack she has left and the tinderbox. I take it all into the cover of the trees, thinking to myself how much better I am already to be able to walk around like this and what is a bit of pain to a True Path Initiate?

As soon as I bend down to light a new fire though, the weakness and pain hollow me out again and I have to sit down before I faint.

Still, she'll be impressed when she comes back. I've been helpful, and I'm taking charge of things, which she'll probably find is a big relief. You could see the stress she was under, having to make all the decisions. I imagine her coming back with maybe a rabbit or two that she's caught with her snares and she'll see what I've done and put the rabbits down in front of me and thank me and then I'll say that she's been good and she'll be rewarded.

She's got another thing coming, though, if she thinks she can just run off, as soon as I'm better, and try and find her own family. Her duty is to the True Path. To me. She took an oath the day she joined the Colony.

When she finally returns, instead of the two rabbits I had been hoping for, she has a small duck by the neck, its dripping blood leaving a trail of spots behind her. Careless: those men could still be close by. She has the bulging water sack looped over her shoulder. I force myself up to my feet. The duck's eyes are wide open, like it's surprised to find itself caught.

She stops at the clearing before she notices where I am. I don't see the look of relief and gratitude I expected. Instead, she quietly appraises the pile of sticks I've assembled in a space just about wide enough for us both to sit. There aren't very many sticks or branches on the fire. I can see that now. It had seemed a lot more impressive when I gathered them up.

'The sun,' I say. It would be better if she just laughed. 'We could have burned out there. You should have thought about the sun.'

She looks at me. Those lips tighten again. That's all I get as a reply. Soundlessly she lays down the water sack and scours the clearing, picking up the rest of the firewood and loading it up in front of me. When she has everything gathered, she squeezes between a tree trunk and the wood pile and crouches down and takes the tinder box and scrapes out sparks that leap onto the kindling, setting it instantly alight.

She gives me a weak, self-conscious smile. 'Sit,' she says. 'Rest.'

She likes taking care of me, this Rus divvy. Thinks she can go off for a while into the forest and come back to find me tamed. I don't sit. I guess the duck must have come from the river where we hid from the gunmen. Her stories come back to me, about her home in the North and the crossing of the straits. She is my age and yet her stories seem ancient.

As she stokes the fire she starts to hum and then to sing. I can't really hear words, only that there are words, in her Rus language. It takes me back to the Colony, to hear it, crossing the yard to the mess hall at mealtime. The sound of the divvies singing in their dorm, sometimes all of them, more often just one or two, their voices in the still air. The Rus words. It was often part of the gentle easing of sundown. The day done, the air cool and loosening. It made me wonder what they were singing about. It makes me wonder now.

'What is that song?' I say, after a while.

'It's an old one. From my town.'

'What is it about?'

'Oh,' she says, turning dreamy. She laughs. She sings again, pronouncing the words more clearly, while the duck loses his feathers with alarming speed. She uses my knife to slit the carcass open and, tucking her fingers under the flaps of skin, scoops out the organs and the guts and loops the cords of meat over the fire.

'What is the song about?' I say again.

'Murad and Sophia,' she says.

'Who?'

'It's a silly story,' she says. 'Long time ago. It's not a Ukraine song, it's a song from America, but my people sing it in Rus.' She avoids my gaze. Her smile has gone.

'Who were they?' I say.

'I don't know,' she says.

This is the longest conversation I've ever had with her. I want it to continue. Like the entrails puddling beside her on the forest floor I want to draw the words out. Everything that is in her head, that was locked away there all this time when I had no idea she could speak at all. 'But the song is about something, right? It's a story.'

'Yes.'

'So what does it say?'

Ulya's eyes are deep in their sockets and heavy lidded. Even when she grins it is hard to tell if she is mischievous, or afraid. She keeps working with the knife, dicing the meat.

'Sophia loved Murad, from when they were children and when they took him away she spent many years looking for him. She went all around America and many bad things happened but she didn't die. Men tried to kill her; take her to bad places. She was not afraid, because she thought she would find her lover again. Then, in the end of the story, she finds him,' she says.

'Who took him? Where was he taken?'

'To a special place. He had a mark on his neck and because of that he was special. So they took him to be with the other people who have this mark, and the girl couldn't come. She had to stay at home.'

'I don't understand'

'It's not what I say, it's just a song.'

'Say what?' I have to keep the impatience out of my voice. She will find a way, with all her divvy cunning, to avoid telling me this story if it is going to put her in danger. 'Ulya,' I say. 'Tell me.'

'It's just an old song.'

'I know, but say it anyway.'

'Murad had mark on his neck. They call it Jacob's Ladder. That meant he was going to Thule. In Rus we call this person a *sechnick*. Sophia couldn't go to Thule because she didn't have Jacob's Ladder. She cries and cries because of this. Her lover going away to another planet and not her.' Ulya gives a weak laugh.

'Jacob's Ladder – I heard that name. The man – ,' I touch the back of my neck. I had forgotten the spike that woman jabbed me with that night. 'You're making no sense to me, what mark are you talking about?'

'Jacob's Ladder. It is the sign that you are ready to go.'

'That's ridiculous. What sign? When the Fifth Message comes the Saviours will choose the strongest and the fittest to go to Thule.'

'I know. It's an old song.'

I think about this a while. I am not Theo. I'm not going to open my ears to every story from beyond the valley. 'They only had one or two of the Messages at that time, so they didn't know about the test,' I say, softening my tone. 'They didn't really understand the whole truth, about how to prepare and how people would be chosen.'

'No,' she says, looking relieved. Her shoulders sag just a fraction. I hadn't even noticed how tense she was.

'It's funny though, that they believed there was a mark.'

'Yes,' she says, a little too quickly for my liking.

'So the people who had this mark, the Ladder, went to this place?'

She nods.

'Seems like they didn't get it, in the Time Before. They didn't get it at all. What happened to them? To Sophia and Murad?'

'It's sad,' she says.

'Why?'

'They died. Sophia killed him and then she killed herself.'

'Why the hell did she do that?'

'Because she didn't want him to go to Thule.'

'That's crazy.'

'Yes.'

'People are stupid.'

'Yes.'

'That's a stupid song.'

She doesn't say anything to that. The scent of roasting meat has entered our cramped corner of the forest. My stomach is beginning to recognise that it is empty.

'What else did people believe back then, about Thule and the Messages?'

'I don't know,' she says. 'This is an American song, not Ukraine. We don't tell stories about these people long ago. We learned this song when we came here.'

'Didn't they understand anything though? It's so simple – *There will be five Messages of which this is the first.* How hard is that?'

'Three messages,' I think she says, in such a tiny voice I have to lean uncomfortably close to the fire to hear it.

'What did you say?'

'They said only three messages. Not five. True Path say five. Ukraine, America, Turk, Rus, they say three.'

'There will be three messages of which this is the first?'

'Yes.'

'That's a lie. That's not what the message said. Why would they change the message?'

Ulya removes a lump of meat from the fire and examines it, before setting it on the heat again, a little higher than it was.

'Well, that world and those people aren't around anymore so it doesn't really matter what they believed,' I say. 'They're all gone.'

'What about that woman?' says Ulya. I look across to her and catch the tail of a glance, more insolent than a divvy in the Colony would usually risk.

The mention of my Bind, Vanesa, startles me. I had almost forgotten about her as well. My mind had somehow pinched her out. I haven't really begun to piece together what I saw and heard in that hideout and those men with the guns.

'Sure,' I say. 'There are plenty of people left, scattered around, especially in faraway places where they could keep out of trouble, like the villages. Not cities, though, and not Esperanza. Esperanza fell. So whatever's there, it's not a city.'

'Maybe they built it again.'

I rub my forehead. Now it's my turn to sigh. 'I'm sorry, Ulya. I really am. But that world is dead, outside the valley: Esperanza, New Brazil, all of it. What's left is not worth saving. What matters is the future of mankind on Thule, and only the True Path are ready for that. It's a hard reality, but it's the only one.'

For the first time in my life, these words sound strange in my own ears. I'm not really able to make them sound like they should sound; like they've always sounded to me.

'I don't expect you to fully understand,' I say. 'You're just a divvy after all.'

'Okay,' she says.

Now I really want to hit her. 'If you went out of the valley, you'd see,' I say. 'There's nothing left.'

She goes quiet for a long time. The meat sizzles and the smell is intoxicating. My dry mouth craves it. Which is a sign that I'm healing. She gets the water skin and empties some into our one remaining utensil, a tin cup, and sets it on the fire to boil.

'Where are you going to go now?' she says.

'I don't know. I can't go back to the Colony,' the moment I say this, I realise it's true. Even if I did return and managed to pretend, somehow, that I had Risen, and they couldn't see through my lie, they would still be able to see that I had one.

'I've got to find those men,' I say, doing my best to sound like a leader again. 'And kill them.'

Ulya says nothing to that. Her eyes narrow in the firelight.

'What's wrong?' I say.

She shakes her head.

'I have to regain my honour, somehow. I can't go back and those men are still out there.'

'With guns,' she says.

'Yes, sure, with guns. If I die, at least I die doing something.'

'It doesn't matter to them. If they shoot you.'

'No, but I won't let them. At least, maybe, I can take one or two with me.'

Ulya draws one of the sticks away from the fire and carefully prods the sizzling meat off the end. She juggles it, on her fingertips, over to a stone and rests it there, steaming in the cold evening air. I notice the way she hangs her head to one side when she is busy. Even this thoughtless gesture, has something in it. She's working on me somehow. The General warned me about women and how they can dominate even a strong man. She controls the food supply. The fire. What if she is controlling my infected wound? Treating it, but not letting it heal?

She scoops up the meat when it cools. At first she makes no move to pass it over to me and I actually think she is going to take the first bite. She is staring at it greedily.

'Martha,' I say.

'You need to be careful,' she says. 'You have fever and you haven't eaten for many days.'

'Ulya,' I say. I will give her that. I'll give her the name she wants, but she must give everything else back to me: My food, my strength, my position as captain in this shrunken, pathetic squad.

She lets the meat cool a little more and then she tears the pieces into smaller chunks and edges around the fire and passes them to me. she is Martha again, nimble and efficient. She goes back to her place and sits down and watches without comment while I pop the pieces into my mouth and feel the hot juices on my tongue. There's a moment of pain as each one slips through my throat, but oh they are good when they reach my stomach. She comes again, a few minutes later, with more meat and the boiled water.

'You don't think it's a good plan, do you?' I say, after I have finished my portion. 'To go after those men.'

She doesn't reply.

'You can speak your mind,' I say. 'Do you think it's a good idea?'

'No,' she says.

'What do you think I should do? Lie here and die? Go off with you to New Brazil?'

'No,' she says. 'But that would be nice, if you did.'

'Well, I'm not going to.'

'No.'

'So what then?'

She prods at the spiky new growth on her head with the palm of her hand. 'I think you must go to Esperanza,' she says. 'Because they called everybody and they told you to come.'

18

In the night I wake suddenly. There are fingers at my throat.

Before she can react I have the knife out of the sheath at her belt and I grab her and fold her to the ground just inches from the flaring embers of our dead fire. She goes snared-rabbit-still. I raise my fist. It's then I notice that my shirt is pulled up over my shoulder and my bandage open.

'What the hell were you doing?'

She blinks. A marmot whistles into the darkness. A cold wind, a northerly, gibbers in the tree canopy above us.

'You had pain,' she says. 'You were screaming.'

'No.'

'Yes.'

'No.'

'Okay.'

Her small eyes peer up at me, trying to make me out. She could be a tiny forest creature: a hedgehog or a chipmunk. I shove her away and slump down. She waits a moment and then makes her way back to me on her hands and knees, to finish what she was doing. I let her. No more protests. She rewinds the bandage and takes a few chunks remaining from our dinner and pushes them into my mouth and follows that with another cup of water. Has she eaten yet? I didn't see her take anything.

'Is it painful?' she says.

Let me die, I want to say.

I try to find some tiny indication of what she's thinking in that unreadable face. Several fathoms down, below those cautious divvy eyes, certain feelings are kept just off the boil. One of them, I'm sure, is contempt.

'I had to kill her,' I say.

'Who?'

'That woman, Vanesa. It's what had to be done.'

'Oh,' she says. She finishes with the bandages and helps me pull my shirt back on.

'You gave me a look, I saw it.'

'What look?'

'Don't pretend you didn't give me a look.'

In the dark there is no way to see if she is tense or relaxed. Not that it matters. It's time to have this out.

'Maybe you didn't want to kill this woman,' she says.

'I didn't have to want it. I just had to do it, and you stopped me.'

'I'm sorry,' she says.

'Why?' I don't hear any sincerity in the apology. 'Why did you do it?' I hiss.

'I'm sorry.'

'I would have slit her throat. I wasn't scared.'

'Yes.'

I'm about to reach out and grab her and try and shake some meaningful answer out of her when she does something that takes me completely by surprise. She slips her hand under my shirt and up over my heart and presses it against my breastbone.

'You must not die, Leon,' she says. She uses my name. I'm about to say something but don't. If I mention it I will acknowledge her cheek, or her bravery.

Her hand is cold. When she takes it away again, she puts her left hand briefly on my cheek, before she slips off once again to her side of our smouldering fire.

I don't know how long I sit there, absorbing what she's done and the line she's crossed. She curls right up and goes off to sleep as if nothing has just occurred between us. In the Colony, she would lose her place as a divvy for this, banished to the kitchens, or exiled to the Citizen's village, a servant to some low family. But we're not in the Colony and I'm not Risen, and so those rules don't apply any more. Out here, apparently, a divvy can think about eating first, dole out rations as she sees fit. Even touch her superior without permission.

19

If only General Hilles could see me now. Talking away to a divvy. *A divvy*. Asking for her opinion on my plans. Letting her decide when and how much I eat. And when she looks at my wound again she tut tuts and says, 'Oh Leon'. She's very good at this; it seems quite natural to her to take charge of things.

Sit up. Let me look.

Keep the pressure on it. Keep it clean.

Walk around. Clear your head.

Lie down.

Sit up.

Drink this.

Eat. Why don't you?

She'll mutter darkly one minute, drop right into a soothing voice the next and then dish out the silent treatment, her favourite because she knows I hate it. I have discovered that trying to find the right words is like stepping around a field full of clickers. She prods her fingers around the uneven, frowning edges of the wound and she asks me if it hurts. And it does, but as long as I have that pain, other nasty things, crowding around the edges of my thoughts and dreams, have no way in.

The fever has come and gone and the infection lingers, but really Ulya has done her best to control it with what she has found in the forest.

What she has achieved is a minor miracle. At dawn on the third day, I feel strong enough to walk.

'It's time,' I say.

'Maybe one more day.'

'No more days.'

I won't let her prop me up. I'd rather be slow than held by a divvy, though the pace is maddening. Those men are on horses and they have days on us, while I grope, Sully-like from one type of pain to another. We head for the highest ground we can see, a bare, black hill that was visible from the house where I lost my men, but though it seems close, no more than a couple of miles, we go the whole morning without getting much nearer.

'What do you think those men want?' she says, waiting patiently while I take one of my rests.

'The gunmen?' I say breathing hard. A vein pulsing in my head.

'Yes.'

'They wanted my Bind. For what I don't know.'

'For the message. What the man in the box said. The good news.'

'He was trying to save my Bind. He would have said anything.'

She looks unconvinced. Her hands on her hips, like she's annoyed at me for another of her many unfathomable reasons. Then her eyes narrow and she jerks around. She has heard something.

'What is it?'

She goes rigid and watchful. Her responses are so sudden; so instinctive, it wouldn't surprise me to see her ears pricking up. I strain to hear what she's hearing over my own laboured breathing. The ground to our right falls away steeply into a grid of pines wrapped in thick skirts of undergrowth. The more I stare into it, the more the gloom in amongst the trees seems to ripple with darting, silent movement. Ulya and I try to separate distinct shapes from the shadows, but it is only when I turn to leave that Ulya draws my attention to a pair of long, pointy ears poking out above a clump of wild holly.

'Forest dogs,' she says.

'Probably.'

I'm not scared of these animals. I know they will not attack anything that shows a willingness to fight back. And yet, I'm carrying a wound and they can smell it. Just how hungry are they? They could come at night and make off with Ulya.

Theo said they were tame once and used to live in people's houses and those people combed their hair and treated them like they were their children. If that was ever true, it's not true now. These night stalkers are the valley's predators.

The longer they shadow us, the less shy they become. When I take my breaks and sit down, Ulya goes back along the trail to see where they are and they are quite happy to stand out amongst the trees and let her look at them. There is a tall one, the one with the ears and a small, stocky thing, with a jaw as wide as the lintel on the council chamber door. All of them have a similar, mottled, mostly rust coloured hide with the same, blank, indifferent eyes but the traces of the animals they once were are still visible, in the funny mix of sizes, shapes and body parts.

We are hungry. They are hungry. It's a question of who eats first. I have to admire them a bit. They are creatures of pure and simple purpose.

They have no dens in the forest or the rocks. They are always on the their feet in the wilderness, endlessly alert, following scent trails, with one eye on the weather.

They are our only followers. Ulya has done lookout duty a few times along the way, climbing up into the most scalable trees. She has spotted no smoke and no sign of movement. The True Path won't go looking for us for a couple of days yet. If those gunmen are around, they could be avoiding fires, keeping to dense cover, but why would they bother? If they wanted to take me they could do it. Whether I saw them coming or not.

A day and a half out from our first camp, we hit a cut in the forest that goes due west. It is the remains of some ancient way, mostly meadow grass and bindweed and kudzu now, eating through the last chunks of concrete, and trees that have straggled out into the open to break its neat, engineered lines. A giant metal hulk is rusting at the side of the road, now home to a young chestnut tree that has pushed its limbs through holes in the roof.

Ulya and I decide to rest here for an hour once we find a suitable place for a fire. We follow the old route through the cut.

Some distance on we find a few sets of prints in the dirt. It looks like five or six horses, along with the twin drag marks left by something heavy they were pulling behind them. From the dry state of the horseshit scattered close to the prints, I figure they are two, maybe three days gone.

This is my last failure. I have only my divvy left and I am not going to catch these men. Wherever they are headed, they don't have to worry about us. I slump down beside the hoof prints and there I sit until the sun goes down, my head on my knees.

The world can come and go.

I wait for some choice words from Ulya, either hard or comforting, but nothing is said. Instead she combs the edges of the road for wood and starts a new fire. We have nothing to eat. We need to hunt. Those dogs will have us if we don't keep our strength up.

She approaches me, while I'm still in this vegetable state, and puts her hand on my head. This is her way of trying to help me, but it's a mistake. I snatch it up in a firm grip and shove it at her own face.

'What the hell do you want?' I'm half up off the ground without even thinking. A rapid, sturdy twist would snap a femur cleanly or badly, splintering the bone into fragments. Then she would know who I am.

She doesn't react. Stays still. Instead, she concentrates hard on the ground at her feet, showing me only the dark spot of Thule, furred with new hair, on the top of her head, like she always did when she was a proper, well-behaved, divvy.

'Do you want this? Do you want me to feed you to those curs?'

Ulya leaves her arm in my hand like an offering. All that bone weariness that had me consumed and beaten a moment ago has simply vanished, like it has been slaked clean. At last, she has got me moving again.

I use the side of my hand to jam her sleeve up so I can get a better grip. As I do that, my own sleeve slips back from my wrist, revealing a weird discolouration in my skin. It makes me think of that nightmare – my hand melting in front of my eyes. Only this is worse. My arm has gone an unnatural shade of white and my tattoos have simply vanished.

Ulya gasps. I'm too stunned to speak. I let go of her and she takes my arm immediately and examines it. The white growth is up to my elbow and possibly further. There's a slight smell from it, not like the reek from the shoulder wound. It is different, a disease I've picked up in the past few hours. A Sat worm. Something.

'Get away from me.' I shove her back. She is surprised but not horrified by this the way I am. 'It could be contagious.'

I've never seen an infection like this. It must be a Sat worm. Once you have one of those inside you there is nothing but a bad death ahead. I've heard the stories. The white skin glistens horribly. It's like a living thing has been grafted on to me. There are Sat worm eggs swimming through my bloodstream now, just looking for a place to settle: my stomach, my brain. Tiny hatchling maggots about to burst out all over me.

Ulya tries to approach. I back away, holding out my hand. 'Don't be stupid,' I say. 'This is it.'

I look pointedly at the knife at her belt. She notices, but shakes her head. 'You're not dying,' she says.

'You can't know that.'

'I do. It's not your wound. It's Thule.'

'Thule?'

'You're marked. Like Murad. You are one of them. A sechnik.'

Sechnik.

I look at my altered skin. It does appear strangely undamaged. There is nothing organic or rotten or sweet about the smell. It is faintly metallic.

'You are not going to die,' she says again. 'You are going to change and then you can't hide what you are anymore.'

'What am I?'

'You are one of them.'

She's not scared of it. She's not frightened of me or that I might give her this thing, whatever it is. If she has poisoned me then her initial gasp was just an act, or the infection had spread faster than she expected. But she would be afraid of a Sat worm. Anyone would be scared of that.

I want to shut her voice out. I want to see the clear truth the way I'm supposed to see it but my mind is confused with the injury and starvation and my witch divvy has been working on me all this time, making me easy prey for her lies. She's been taking me gently, carefully down this road.

'Leon,' she says. 'You must listen.'

'Listen to you? Why should I listen to you?'

'Because I know this thing.'

'You knew it was coming, didn't you? You're not even a little surprised. You were just waiting for it.'

Ulya is agitated. That well managed face has now broken out in a wild play of emotions. I have found out her scheme.

'Yes I thought, maybe…I waited.'

'Why, what did you do to me?' I raise my arm up to her as a demonstration of her handiwork. 'Is this some kind of joke? Are you getting even with me, with the True Path, for making you a divvy?' My throat catches. Almost cuts off the words.

'I didn't do anything. I thought because I saw the mark on you. You have it on your neck. I saw it that night in the room under the ground. Everyone saw it. They tried to tell you.'

'There's no mark on me,' I say.

'Yes, on your neck. I don't know how but it first showed up on the night with the guns.'

'What mark are you talking about?'

'Jacob's Ladder.'

I feel around the back of my neck once again. There is still a tiny lump, not painful anymore.

'My Bind,' I say. 'She did something.'

'You don't understand. She can't make it. It was in you already. Since you were born. It must have been hidden some way. The True Path; they hid it. But that woman brought it out of you. She gave you something powerful, to make is show and now its there, clear: The mark.'

'From your song?'

'Yes.'

'But you said that was just old and stupid. I thought you didn't believe it.'

'It's true though.'

'It's true? Then prove it.'

Ulya is quivering. She takes a long deep breath. The Leon-dog has shaken off his muzzle and torn up the leash.

'Okay,' she says. She scoops the water sack from her shoulder and unties the nozzle. 'You must put your arm out,' she says, and she rolls her own sleeve back and stretches out her arm to show me how she wants it done.

'What are you going to do?'

'It won't hurt. It's okay.'

'What is it? What's okay?'

'I promise,' she says. 'It's strange, but not painful. I did it before, I –' she stops. Looks at me. 'I know what I'm doing.'

I let her have the arm, which she takes gingerly in her shaking hands. She tips the water sack and lets a thin stream of our precious water trickle from just above my elbow down the gleaming white surface of my altered flesh. I brace myself for a sudden sting, or some reaction, but there is no sensation at all, not even the cold trickle of the water. At least, not for the first few seconds.

'Try not to speak or breathe,' says Ulya. 'When it drinks.'

'Drink. What do you mean – ?'

All at once, my arm comes alive. I feel it first, before I see it, as though a thousand tiny hairs were rising out of my skin. A swift, gentle bristling, from above my elbow to the heel of my hand. Under the white skin a dense black layer emerges and these things spring from it. Not hairs so much as feelers, antennae, tiny but muscular, flexing back and forth like tongues. As the water streams over them they stiffen and then begin to suck. I can feel the hairs tug on the water and the water's soaking into my vessels. My body tingles with it. Cool water pools in my stomach. I jerk my arm away from the water sack, but the water follows me, arcing out from the hole as if drawn by gravity.

The hairs – if that's what they are – are black and sharp like nail heads, springing and coiling from this dark mass deep in my arm.

The revolt starts in my stomach. The water and anything else I'm holding down there, comes shooting up in a violent rush and I hurl a wadge of vomit several feet into the air, followed quickly by a knotted string of drool. I am drowning. Spots appear like footprints across my vision. Still the arm sucks, the lipless mouths pulling hungrily on the water.

'Ulya,' I splutter.

She's there. She has stopped pouring. She's got me around the waist and pulls with all her strength. The water spills out of my mouth. My body doesn't want this. Fights in every corner, in my spasming muscles, my straining heart.

My head hits the old road. I'm biting at the mud. My arm is sucking, sucking, sucking.

She is saying something. Her voice booms in my ears but her words are just broken, far away calls. I lift my head to hear her.

'Breathe now,' she's saying. 'Just breathe. You can do it.'

I let go of everything. The water bursts out of me in a single lurch. My arm has stopped drinking but is still making that hungry noise and my throat is hot and painful and I'm on all fours moaning like Sully the day the rain burned him.

'It is good news,' says Ulya, breathless and hauling me off the ground. 'You are going to Thule.'

20

I am crouched at the side of some ancient, ruined road, balled up and shivering. Like something freshly gutted. A skinned animal set on the fire to smoke.

I have pulled my sleeve back over my arm, without looking at it, and no water seeps through the cotton; it's perfectly dry. My new skin has absorbed every bit of moisture. It has stopped sucking. That horrible sound is finally gone, leaving only these faint sensations on my arm like bubbles silently winking out.

Ulya knows better than to talk to me and busies herself with making camp. She leaves me to sit in silence until darkness has swallowed the road and all but the closest trees, and we have only the sound of the crickets to keep us company. Puddles in holes and ruts along the road reflect the writhing aurora. I watch them. The colours in the muddy water are sickly, alien.

When Ulya has the fire going, she begins to carve a small oak branch with the knife, paring one end away with shallow strokes and dropping curls of wood into the fire.

'What's that?' I grunt. The only way I can hide the tremor in my voice. She looks up. Startled. 'Nothing,' she says. She puts it down quickly. 'Is it a tool? Something we can use?'
'No, I was just playing.'
'You can tell me,' I say. 'Out here. It doesn't matter.'

Ulya looks thoughtfully at her work. She is trying to decide something.

'I wanted to make the necklace again, that my brother made for me. But it's silly. I can't make it. It's wood, not beads. I just thought …'

'Maybe they still have it somewhere in the Colony.'

She gives a half smile. Now that her anxiety has passed, I cannot see what Ulya is thinking, but I have learned to tell how far away from me she is. How deep into her own daydreams she has retreated. Right now she is some great distance away, in some valley in her own mind where there is no beast called Leon waiting to snap her arm in two.

'It happens,' I say, clearing my throat. 'When a divvy has been loyal or they have done something brave, like risking their lives for the Colony, then she can be raised up to citizenship early. There's a ceremony. I can't remember all the details, but some words can be said and that's that. You are a full Citizen. You can live on the farms, marry, have children.'

She considers this news for a while – long enough to make me regret mentioning it – before she replies: 'You're going back to the Colony?'

'One day, maybe,' I say.

'You can't go back.'

'I know it.'

'How can you go back?'

'I can't.' I lick my teeth. Watch the sparks thrown out by the fire and the embers, bellied and then abandoned on a fitful breeze. 'If I could get the message,' I say. 'Then they might take me back.'

We both know that nobody is going to take me like this, with my pale, hard, water sucking skin. Not the Colony, not the imaginary city of Esperanza, not even the people in the villages.

'Will it spread all over me?' I say, flat as I can, like it was just a fact I wanted to clear up.

'No,' she says, again so definite. So certain. 'It might be gone tomorrow. Then it will come back in different place. Your leg or your face, sometimes.'

'You said you've seen it before?'

'Yes, there was a boy, in my village. Other people sent him because they thought he would be safe with us. The sechniks were always in danger. People wanted to take them, or kill them. This boy stayed with us for a few months. We saw him drink like this. He let us. He didn't mind. Then he was gone. I don't know why. I think maybe our leaders didn't want trouble. I don't know what happened to him in the end. Probably he died.'

'They never spoke about this in the Colony.'

'No.'

'It was never mentioned.'

'No.'

'It must be some kind of disease. It's got nothing to do with Thule. You know how people got things mixed up back in those days. They thought everything was about the Messages. But this is some kind of skin disease.'

She doesn't answer that. She lets the silence do its own work. A disease that drinks water through the skin. I reach under my sleeve and feel along the edges of this thing, this growth, with my fingers. It's harder than my skin and yet just as flexible. I'm not aware of it unless I touch it.

'It's just a story,' I say. 'In the song. There was never any Murad or Sophia. *You will be tested before you are taken. If you fail the test, you will not be chosen.* Do you hear that? *If you fail the test, you will not be chosen.* Nothing about marked people.'

She nods a divvy nod. Yes, sir. Whatever you say, sir. I pull a branch out of the hottest part of the fire, take a second to watch the burning end fizzle and crack and then I lob it high over the fire. It lands in the undergrowth behind her. She straightens and rolls her shoulders without for a moment taking her gaze from the flames.

'If you fail the test, you will not be chosen.'

I wait for Ulya to come out, the talkative, insolent one, but she's gone for now. Slithered back into her hole. It's just Martha and me here, by the fire. We don't speak again that night.

I wake much later to find the temperature has dropped and a deep cold has gotten in around my bones. The fire has gone out and the soft panting of the forest dogs animates the darkness all around us. I lift my head, only to realise that there is something wrapped around my torso and pressed against my back. It is Ulya. During the night she must have crawled up to me for body heat.

I don't move her arms or push her away this time, because I need the heat too. Instead, I try to manoeuvre the infected arm a safe distance away from her, so it won't touch her body. She is not afraid of my grotesque skin. The squirming black shape that rises inside it. Fear doesn't eat into her dreams like it does into mine.

I listen to the panting dogs – that might in fact, just be rain or wind in the distance – and let her hold me. She makes quite a lot of noise in her sleep and I find it comforting. Like being in the dorm again. She snores, mumbles and at some stage during the long night – I'm not imagining it – she actually giggles.

Ulya is up before me as usual.

I blink in tea coloured daylight, the smell of tree sap and pine needles and smoke.

She raises my shirt over my left ear before I realise what she's doing.

'No,' I say, clamping a hand down on hers. I have heard the stories. Men infected by Sat worms are open to suggestion, easy to control. She can't try that on me. I would see that witchcraft a mile off.

'I must,' she says. 'Please.'

Her hands are warm. She has been building a new fire. Her long fingers are not callused and dry like her palms and knuckles, but soft, caressing. She knows that I like the feeling they give me all down my body when she brushes those fingertips over my skin. She uses it.

'No,' I say.

'You must learn to drink like this, or you could drown. You must practise, like speaking the Russian words. Practise drinking.' She meets my gaze directly.

She puts her hand on my hand. 'Leon,' she says. 'I have to.'

She takes her rag and empties the last of our water from the sack into it until it is dripping wet.

'No,' I say. 'No way. You should drink. I'm fine.'

'I drank some. I'm okay. You are injured and if you don't get better, then you won't get the Last Message and then maybe nobody will.'

'That's what you're keeping me alive for? So I can get the Last Message?'

'No.'

'Then why?'

'Because I'm your divvy and it's my job.'

'That's not the real answer.'

'The water will dry up,' she says.

She reaches for my sleeve. I pull back. She reaches again. I put up a warning hand.

'I'll do it,' I say.

I straighten my spine, burying the horrors of the previous evening before I roll up my sleeve inch-by-inch. It is still *my* arm. It responds to me and I can bend it, twist it. There is nothing in there, that is not me. And yet –

Ulya watches me as she lowers the cloth on to my forearm.

'You will get used to it,' she says. 'It comes and goes for a while, but it will settle.'

'I won't listen to your crap about Thule.'

'Okay.'

I hold down the first surge of emotion as the suction starts, but even when I'm prepared for this, the sound is bizarre and threatening and sickening all at the same time. The water filters into my stomach. This time, it is not rejected and I don't go into a coughing, vomiting fit. Instead, it percolates through me, clearing my head, cooling my body.

When she pulls the cloth away the arm and the cloth are dry. Tiny black points all up and down the surface of my new skin white out, one by one, forming a seal over the extracted water. The black underskin sinks away.

'See?' she says. 'It doesn't hurt.'

When we finally get on the move again, with the sun already high over the trees, she tells me that my condition has to be managed carefully, but I will survive.

'You will go blind for a little bit,' she says, keeping a few steps ahead of me. She talks more freely when her back is turned.

'I can't go blind. Not out here.'

'Don't worry, I will be with you,' she says breezily, as if she was happy about it. 'It won't be for long and then most of the time, you will be normal. Like you always were.'

'What else?'

'Your skin changes on your face. Your eyes change. You'll hear new things. Things you didn't hear before. Different stuff like this. None of it is very bad. It doesn't hurt, but you need somebody to help you.'

'Blindness is pretty bad.'

'Only for a little while.'

'Long enough to walk off a cliff. Or into a dog's mouth.'

I turn to check on our camp followers and they are still there. The long-eared one out in front. He stops when I stop, like the moon, and watches me with his mouth open. Would he eat me now, with this arm of mine? It makes me smile to myself to think that he might have come all this way for a bad meal.

In the afternoon we rest on high ground, with a good view of the mountains. Ulya is gone a while and when she comes back she has a writhing heap of bugs stuffed into the tin cup.

'Lunch,' she says.

'Couldn't you do better than that?'

'Not today. There's nothing.'

She pounds and grinds them up, and then boils them with some water on a new fire. Her face is fixed in concentration. I think this is Ulya happy.

I take every morsel from the cup and clean the sides with my finger and when it's finally empty I put it down beside me. Ulya is opening out that rag again.

'I'm not thirsty,' I say.

'You just ate.'

'I don't need it.'

I look down at the cup. 'You're not eating?' I say.

She shakes her head. She puts the rag down and walks up the slope behind me to the edge of a rocky ridge.

'Do you know where it is?' she says, looking out at the horizon.

'Where what is?'

'Esperanza.'

'No. It's south. Somewhere south.'

'People will know, I suppose. Out there. We could ask them.'

'There aren't any people.'

'There are some.'

'Yeah, well. They might know. They might not.'

'We can make it there, I think, if we can get to a better place with more food. There is a river near here.'

'The South Divide.'

'Can we get there?'

'All of a sudden you're in charge now? Deciding where we go?'

'No. Never.'

'Sounds like it to me.'

Her face is turned away from me, so I can't see what effect my words have. I'm not angry about her planning our route; I'm angry that she sat there and let me finish the stew like that, without leaving any for her.

'We can make it to the South Divide,' I say. 'Two days, maybe three. At our pace, probably three.'

'There will be fish, and water. Better for us.'

'Esperanza could be months away,' I say.

'If we stay alive, the time isn't important.'

She shifts her gaze to the east, roughly where the Colony is. The True Path will come eventually, with bloodhounds, even if we haven't spotted their campfires yet. They have probably already found the scene of the crime: the ruined house and the dead Initiates in a hole in the ground. Theo in the grass.

They would have counted the bodies. No Leon. Leon is missing.

21

Another evening out in the wilderness, huddled against the weather, cold and hunger steadily chewing through our minds like maggots. Ulya is wet through from gathering firewood. I have to watch her shiver in the black smoke released from our dismal heap of smouldering sticks, her arms around her knees.

'Stop doing that,' I say.

She scrunches up her body and tightens her grip on her knees until the shivers are under control. The rain gutters over the lip of rock above us and drums and spills all around us in a constant, sluicing roar.

At least it is better here, than out in the open. Stumbling along, our heads down. The last thing we ate was a snake Ulya coaxed out of its hole. That was two days ago.

'Now listen,' I say, through the din of the water. 'We are going to find out what that man in that machine was talking about. There is no Esperanza, I don't want you talking crap like that anymore. But something is going on. General Hilles said he questioned my Bind. There were things he was going to tell me later, when I came back from my Rising. So there is something happening and we have to find out what. We go south. We look.'

She stays as she is, her eyes mirroring the ash flakes and the sparks travelling on the tail of the breeze over her head and out into the open sky. It's not long before she goes back to paring out those damn beads for her necklace. There is something she is telling me, in the effort and concentration she puts into the task. Scraping along the grain, peering at the shapes, turning them in her fingers. She is so consumed by it that her body has gone still, impervious to the cold. Each peel of wood a breadcrumb trail to somewhere far away from me.

I sit examining her and reading that mask-like face, until the scratching noise starts to play on my nerves. Then I creep around to her while she's busy carving and wait until she looks up at me. When she does, I stamp down hard on the wooden beads she has assembled in a neat pile on the ground beside her. I crush them into the soil and I twist them down, good and deep, with my right heel.

She watches this impassively, the knife paused in mid-air. When I go back to my place and sit down she puts the knife away and the last bead down and goes back to holding her knees and shivering.

She sleeps wrapped around me again. She never asks me for permission. She creeps up to me when I'm asleep. When I didn't beat her the first time she must have taken it as a sign of approval. I listen out for giggles during the night and when the shivers come again, I hold her against me, as if I could squeeze them out of her. I'm surprised by her smallness. It feels as though, rolled up, she would fit into our water sack.

When we break camp the next morning, I notice she has dug a small hole where I stamped the beads into the earth and, most likely, she has found them all again. Like the dog pack, she goes around me, not through me. She wears me down. A patient, steady circling.

We walk all morning in silence along the damp ground until I realise something has changed. It's not the forest dogs, they are clinging to us as surely as ever. It's me. I roll up the sleeve of my left arm: Nothing. The infection, skin disease, whatever it was, is now gone and my old skin is there: my hair, my freckles and my tattoos. All restored.

A quick inspection tells me that the growth, has not turned up anywhere else on my body. I look at Ulya. She smiles at me. I'm tempted to smile back, just for a moment.

'Will it come back?' I say.

'Yes.'

'So why does it..come and go like that?'

'It takes time to settle. For children it takes many years. I don't know about you.'

'You've seen this?'

'Yes.'

'That boy?'

'Yes.'

'I don't know what to believe.'

'You have to trust, then.'

We go more quickly after that. There's a spring to my step, even as the way gets steeper. We climb steadily out of the valley, until we are above the treeline and can spot the roofs of the houses in one of the villages, out to the East. We cross into an open area of thin, birch forest, when we hear the rush of the water. Ulya smiles at me again.

'Hear that?' she says.

I hear it all right. A swift flowing river in the distance. We climb faster and faster over the rocks and scree until we are running. The growing thunder of the river is driving us on.

I can't tell if the forest dogs are following and I really don't care because we are about to lose them completely. There is no way they are going to pursue us over a river and even if they sweep around these mountains to a place they can cross, I'm sure they will have lost the scent. They are not bloodhounds after all.

We come out at a ridge that looks straight down into a canyon. The white water slides along the bottom, between sheer rock walls sixty feet tall at least. That's not going to stop us.

We charge along the edge of the canyon until we find a route off the ledge and down. A snaking mud track. We run, slide, stumble and sidle our way along. Ulya's laughter jars against the limestone with each footfall, making a funny lurching, stop-start clatter. She and I both know what this river is. It's the South Divide. The boundary. The very edge of the valley.

We emerge at the base of the canyon and follow the river bank until we find a circle of quiet water ringed with boulders and the debris of branches and leaf matter snagged out of the current by the rocks. Around the bend, deeper into the gorge, white water roars unseen. Here the spume foams around the boulders, but the little pool is deep and still.

I feel brave. I don't fear the water. I strip quickly. Plunge in, up to my shoulders.

'It's freezing. It's Goddam freezing.' I shout. Nothing sucks. I never thought the feeling of water on my skin could be so good. It's *my* skin. The cold on it. The tiny hairs prickling. All of it is *mine*.

Ulya frowns at me. 'Turn around,' she says.

I turn. She slips out of her things and into the water behind me. It's only then that I look up to the ridge we just left. Along its edge is a ring of spindly shapes, barely standing out against the tree line.

I can only imagine their frustration and disappointment. I have felt that too. One of them turns and lopes back into the forest.

22

The water makes my wound throb. I unwind the dirty bandage and let the spray rain over it. It is puckered and discoloured still, but the infected area has receded leaving faint rings, the ripples of trauma, under the healing skin.

Ulya is doing the doggy paddle, as if she was mocking our spectators up on the ridge. She laughs, thrashes her feet wildly, her naked body a shadowy blob under the frothing water. She catches me staring.

'What are you looking at?' she says. She goes to where the foam is thickest and rests her arms on a boulder. After a while she lifts her foot out of the water and bends it around toward her face so she can examine her wound. It's the first time I have seen it, a thick red tear through the sole of her foot, scabbed over with a rind of curled, dark skin.

'Let me see,' I say.

She eyes me warily for a moment, and then she lets me take the foot in my hands. It looks like the wound has healed and then re-opened. She has not once complained about it though the strain in her face sometimes tells its own story. I run my thumbs over the flesh either side of the wound and watch her reaction. Instead of flinching, she leans back into the boulder and closes her eyes. I push my thumbs deeper, feeling a little light headed all of a sudden. She sighs with pleasure and laughs and her toes wiggle.

I recognise this for what it is, a key moment between Ulya and me.

Little by the little, the proper order of Initiate and divvy has been falling away like old skin. I can stop it right here, but I don't want to. I look up from her feet and study her face.

'Ulya,' I say. 'Are you pretty?'

She opens her eyes and gives me an exaggerated, comical frown. 'What?' she says.

'I mean I don't know. About girls. I haven't seen many of them. Theo could always tell you: that divvy is pretty; that divvy is a dog. That's what he'd say. But I could never tell and you're not supposed to say that about divvies anyway.'

'It doesn't matter then. We don't count.'

'Be serious.'

'I am serious. I'm not pretty,' she says. 'Lena is pretty. And Maria. She is tall and she has long, beautiful legs. But this is not a good thing, to be a beautiful girl in the Colony. Alot of bad, evil boys around.'

'They wouldn't touch you, that's forbidden.'

'Oh,' she says. 'You don't know everything that happens in the Colony.'

I stop rubbing. 'Why did you shake your head at me, in that hole?'

She draws her foot out of my hands and looks at me, seriously now. 'What are you talking about?'

'I'm talking about that night. You know what I mean. You shook your head like you were telling me not to do it. You knew I had to.'

Ulya pushes her hand through her bristle of hair. I wonder what it will look like when it grows out. 'I don't want you to go all dead, like the others.'

'What others?'

'The boys. The boys that Rise. Some of them, you see them in the mess hall after. They're not the same. It's like somebody killed *them.*

Even if they look happy and people shake their hands and cheer for them; even then, you can see it.'

'See what?'

'They know it's wrong.'

'It's not wrong. How can you say that?'

'Because it is. They know the devil is coming for them.'

Ulya then jumps into a long description of Hell, which is a place the divvies believe bad people go after they die. Those bad people boil there for thousands for years in giant vats and fires stoked by devils. Forever.

She brightens up when she talks about the opposite place, Heaven. Up in Heaven is Vanesa, her face and her skin all fixed and pretty again and she is safe from harm. Safe from me.

'Where are we now?' I say.

'In the middle,' she says. 'And when we die, we will go to Heaven with Jesus.'

'And will I go there?'

'Of course.'

'But what if I go to Thule?'

'The people on Thule go to Heaven as well.'

'Don't I deserve to go to Hell?'

'No,' she says. She's on firm ground with this Heaven and Hell stuff. 'If you bend your head, I can do something.'

'Do what?'

'Help you go to Heaven.'

'Why?'

'It will only take a second.'

I look at her for some trace of mockery or insolence. She is smiling and when she does, her eyes get long and narrow. I bend my head towards the water, keeping my eyes on her as best I can. She eases over from her bed of slimy rocks and stands behind me.

'What are you doing?' I say.

'Just wait,' she says.

I feel water trickling on the top of my head. She is murmuring in Rus, rapidly, her voice soft and rhythmic. After a moment, there is a gentle splosh and she paddles back to her rocks.

'Now,' she says. 'You are free. The bad things you did in the True Path are forgiven. You are a free man. Free to be good.'

'What does that mean?' I say.

'You are going to go to Heaven and then you and me will meet again and you can tell me all about Thule and what you did there.'

'Why would I go to Heaven?'

'Because you didn't kill Vanesa, of course. And you try to be kind.'

'Kind? I'm not kind.'

'Not kind maybe. Kind is the wrong word. I mean that you find it hard to be cruel. You work at it and work at it and you hit me sometimes, like they tell you, but I see the way this hurts you.'

This makes me sit up, because she says it like it's an obvious fact that only a fool wouldn't grasp. A fool like me.

'You're a slave like me. You don't see it, but you are.'

'I'm not a slave and nor are you. You chose to serve.'

'Serve or die. That's the choice I got. When a man with a knife asks a question, then you tell him what he wants to hear. Just because they don't say this word, slave – it's my choice every day, every morning, to go where they tell me, to wear these things on my skin,' she touches the section of her crescent moon tattoo poking out above the water line. 'I choose to wake up breathing. That's the choice I make. And you're just the same. Every bit. Like a divvy. You do what they want you to do.'

'I'm no slave. You can't talk to me like that.'

'If you aren't a slave, then stand up to them. Don't hit me. Don't call me divvy.'

'This is some kind of trick. You're messing with my head.'

'Do you want to hurt me?'

'It's not about hurt.'

'But do you want to?'

'No.'

'Well then. Don't do it.'

She trails off and for a moment, I think she's not going to say any more. I want to hear and yet I don't want to hear, because I'm getting a fuller picture of my failure. That little voice inside me, the doubter, it was right all along. This scene here – me, Ulya, the river – this was always going to happen. I was never going to be a man, like Joel.

'I believe you will change, Leon. You can do it. You just have to get the chains out of your head. It's little things,' she says. 'Sometimes it's the way you look at me, like you see me. You see Ulya. Not Martha. And now, since Vanesa pricked you in that hole underground, I know what it is really. You have Saviour in you. You have Thule in there, in your blood.'

'I've had trouble with Right Thinking. But the General says I'm getting better. He promised me that I would be able to overcome my feelings.'

'The General never saw you go in Four Walls when there were children there, crying. Every time you hear them, you go. Why? You can't listen to the crying and not go.'

'No, you're not right,' I say. 'I go sometimes, it's true, just to stop them from crying. I tell them to get themselves together. Man up. It's my job to put some steel into them.'

'You feel it when they hurt. You can't leave them alone with it,' she says.

'You're wrong.'

'Listen to me,' she says. 'You must understand. They lied to you. Everything in your head is wrong. You have to learn a new lesson. The Saviours didn't make a test. They want to help us. You can't survive on your own, like this, being a tough boy. You need other people. You need me. If you treat me badly I will go and leave you and you will die, because you're a sechnik. Sechniks don't live very long on their own.'

'Why didn't you run away already? You had your chance, more than once.'

'I have a reason,' she says, suddenly dropping her eyes, her voice catching.

'What reason?'

'It's old. Doesn't matter now.'

I turn and climb out of the river and drag my clothes on over my wet limbs.

'Where are you going?' she says.

'You don't know me.'

'No.'

'We should go.'

She follows me soon enough and we walk the bank until twilight, when we climb again, to a wide ledge in a windbreak of pines, where we can settle.

I leave her while I go in search of firewood. There is not much here that will burn well and I have to spend quite a while scouring the area.

All the time, I argue in my head with Ulya. Why should I listen to the whispered conversations of divvies in their dorm at night? What do they know? They don't even know the Messages. They don't understand about Thule and they are not part of any plan for the world to come. So what does it matter if they think one Initiate is softer than the others?

But she has planted these things in my head, and I can't get rid myself of them now. She's another accuser, like Theo and his hints and suspicions on our first night out on the hunt.

My head is so full of these things, with several running arguments going on at once, that when I return I actually drop the wood, rub my hands on my sides and prepare to say some important things to her before I even notice the three dogs standing just a few feet from me, the others set back in the undergrowth and Ulya, with the knife in her hand, and blood running down her arm.

The dog with the wide jaw has received a slash along the top of his head, that has lopped a half-inch of flesh from his ear. There is blood on his teeth and along the bottom of his mouth and he has his feet planted wide apart, ready to go in again. There's a standoff. Ulya is panting.

How did I not hear this? But then, these dogs are weirdly soundless. There's no barking in their attack; not even any growling. Now that I'm here, the wide-jawed beast has to decide which way to go. The others move closer, as if to get between Ulya and me.

She looks scared. Ulya actually looks scared. These are not the scrawny, cowardly forest dogs they seemed to be only a short time ago. I stay still. Reach out my hand.

'Ulya, the knife.'

She scrunches her face in confusion.

'The knife. Throw me the knife.'

For the first time, in a long time, I know what to do. I've been here before in my seventh year, my standoff in The Four Walls, Initiates on every side, armed and approaching.

Ulya looks down at the knife in her hand as if she had not realised she was holding it. She throws it. It thumps softly into the ground close to my feet. The wide-jawed dog shows some more of his blood-stained teeth. As I lift the knife, his breath vapours in the gathering chill and he comes on now, low slung, all shoulders and teeth and eyes.

I run. He leaps. I go right under him and he hits the ground with a thud that makes him whine. It takes him a second to get his bearings and push himself back up on four feet. That's my chance. I dive on his back, slashing with my knife. This is not the precise, neat kill I've been taught to make, but then he's no pig bleating in terror in the Four Walls. He's pure muscle and ferocity. With a speed that takes me by surprise he manages to pull out from under me, and get his jaws into my thigh.

Ulya is not coming to rescue me this time. I can't hear her.

The dog has snagged some of his teeth in my belt and is having trouble getting his jaw free. I almost white out. There are others approaching. Right now, they are choosing what point in my body to go for. They are a pack, so they will co-ordinate, somehow.

My attacker shakes his powerful head and pulls away. The blood on his jaw – Ulya's blood and my blood – drips down onto my face and neck and an elastic stretch of drool dangles from his slavering mouth until it is just an inch away from my eye.

He plants a paw on either side of my head. Claiming victory. Inviting the others.

I use the pain from the bite as an anchor, a grip. Clench my mind around it. My knife hand takes a neat line from the ground to his lower jaw and drives the four inches of steel all the way up into his brain.

His moment of death is as quiet as his life. His eyes bulge; his body stiffens, before it falls slack. His full weight comes right down on top of me. With an immense heave and a lot of hip wriggling I manage to squeeze my way out from under him and stagger up onto my feet. The dogs in the undergrowth have retreated and the others pause, mid-approach.

'Leon,' says Ulya.

She's frightened of what she sees and I'm thinking: *so this is what it takes to survive? Kindness?*

The pain in my thigh feels good. The dog blood all down my fist and my sleeve feels even better. My mind is finally clear of everything and I am in that place I was always meant to be. Even these dogs know it when they see it. Their circle is widening, pressing outwards and away.

I lunge. A dog retreats and whines. I lunge again. When I dart forward, this time I get my prey and bring him down, pinning his face to the dirt with my left hand. His squeals are high pitched and desperate, and it takes eight or nine blows to silence him.

When I stand up from the task, all order has gone from the dog pack. They scramble over each other to get out of the way, using arched backs as springboards.

I target one of the smaller ones, who has not run and is baring his teeth savagely, but as soon as I go for him he bolts, like a hare, into the trees.

I tear after him. My mind is pure red, full of the stink of hot blood and dog urine. I am letting myself go, letting the fury take hold. And here I am. Here's Leon. Bursting out like a bug from a chrysalis.

I charge into the thick foliage. His tail flicks as he bounds over the rocks and shrubs, darting in and out of view, crashing through undergrowth at high speed. The tail is my target, my beacon. I lose him constantly, a blur in tree shadow, though the woods seem to be filled with his wheezing breaths and the violent effort of his little struggling heart. When I lose sight of him I stop, only to spot that tail again, like a reed light swishing through the gloom.

He's the unlucky one who has to face the reckoning for everything that has happened. I'm going to grasp that small skull in one hand and twist.

He goes left and right, trying to shake me. There's a sheer face of limestone right ahead. A dead end.

He is so blind with fear he goes right at it, at full tilt. He makes a very late turn that sends his back feet into a mad scramble in the dirt and his hip smashing into the rock. He moans with the pain. Yips in terror. Drags his injured hindquarters off the ground with his tottering front paws.

I stop. Put my knife into my belt. He doesn't meet my eye, but we both hear the scream from behind and we both look to see what it is.

Ulya.

23

So clever. So Goddamned clever. This isn't the first time this little squealer has diverted a predator. That's his job in the pack. He does it well.

He's no longer cowering in front of me. Instead he slumps to the ground, tongue drooped over those spiky little teeth, getting his breath back and waiting to see what I will do.

I'm dizzy. That surge of energy only lasted long enough to bring me here. I left her without even the knife to defend herself. But she is screaming and as long as she is doing that, she is alive.

I leave the self-satisfied dog to his gloating and race back to our camp. I can hear the dogs making low, guttural sounds. They are busy with their prey. They knew if we crossed the river we would be gone and so they had to act quickly.

Right now, I can imagine they are taking big bites out of Ulya. They reckon that if she's dead I'll leave her. If she's dead, they can have the whole carcass.

I burst out onto the ledge. It's empty. Drag marks through the leaves and soil lead down the trail in the direction of the river. Not much blood. At the lip of the ridge I find evidence of a more serious struggle, which tells me she lay quiet while they pulled her along and then suddenly sprang to action. There's more blood here, and plenty of fur. Maybe she tore a handful out of a forest dog pelt or, this being Ulya, maybe she took a bite.

They got her into the trees, off the path. I find a spatter of blood on a knotted tree stump. She's not calling anymore.

The panic comes cold and thick through my blood. I want to grab her. I want to say sorry, sorry, sorry for letting her down. For another failure.

I hit the undergrowth like the little dog did. The ground getting sucked under my feet.

There she is, in amongst seven dogs at least, her left leg trailing through the leaf litter as they pull her by her clothes and her arms and anything they could get a good hold of.

'Hey,' I shout.

They instantly drop her. Three of them turn to me. Just like the wide-jawed dog, they show their blood-stained teeth. Such a change in them. The eyes are needle points. The vague, lazy creatures that trotted behind us for days are now like one black maw you dare not put your hand into.

I draw my knife out of my belt and let them see the steel for themselves. One or two back up, revealing more of Ulya. Her mouth is open; her arms outstretched. Tears and claw gouges on her arms, her clothes, blood everywhere, but they have not torn into her neck.

They are not afraid of me and they need to be. I walk right up to them and hunker down in front of the long-eared one, the pack leader, so I can look him right in the eye. The others let go of their prey and align themselves behind him. He looks at my knife. His measuring glance reflected in the steel.

Does *he* have doubts? Does he wrestle with a *lie*? Does it ever cross *his* mind that he might not be able to do what needs to be done?

This is another trick. While the pack leader and I try to outstare each other, another lean hunter has looped around behind me, and now he attacks: locking his jaw onto my right arm, below the wrist, and scrambling over my head. His front paws scratch at my skull.

The long-eared dog bears his teeth in what might be his version of a grin. Instead of a growl he voids a long, earthy breath, like the smell from an uprooted plant. He watches my struggle to hold on to my knife and battle the other dog, waiting for the right moment, for an opening. I can still use my feet to defend me and though my knife arm is disabled, the other dog is far too light and small to do damage. With a brute thrust I lift him, mewling, off the ground and bring him down hard into the dirt.

Two more dogs approach on either flank, as silent as foxes. I kick out, making only glancing contact with the leader's chest. It hardly slows him down. He slips past my outstretched leg, pauses to let me see those teeth again and then he lunges.

The next moments are made up of impressions only, like scraps of a dream. I face into his lunge and make contact with my left arm; everything else: the forest, the other dogs, Ulya, swing out and away in a great dizzying arc, as if I've stumbled and fallen, cartwheeling from a cliff. A weightless tumble.

I am cold, cold, cold despite my surging blood. I see cave walls, tunnels, a gleaming ocean dotted with islands, a steel red sky. All spinning, altering as it goes, from dim, grimy daylight to night to dawn. My blood, swollen and gushing, bulges through my veins. All my senses heightened, sharpened, but in nothing, in a void. The spin goes on for a long time – long enough to wonder if I'm dead – the visions careen around me, until they gradually lose speed, a little at a time, and my surroundings return: the dogs, the dog stink, the light and shadow of cloud and trees.

I find myself rising off the ground, the wheeling vision washing out. I'm back in the forest. The dogs are here but the pack leader is falling in front of me. His back legs have gone from under him, and he's already dead.

His body keels sideways, bringing me with him, since my left arm with its shredded sleeve is tethered to his pelt, connected through wire like hairs that run down my forearm in several rows, like the comb on a brush. Some of the hairs in the rows are missing, others project straight into the dog leaving tiny wounds that spritz and sizzle in a white acid bath.

Smoke curls from his torched hair. Patches of his legs, stomach and throat have turned black. His left eye, bloodshot, has come adrift from its socket. Dark bile and vomit run in a stream from his slack open mouth.

The stink is blinding, like rotten flesh set alight. That and something sinister and unearthly that sends the other dogs into a goggle eyed, crouching retreat. They are not showing their teeth anymore. The attacker to my left has abandoned my good arm and fled.

The eyes of the cauterized pack leader still show the astonishment he had just enough time to experience before he died. The bubbling wounds, where the hairs pierced him, continue to fizz. It is the only sound here now, apart from the river. All birdsong has stopped. All life seems to have retreated and slipped away.

Slowly I work the hairs, like fish hooks, out of the smoking flesh. Once out, the remaining hairs withdraw, leaving the dark lumps under my skin from which they sprouted. The smell lingers.

I can hear my own blood. My ears throb with it. The stink of the corpse, the seething acid – they are *my* smells, they are on *my* skin.

There is one more noise here. I become aware of it only gradually: a low, wretched keening. The sound of my own tears is as strange to me as my alien skin.

Ulya lies where the dogs left her. When the sun drops finally behind the mountains, we are as we were: the girl unconscious and bleeding; the boy on his knees, his arms laid out before him on the ground.

She stirs slowly, fitfully at first, as if she was under attack again in her dreams. When she pulls herself up on her elbows she absorbs the scene. What does she notice first? The weird silence? The smell? The dog corpse? Me? She doesn't say anything for a while. She mouths my name. She is unable to hide her horror at what has happened. What I've done.

No night predator or scavenger has crept out of the undergrowth to check the dog carcass. Even after this short time, you would expect some flies, or other interested parties. At least a few buzzards circling in the sky over the treetops. The corpse is the only busy thing here. It undulates gently and now and again, gasses or foul air are released out of the mouth and every other orifice, including the wounds left by the poison, that continue to pop and wink in the gathering dark.

What will she say to me now? She twists and looks around her for the other dogs.

'They're gone,' I say. 'Fled.'

'They might come back,' she says.

'They might.'

'You didn't leave me,' she says, after another, longer silence has passed between us.

'I did.'

'You didn't. You came.'

'Too late,' I say.

'We're alive for a reason,' she says.

'What reason?'

'I don't know. But it's true.'

I look up at her. Meeting her eyes for the first time since she woke up.

'What is this?' I say. 'What's happened to me?'

She rubs her eye. Blinks. 'It's a good thing. I promise. It's a gift.'

The dog-corpse sighs. Its stomach sinks and folds in on itself.

'More lies,' I say. 'When will you stop with the lies?'

I get up when she does. She gives me a wide berth. I follow behind, my arms hanging at my sides. I look back once, to where the remains of the dog steam in the night air. It is becoming shapeless, its bones and muscles dissolving away. If I came back in an hour or two, would there be anything left at all?

We return to our camping spot and gather our things. Ulya winces as she stoops to pick up the water sack. She sits on her haunches, breathing hard, looking out over the ledge to the river. She takes slow blinks.

I watch the trees. The dogs remain a threat. How quickly might they recover from the violence of my attack and regain their courage? Hunger is a powerful motivator.

I lead the way down to the river to the point where we swam earlier. She waits while I wade out a little ways beyond the pool to test the depth, my feet sinking into the silt. It is wide and dark, a threatening sinuous current. Not like Glass Lake in the mountains east of the Colony: a calm, bright stretch of water. I am confident in that water. I know the depth and where to find the cold and not so cold stretches. I'm a lot less sure of the dangers that might lurk here.

Ulya has talked of crossing rivers in the past, but can she swim?

A short way out, the river bed shelves suddenly, way beyond my depth, and the reddish sediment evaporates into impenetrable black. I had hoped to wade across, most of the way at least, but it is a long swim. I can't go out too far with Ulya still on the shore and vulnerable. I try to judge the speed from the flotsam carried on the river. Leaves and branches ease swiftly by. Too quickly for the weak and the injured. The current would carry her around the bend in the gorge to the whitewater that waits there.

I go back to Ulya, all the time scanning the trees for the dogs. I know they're in there. Still too wary to show themselves.

'We must get to the other shore,' I say.

She nods. We have to recross our camp ground and through the trees, along the ledge, before we find a tight passage back down to the river where the rapids start. I'm looking for some narrow, fordable spot. I need it to come soon, while I still have strength.

The spray from the rapids is welcome, the pallid vapours mist the water and cool my skin. We have to climb once more, up another steep incline, until we finally come down into flood marsh: reeds and grasses and mud. The river seems slower and more manageable here.

Ulya and I wade in together, up to our knees in the treacherous sediment. I spot a snout above us on the path. They have not given up.

'I can't swim it,' she says, sullen with fear.

'We'll do it together.'

The far bank is a dark line against moonlit water. It is a short way really. A matter of minutes. A few strokes out of our depth to the mud and safety. The doggy paddle she did in the pool earlier would surely carry her that distance.

'I can't,' she says. 'I can't do that.'

'You can.'

Two or three of our furry companions now top the ridge and regard us with their moon tinted eyes. Maybe to say goodbye, this one last time. Maybe to wonder what I'm going to do with a nearly dead girl. Will I eat her myself, or melt her down with the arm that scalds living flesh?

They can still smell it I'm sure: the smoking body of their leader and the other tang that came with the acidic poison – a scent so unfamiliar, so alien, of plants and water and air, stones and elements unknown. New things under the sun.

24

We find our feet in amongst the reeds. I take all the weight: the saddle bag and water sack and knife and go in front. I use a stick to hack a route through the grasses and test for hidden threats and to prod the river bed for changing depths. A blurred shape, possibly a water snake, glides past us, just under the surface. It gets my hackles up. I raise my stick over my head, ready to strike.

Ulya follows with her head down, swishing her hand in the water and watching it run through her fingers.

At last we get clear of the reeds and into open water, where the going is easier and I can get a decent look at the challenge ahead of us. A bit of current is a good thing, we don't want the dogs following us after all, but too much would bring disaster.

'It's just a short way,' I tell her.

She shakes her head, glaring at the far bank. It's actually a good bit further than it looked from up on the ridge.

'Can I hold on to you?' she says.

'No,' I say. 'Best just to go quick. It'll be cold.'

We inch out until we are up to our necks. One more step and the river bed is gone from under us and we are out into black water. The cold is a shock. No sooner are we off our feet then it flashes through my body. A sheer muscle tightening bolt. Ulya yells. She is already struggling to keep her face above the surface, gulping at the air.

'Help me,' she yells.

'I can't. I have the bags. Turn on your back. Kick with your feet.'

She tries that and manages to get her legs up into the air. There is a lot of noise and effort with very little effect. Eventually she rolls to her stomach again and tries to ape my breast stroke.

I will not touch her or allow her to come close to me. Her skin against my skin. To feel the acid fizz. To hear her burn.

Out here, only a few yards from where we launched ourselves in the river, I have quickly lost sight of the far shore. At least I have the noise of the rapids off to my left to help orient myself. My feet are so cold they feel hot. It is that cold we have against us now. The longer we spend in this water, the greater the danger. The cold will sap our strength, suck the energy out of our muscles.

With that thought I take quick, powerful strokes at first, thinking I can get the bags to the bank and come back for her, but when I shift around, trying to spot Ulya, she has fallen well behind and now she is floundering badly. Only her nose and mouth break the surface. Her lips have turned pale.

I strike out for her, in the grip of my own hysteria now. Two or three strokes out she goes under. A momentary flicker of her hand is the last I see of her before a deep current drags her swiftly down.

I hesitate. My mind is blank. My feet numb. The black water slops on the shore, a thousand miles away. Everything seems suddenly impossible. Beyond me. I'm going to drown as well. This was a mistake. Our lack of food and our lost blood have weakened us.

I plant my face in the water. Catch a flicker of grey: her face flaring luridly in the gloom below. The sight shakes me out of myself.

I abandon the bags and dive down and snatch her arm, half expecting the poison barbs in my flesh to come streaming out. She is frozen, stiff, limp. Already a dead weight in the water. It takes several furious heel kicks to get us to the air again.

I have her under the chin, feel a gulp at her throat. A sip of breath.

'Ulya.'

Water leaks out of the side of her mouth. She is ebbing away, the cold eating her insides while I pull and pull and pull against the water and the bank that won't come any closer. I don't dare look for it. I keep my eyes on the bobbing surface, my legs pumping, my right arm carving out strokes. Water that had seemed so cool and unresisting is as thick as oil.

The world has shrunk to a tiny little patch of space. Just this stretch of river and the grunts of my effort and Ulya's slackening pulse.

I screw myself up against the drag, the tranquillising cold, and pull and pull and pull.

One more furious effort takes me to soft ground. Another stroke and I can wobble and then stand. I haul her by the armpits until we are clear of the water and I can let her flop down on her back.

Her arms are goose pimpled and grey. Her wounds have stopped leaking blood.

This should be easy. How many times have I seen a living thing go still – the quicksilver moment – under the force of my knife? Instead here I am pumping her chest, blowing air into her mouth and yelling obscenities at the unknown, undefinable thing that has done this to us.

'Ulya. Listen to me – Ulya.'

Her body jerks. Her mouth flies open and with a couple of heaves she vomits river water over her chin.

She is not by any means, out of danger. I cannot build a fire. The saddle bag is gone, along with the tinder box and any trees that might supply firewood are a long way off, across a stretch of marsh and flood plain. The past hour has been a disaster.

I sit by her as she slips in and out of consciousness.

'Hold me,' she mumbles, with her eyes closed. 'I'm cold.'

'I can't,' I say.

'Please hold me.'

'No.'

'Leon,' she says.

'It's not safe.'

'Leon, please,' she says.

She takes shallow breaths in a vain effort to keep her body still. She is turned away from me, so I can only see the convulsions of her back and hear her struggling lungs. A sound like steel wire dragged out of damp soil.

Eventually she twists around at the hips until she can see me and her eyes, glimmering green like fish bellies in the aurora light, study me without fear or divvy carefulness.

'You won't hurt me,' she says.

I hold my arms up in front of me in the dark. They are shaking too.

'Leon.'

'What is this?' I say. Staring at my arms.

She doesn't answer. May not have the strength.

'What have you done?'

I gaze out across the river, at the distant cut outs of the mountains and then I get up, mutter something incoherent about finding wood and leave her trembling there alone while I walk out across the marshland. The bands of aurora light throw ghostly shapes all around me.

I take long strides, as if there was someone coming after me and I didn't want to look like I was running or that I knew that they were there. At first I have no idea in my head at all, only to walk to the trees, but then a recklessness takes hold of me.

I ignore her calls – easily done when they are so faint against the din of the river – and just carry on walking.

'Leon.' Confusion and pain in her voice. A pinch at my heart each time I hear it, but I keep going. Keep striding.

No idea how long, how far but soon I am out of earshot. All sound is gone. There is nothing. Not even crickets. Chill air. The distant burning of stars and aurora. This is what it will be like: the last days. It will be a desert without sound or smell.

Nothing is holding me now. Nobody would find this girl on the shore until she was just bones, and perhaps not even then, if her bones were washed into the river or buried under the mud and so no one would ever hear how I deserted her and walked away into the night and never returned.

I shiver in the dark and peer as far as I can into it, thinking of Theo and how I might have stood in a place like this with him, if things had gone as they were supposed to and he had lived and I had Risen. I would give him his choice to make and he would make it and either he would come with me to the Colony as a Citizen or walk off into the wild. Not such a bad thing, surely, to be out there alone. If I just put one foot in front of the other…

I turn. Look out for her shape and the moonlit strand of the river, but I can't see it. It's gone. How far have I walked? I am lost. No markers to use but the mountains. What a fool.

I call her name. Run. Through black, formless land. No river.

Twice I go back on myself. Stop. Twist and turn. Where is the North? Where did we come from? Even the sight of the dog's eyes might help.

She will die thinking I deserted her. Left her alone in the cold after everything. I would call her name again but I feel stupid. Ridiculous. Lost in the wilderness.

So I stride on in a hopeless, despairing state until the sound of water sends my heart racing. I squelch through the muddy ground to the shore. Circle with my head down like a dog.

Eventually I find a lump on that ground, unmoving, lifeless.

This time I don't hesitate. Don't look at my arms. I lie down beside her and pull her close to me, placing one hand on her heart so that I can feel the rise and fall of her ribs.

I do not burn her. Nothing stirs in my blood.

Hardly any life there under those ribs. An assemblage of bone and muscle clinging to this last unburned inch of a taper, and yet such strength: a white knuckle grip. What does she hold on to? Why so keen to live?

I make all kinds of apologies to her in the night. I tell her I'm sorry for the way I treated her in the Colony. For being the reason she came down here in the first place and didn't go straight out east, where she wanted to go. I make her a promise that if she makes it through this night I will help her find her family, when the time comes, and she never needs to call me her sir again. We have to go look for the message first, because that's too important, but after that.

I'm not sure if she hears any of it, probably not, but if she were awake now and listening she'd have a big grin on her face and she'd say that I was babbling, which I am, and that I was an idiot, which is also true.

I go in and out of scraps of sleep. During the night I feel a movement from her. She is still alive. I won't sleep then. I sit up. If she is going to die then I want to be there at that moment.

I wait for it to happen. Checking every few minutes.

At some hour beyond reckoning she shivers. It happens again a moment later. I'm so happy for just this little hint of hope that I actually start imagining our lives together on the river.

Her shivers become more frequent and her indestructible heartbeat builds, steadies. I have done nothing, put my arms around her, warmed her a little maybe, and she has climbed and climbed and climbed and climbed through the dark. Heaved herself back to the surface. The girl who crossed the ice.

I think about what she said in that clearing, about a reason for our survival and as I watch the light spreading over the mountain peaks, I wonder what that reason could possibly be.

25

I don't wake her. I let her sleep until the sun can dry her. I won't dare go off to look for wood, in case she needs me. Even though we have the river between us and the forest dogs, I cannot rest easy. They might find somewhere downstream to cross.

I lie down close to her and get some more sleep myself. When I open my eyes again she is up and standing on the gravel wash, letting the water run over her feet as she peers down at them.

She is deathly pale and quivering, her divvy's tunic hitched up over her knees. The light on the water makes jiggling patterns on her face and her legs. It's as if she died in the night after all and some new soul had entered her body and was trying to find out where it was and what had happened to it.

I let her stay where she is until I start to worry that she is getting cold again. Then I go over and wrap her in my cloak and bring her back to where she lay through the night. She has always been a scrap of a thing, now there are sharper angles to those bones, her eyes more sunken, a pattern of scars like a new set of tattoos. The crescent moon on her breast bone has been slashed by a dog, as if he was making his own claim on her. There is hardly room left on her body for my Five Stars.

In a trembling voice, she tells me about the river that she remembers near their village in the North and how it was frozen for much of the year and they were able to ride along it on sleds.

'Alexei was clumsy on the ice,' she says, 'But he got so angry when I laughed at him. I remember taking Lena out the first time – she could hardly walk – and swinging her by her arms, like this – ' she stretches her arms out as far as they will go and rocks them from side-to -side. 'She could make her body flat like a board. Only small children can do it.'

She speaks haltingly and it takes all her concentration, as though she is picking her way over treacherous, broken ground.

'Where are we going?' she says, peering down the river valley to where The South Divide flows out of sight.

'The beacon,'

'Do you think we'll find it?'

'I don't know.'

'If we do find it, or if we can't find it and we give up. Then I want to go to New Brazil.'

I don't say anything to that. To me the East is only a vague shape, full of the stories from our history lessons. The wars between the Satz and The New American Army. Bodies heaped in fields and the streets of the cities choked and ruined. I wonder how much she heard of my babbling when she was supposedly unconscious.

'Leon,' she says.

I don't answer. I scan the shore for the telltale, slinking forms of the dogs.

'You don't trust me,' she says. 'You think I'm lying, about the Ladder and everything.'

'I don't know, Ulya.'

'Yes, I can see it. You've got bees in your head.'

She struggles up to her feet, despite my attempts to hold her down. She hands me back my cloak. Straightens her spine.

'Stand up,' she says.

'What?'

'Stand up here, with me.'

I look around, as if there might be some trick going on. Slowly I lift myself up and attempt a smile.

'Now,' she says. 'Take my hand.'

She puts her hand out. Tightens her mouth as a tremor goes through her outstretched arm. 'Take it,' she says, biting the words out.

As soon as I touch her palm she grasps my fingers tightly.

'It doesn't matter who we were before, or what happened to us,' she says. 'You have to take care of me. I have to take care of you. One day you will go to Thule and I will go with my people and that will be that. But now, we have this. You and me. I will tell you everything about the Ladder that I know. You don't hit me. You don't beat me. Don't call me divvy or bitch. I'm not your enemy.'

'I don't remember releasing you from your oath.'

'Who cares about your stupid oath? I was a girl in a village once, and your people had no right, what you did. You can't own somebody's life.'

There are tears in her eyes. They drive her mad. She doesn't want them. Presses them out with the heel of her left hand. This is Ulya shaken and wounded, but victorious over death. All her fear gone in the night as if the ghost of the former divvy, Martha, has finally fled into the marshlands. Is this what she has been waiting for, to cross to this shore? The point of no return.

I wait for the anger that seized me only yesterday. It should be there now, but the night has taken it from me as well.

She shakes my hand. I shake her hand. She looks into my eyes and I return her candid stare. I wonder what this means. Can I be held to it? A pact with a divvy.

Since we have no way to make a fire, we get moving in the afternoon, going as slow as we need to. Her wounded state has made her limp worse. She straggles along, eyes to the ground, as colourless and lank as a strand of cut barley. Her clothes are shredded, there are rough bandages, made out of strips from my sleeves and hers, tied loosely around her various cuts and tears. We stay by the river so we have clean water to wash them. We can only hope the dogs weren't carrying diseases.

Down here, out of the mountains, there is noticeably more heat in the sun. It dries us out quickly. The danger the cold brought in the night is almost forgotten in the bright, warm afternoon.

That evening, I bind my knife to a long branch and go spear fishing in a shallow inlet, cut off from the river by an island of gravel. It's been years since we were taught to fish, but I still have a quick hand, a good eye. I come back with a couple of large, silver fish that turn out to have very little in the way of meat, but plenty of tiny white bones. I have enough assorted pieces of wood to build a reasonable fire and manage, eventually, to get it lit without the tinderbox. A pale moon crawls over the mountain peaks as we pick the pieces of flesh out of the skin. The firelight makes her face glow softly pink and she looks less skeletal. The aurora writhes and flows over her body.

'We're going to be okay,' I say, when I have finished my portion and put it down. I made sure she had most of the fish.

She looks at me from deep inside her thoughts and smiles. The smile is so distant I feel it is not for me at all, but for someone not here. Someone who might have sat with her, at a fire like this one, in some country to the North long ago.

Late in the night I wake to the sound of calls on the north shore. Two or more men some way down river. I can't make out the words, only their wind-snatched voices, which, by some trick of the air or water, seem impossibly close by. They are followed by a crackle of gunfire, gone as quickly as it starts.

I watch the shoreline as far as the point where it turns to the South. There are no more gunshots or calls, but later I hear a single cry that's so distant it might not be anywhere near the river at all. The noises are all downstream. Waiting for us. The river rumbles on as if there was nothing to fear and no other direction in the world but this one.

The next day our little meal has made us a bit stronger and we can manage to pick up the pace, even though the ground climbs into hills. We find an old, ruined building, hidden in a cluster of alders and willow. Only two walls still stand. Rising out of the tall grass is a rusted metal frame that attracts Ulya's attention. She runs her hand along it, lovingly.

'I think it's a kacheli,' she says.

'A what?'

She thinks a moment. 'You sit on it and you go up and down. The thing you sit on is gone.'

She mimics whatever it is the 'kacheli' is supposed to do, but I don't really get it. Ulya pouts. Shrugs her shoulders. She gets excited again when we find another old and ruined thing in the undergrowth, close to the water. As far as I can make out, it's made up of twelve logs lashed together with rope. She tugs at it. It doesn't budge. A rhododendron has weaved its way through the gaps in its half-buried wooden poles. I have a fair idea what this thing could be used for, but I'm not that hopeful we can get it out.

'It's a boat, a boat,' says Ulya, clapping her hands together and jumping up and down on the spot.

'Pretty old,' I say. 'Not good anymore.'

'Looks good to me.'

'All right, then.'

It takes a lot of plant slashing and yanking to free the thing from its resting place, leaving me in a cold sweat. Once we haul it down to the water I expect it to sink and vanish almost immediately but the damn thing actually floats. Which means that it is not as old as it looked, buried in the mud. It is probably a lot younger than the house behind it. Left here by someone travelling the river twenty or so years back, perhaps sooner.

Ulya is the first to clamber on and sit down.

'What are you waiting for?' she says.

I don't trust this thing, the old rope seems unsound. The heavy logs ungainly in the water.

'Come on, quick, before I float away.'

When I finally raise the nerve to jump on the boat, the logs wobble and twist in their bindings and I nearly lose my footing and go straight into the water. Ulya laughs.

'You have never been on a boat, huh?'

Never. It's worse than trying to swim in the deep water.

'You get used to it,' she says. She takes the branch and uses it to push us out into the current. The boat lurches from side-to-side in the swift water and my stomach does the same. I spend the first hour of our boat ride on my hands and knees.

'You are funny,' says Ulya.

After a while, I get my balance and my confidence on two legs. I take the branch from her and tell her to sit down. She insists she is fine, not tired, feeling strong, but pretty soon she falls asleep with her head on her knees.

We spend the rest of the day on our boat and I do get used to it, gradually. Much of the time the river is too deep for our makeshift oar to reach the bottom, so I just have to let us run freely on the current and hope we can get to shore if we see rapids, which we don't. The river flows evenly on its wide bed and its easeful movement seems to run into the cracks and tangles of my own mind like some slow acting balm.

The evening comes. The nighttime noises of the land begin. Just before sundown, as the crickets stir in the long grasses, I see something slide out from the northern shore, drawn by the current, head down, bloated, looking far too heavy to be carried on the water: a body.

26

The body does not travel far, it gets snagged in a twist of water-weed at the edge of a bed of rushes, swaying in the current. There is no blood. The body is bloated and its skin is the colour of the grey water around it. I only see it for a few seconds before it's out of sight behind the rushes.

Ulya is awake. She scrambles up and stands, watching the water.

There is another body, not caught like the first, but it is making slow half-turns in an eddy by the south shore. This time the water around it is mingled with blood that has spread all the way to the mud bank. This man has not drowned. His face is up, his mouth open, his lips blanched.

When we try to bring the boat up close we spot another one – no, two – beached on a strip of shore some distance further downstream. The closest body to us is dry down to his hips, with only his legs in the water. The other lies like a burst water sack barely clinging to the bank, its legs abandoned to the gentle tide of the river.

'Leave them,' says Ulya.

'I can't.'

'Why not?'

'Because we could help.'

'They're dead.'

'Probably, but I have to see.'

'You have to see what killed them? It will kill you too.'

I check my knife is still on my belt and I pole the boat across until the gravel sucks underneath the logs and I can jump off and haul it out of the water.

The first body, the one that is halfway out of the river, is not dead at all, he is moving. The fingers of one hand are walking their way across the stones as if he was trying to reach for something none of us can see. I wait, my hand at Stella's hilt, waiting for some sound from him.

We are on a tiny island, surrounded on three sides by a jungle of reeds and shallow waters. Perfect for an ambush. The reeds whisper and flutter. The water plonks and slops out of sight between them. Ulya tugs fitfully at my sleeve.

'I have a bad feeling,' she says. 'Don't go.'

'I just have to see. You stay here.'

'Leon – '

'What if these are the men that attacked us back at the house? The men with the guns. I have to see.'

Ulya hesitates. Her eyes dart between the boat and the bodies on the shore.

'Stay where you are,' I say. 'It will be all right. I promise.'

Whatever caused this carnage is long gone. There's no way it was the forest dogs; a group of men is too big a stretch for them.

When I'm within a few yards of the injured man, he senses my presence and rises an inch or two off the ground, on his elbow, and cranes his head in my direction. Drool slips out of his mouth as he opens it. His eyes are bloodshot and the pupils enlarged. He is trying to speak.

All around him are strands of a fibrous white growth, like pond weed, strewn in a wide arc, as if he had frantically torn himself free of it and then collapsed with the effort.

The body next to him is a boy, hard to tell how old. His shirt is pulled half way over his head. His left arm has come out of its sleeve and lies naked in the mud. He is not moving.

The man slides his knee towards his arms in an effort to get up. My approach is getting him agitated. His shirt is caught underneath him and he drags it up to his armpits, leaving his torso naked.

'Easy,' I say. 'It's all right.'

He lets out a groan and slumps to the ground again. I kneel down beside him, keeping one eye on the shadows in amongst the reeds. The man's face is unnaturally pale and the cheeks are red and puffy, but the strangest thing is this thin film of fleshy weed that hangs at his hairline, his nostrils, and the corners of his mouth. It is on his eyes too. His enlarged pupils stare at me through a thread-like curtain.

No flu or cancer would do this. I touch the white substance on his forehead. It is spongey and sticky. It is under his skin too. Like a network of veins. His arms and upper body are pockmarked with white-tipped pustules where this substance has leaked out of him.

His mouth opens wider in an effort to form words and the strands of white stretch from lip to lip.

'Don't try and speak,' I say. 'Lie still. I'll get you some water.'

He has a sodden knapsack attached to his shoulders and I find a wooden cup inside. I go down to the water's edge and fill it up.

When I turn back I notice a lump rise in the mud a couple of inches from his chest. It travels smoothly, lifting a soft unbroken ridge of mud over itself. The lump takes a line a couple of feet above the boy's head before it sinks deeper into the ground and is gone.

The man has collapsed again, his arms pulled out behind him. I watch the ground for whatever it was that just tunnelled through the mud but it seems to have vanished.

There is a strange silence here on this island, not unlike the silence that followed my burning of that dog. We are out of the breeze, sheltered by the reeds and kept company only by the gulp and slap of the river.

I can feel Ulya's eyes on me. Sense her agitation. I should leave him. Should never have even touched him. He's diseased. His leg twitches, his head jerks minutely, but he is not shivering. There is no fever.

I watch every step as I bring him the water bottle, scanning the ground for a lump, any kind of disturbance and then I crouch a little distance from his mouth and put the cup against his lips. He doesn't take it, though the lips move, sipping the air.

I hook my foot under his belly and gently wedge it upwards, just to look.

'Leon,' says Ulya from behind me.

I lift my hand to quiet her. The man is surprisingly light, despite his bulk. I manage to raise him off the ground enough to see the fist sized hole just below his belly button. There is a matching hole in the ground beneath it, its rim stained red and purple and brown. A smear of blood marks a clear trail from his chest into the mud.

That's not all. His chest is busy, rippling, as if there was an army of bed bugs under the skin. I look up to see if I can spot that lump in the mud again but instead I see the boy, who a moment ago was lifeless, now propped up on his elbows and staring at me.

Slowly his mouth opens and he shakes his head, flicking his eyes towards my foot. I look down. A long feeler, like a muscular black tongue, has worked its way out of the cavity in the man's belly and probes the edges of the wound. Its v-shaped tip splits, forks, like a snake and prods the skin around the hole. Then it reaches up and sways, curling and uncurling, tasting the air. I leap backwards, sending the torso flopping back onto the beach.

'Worms,' says the boy in a breathless hiss.

The thing inside the man comes sliding under his skin around from his belly to his spine, slipping through his back, over the ribcage. I can clearly make out the ridges in its firm body, even the shape of that tongue. The boy scoops a handful of gravel from below his knee and hurls it at the infected man.

'Get the –'

He stops, mid-sentence, his mouth forming an 'O'. He has seen something behind me. I feel Ulya's cold hand on my arm. 'Leon.' I swivel towards her. A vital moment is lost while I try to unscramble my senses. Ulya screams. A hand is just inches from my face. A swing of my knife makes brief, slashing contact with the grisly, white wrist and a spray of blood dapples the beach.

The creature – it is not human, though it has a basic human shape, almost lost in folds of skin – has emerged out of the reeds behind us. It does not scream. It looks at its fat, clammy hand, a stream of blood now coursing down its arm, as if it wasn't sure who's blood this was.

It gathers itself, lurches at me again, puckering a lipless mouth between vast, mounded cheeks. Its tongue writhes around the colourless rim where its lips ought to be. It swings its injured hand at my head and I duck slashing my knife across its belly, leaving a vicious red stripe the width of its torso that eases apart silently like an opening mouth.

Ulya has a stone in her free hand and, as she makes to swing it at his head. I grab her wrist and hold her.

'Don't touch him,' I yell.

The creature falls to its knees. Its innards spill out of the wound and with them, a nest that was embedded in his guts: a purse of larvae, rocking, fidgeting on the sand. The pink sack rolls back and forth as the maggots try to break out. The stink makes my eyes water.

There are more of the fat creatures coming, splashing through the reeds. The sound of their dry, harsh breathing is everywhere.

Ulya is calling to me, yanking on my arm.

Leon. Leon. Leon.

The thing I just cut open is not dead. It is now attempting to lower its heavy body to scoop up its own innards and get them back into its smiling chest. There is no fear or horror in the creature's eyes but a stream of black urine runs down its inner thigh and makes a little puddle underneath it.

I stagger backwards, letting Ulya lead me. She has her shirt pulled up over her mouth. It muffles her scream when she sees the boy, who is on his knees now and under attack.

A creature just like the one I eviscerated a moment ago is standing on the other side of the boy, poised. At the edge of its mouth, which is about an inch higher than it would be on a human face, dangles the tip of one of the boy's fingers. The wound where the finger was torn is bubbling, seething, and yet the boy is quite still, blinking slowly. The thing behind him opens its mouth, dropping the sliver of meat.

Something wild takes hold of me. All sense of danger gone. I leap over the infected man and the boy and deliver a slashing cut to the neck of the creature, sending it reeling backwards until it loses its footing and tumbles into the reeds with an enormous splash.

Its companion is still struggling to re-assemble its stomach. Before it can react I come charging back and plunge Stella into its neck. It looks up at me, the blood leaking down its naked chest. A blank expression on its face.

I shove my foot into its belly and drive it backwards until it too falls off the edge of the island into the water.

More splashing out there. More noises. I haul the boy up – he is drowsy, unbalanced but not unconscious – and try to drag him to the boat. Ulya comes and helps me. The boy stops suddenly and pulls against us.

'Cut it,' he says.

'What?'

'Cut it off.'

I look down at his wound. A rust brown and yellow corona is spreading through his index finger, below the torn flesh. The creature has cut into the next finger as well and this too is frothing with poison.

'No time,' he says.

I stare at the wound.

'Poison,' he says. 'No eggs. It's not infected.'

I scan the reeds. Nothing else has emerged yet, but these things move fast, faster than should be possible with their cumbersome bodies.

'Look away,' I say.

'Leon, not now,' says Ulya.

'You too Ulya. Look away.'

The boy is not afraid. He stares directly into my eyes.

'Do it.'

I grip him below the wrist and guide his hand down to a rock. He drops to his knees. His face set hard. His teeth locked together.

There is no time for this. A ruckus behind us in the water. The infected man moaning. His body a heaving mess.

'Do it,' says the boy.

I bring the knife down like a hammer, slicing through the rest of the bitten finger down to the joint. He doesn't scream. Whistles through his teeth. There are tears in his eyes, but no grimace. The poison must have numbed the wound. I do the same with the next finger. Same result. There are two dismembered pieces of him sitting on the rock like trimmed fat.

'Deeper,' he says.

'Leon,' says Ulya.

I can hear those things thrashing about. Floundering in the water in an effort to get themselves back up onto the island.

I bend low, examine the stubs of his fingers. How much poison already in his bloodstream now? I take the hand, press it down flat on the rock.

'Don't look.'

He keeps his eyes on me. Doesn't move.

I rest the tip of Stella on the rock and line the blade up with the furthest edge of visible infection, just above his knuckles, folding his undamaged fingers out of the way, and then I press down as hard as I can. It takes two attempts to slice the bone. Now he lets out a whine from the back of his throat.

He looks at Ulya as he has only just noticed her. The rock is already soaked with his blood. He drops his eyes to the ruined hand, his mouth falls open and he swoons. I catch him before his face hits the rock.

Ulya and I take his unconscious body by the arms and drag him over to the boat. Once my feet are off solid ground I already feel safer. I ram the oar into the bank and give it an almighty shove so that the boat glides swiftly out and away from the beach.

I only dare glance back when we are a safe distance from the island and then I wish I hadn't. The larvae have burst out all over the infected man's body, like Initiates at assembly. I can hear the skin tearing and the soft fleshy murmur of small, toothless creatures devouring their womb.

27

What happened to our little dream of peace, out here in the wilderness? First the dogs. Now this.

Ulya is bent over the boy who has not moved since we lay him down on the boat. The bone deep shivers that took hold of her the night of the dog attack have returned, but this is shock, not cold. She has used her own clothes as a tourniquet once again, but there is so much blood, the cloth is saturated and anyway, what is in that blood? What poison did the creature leach into the wound?

The boat is too close to the shore, the current takes us right up to a clump of reeds and I have my knife ready for whatever might be waiting there. In my mind I can still see those things bulging in the man's chest. Burrowing through him.

'Check the boy's skin,' I say to Ulya. 'If anything moves under there, we shove him into the river.'

She doesn't answer me. Her shoulders arch as she takes a deep breath. It would be a simple thing to just lever him into the water and let him float away.

Ulya scoops some water into her crossed palms and pours it into the boy's parted lips. He swallows. He is at least partially conscious.

'Is he dead? That man we left?' says Ulya. She sounds so angry it makes me wonder if I've done something to offend her.

'Yes, he's dead.'

'I hope he's dead.'

'He is.'

'This is not like I remember' she says. 'Out here. I almost miss the Colony.'

'It's all going to get burned away,' I say. 'All of it. In just a few years. All of the trees. All of the plants. Everything. Even this river will dry out.'

I wouldn't mind at all if a burst of solar heat rained down right now and scoured that shore, burned the grasses, the soil, and every living thing hidden inside them until it was just a black, smoking ruin.

'People made this,' she says, her back still turned to me.

'Made what?'

'They made it like this. With the worm and bio bombs, and everything.'

'Maybe.'

'There's no maybe. It's the truth.'

I'm happier when the current draws us away from the bank out to the middle of the river once more. The mud and gravel flats give way to fens, and the grasses come out so deep in places we have to navigate through them, always watching for whatever might be crouched there, waiting to leap, or lurking just below the surface of the dark water.

'You were right to get the boy,' she says. 'You were brave. I wasn't.'

'It was a mistake.'

'No. You saved him.'

The boy stirs now and again. He moans, mutters. His fists clench and then relax. Ulya kneels at his side, stroking his cheeks, whispering soothing words in Rus as the evening closes in around us.

This is beyond her. The bandage, the water: these are half-hearted gestures. She knows she can't help him. I should tell her that he won't make it, so she doesn't hope too much. He has lost a lot of blood and will lose more still in the night, no matter what she does. Whatever is left in his veins is poisoned. There is nothing that can be done. Better to just nudge him back into the river and let him finish the dying he has already begun.

Eventually, she leaves him and sits down beside me, her chin on her knees and her hand trailing in the water. The air is all moonlight. Benign moonlight that does not burn us secretly while we bathe in it.

'You're very good at cheering me up,' she says. 'You say such nice things.'

'Yeah well, it's Right Thinking.'

'Will they like that, on Thule?'

'Yes, that's how they do things.'

'You're going to be safe, up there.'

'*If* I go. There's no guarantee of that, and anyway, I never Rose so it's pretty unlikely.'

'Are you going to think about me?'

I stare at Ulya. Her voice is a whole mix of things: disappointment and shock and outrage. Martha and Ulya.

'I suppose.'

'Will you tell them about me?'

'Who? The Thuleans? I don't know what we'll talk about.'

'What will you tell them about me?' she says, her tone brightening now, playful.

'I suppose I could tell them that you are very good at surviving. Good with your hands.'

'A good divvy,' she says.

'Yes...No. I mean you are a strong person. I could say that I knew somebody very good back on earth. Very dependable. Very loyal.'

'Will you miss me?'

'No, of course not. We're not supposed to miss anybody. They told us that.'

'But you might.'

'No.'

'This is why I want to go to New Brazil,' she says. 'You have Thule. That's something. And you will be happy up there with your friends and maybe you'll live forever. I don't know if people die there. I haven't got Thule. I'm going to live here with the sun getting hotter and hotter like you said and I will be on my own. Who will want anything to do with me, covered with these marks?' she runs her hand over the tattoos on her leg, 'like some crazy animal. I need to find my people and free them from slavery. I will only be safe with them.'

This was Ulya's plan all along. Not to bolt as soon as we left the valley, or even to mindlessly serve her master. She wanted to recruit me as her bodyguard. She saw me vulnerable, rejected and hopeless. What use for him now? This spent soldier? He may as well provide the muscle and follow me into the East.

'Will you promise me we'll go. After you find this message?' she says.

'I did that thing, didn't I? I shook your hand.'

'But I want you to promise.'

'I promise.'

'Is it a real promise?'

'Yes.'

'Let me see your hands. So you don't cross your fingers.'

For her sake, even though I don't know what she means by crossing my fingers, I hold my hands out in front of me in the night air. *My hands*. No alien white flesh glowing in the dark. 'I promise,' I say.

It *is* real. I may not want to go east, but I will not let her come to harm. The only honourable thing I've done since we left the Colony was to rescue her from those dogs.

What she hears, in my words or in my voice satisfies her enough that she settles down once again with her temple pressed to her knees, swaying to the motion of the boat on the river.

'Do you know what your divvy name is?' she says. She is difficult to hear with her head bunched between her knees.

'What do you mean, divvy name?'

'The divvies have got special names for all the boys. Your name is Lenechka. A good name for a boy.'

'My name is not Lenechka. You shouldn't call me that. My name is Leon.'

'Leon means lion. You're not a lion.'

'It doesn't mean lion. It's short for Leonidas. He was a king, long ago, and he and three hundred men held a mountain pass against an entire army of thousands. It's a privilege to have a name like Leon.'

'I like Lenechka,' she says. 'I call you that sometimes, very quietly. So nobody hears it.'

'They would have punished you for that.'

She grins. 'I whisper it in your ear when you're sleeping.'

She says nothing else after that. Her head doesn't move from her knees and eventually I decide she has drifted off to sleep.

I'm tempted to wake her. I don't want to be alone with the dark. My body is still shaking. My mind full of those things that attacked us.

The creature clutching at its guts on the ground. The sound of its breathing, like a rake in dry soil. They could be everywhere. Following us along the shore. Can they swim?

I listen to the water gulping at the logs underneath us. Nearby, a dark shape plops into the river, glides towards us and then slips down and away. Unseen creatures rustle in the shrubs and the reeds. Each time we come close to the shore, on one side or the other, I stand upright and ready, tense in every muscle. There is movement everywhere. The aurora makes even the stones flicker and dance.

Just like I did when I faced the Council I try to use the messages to bring some calm back to my fevered brain. I speak them in whispers, defiantly, to anything that might be out there.

We have heard your call …

Our home is not like yours …

I try to imagine I am lining up at the training yard in the morning, the coughs of the men, the quiet, the sand under our feet. Feeling the morning stiffness in my arms and legs and neck and knowing it will loosen as my muscles warm.

Cut away your bonds,

Put aside your history,

Those things will die in the fire.

The repetition helps with my thoughts but not my heart, which thumps away at the same frantic pace. I can almost hear my blood as it gushes through me and something more – as the dark thickens it seems as though my vision sharpens. The clumped forms on the shore have faintly glittering, silver edges.

We pass a grove of wind tortured pines that lean out at steep angles from a lip of shoreline. The boat bobbles and slows on the swirling current. As we make a half-turn close to the mud bank, a shrub suddenly becomes a figure taking a long stride between tree trunks. A man sized glob of shadow but crooked, shapeless. I catch only a fleeting impression of it. Not enough to be sure I really saw anything at all.

Nothing leaps out at us or enters the water. The boat rounds the strip of headland and the current straightens it out and pushes the pines behind us and away.

'Hey, what's that on your neck?'

The strange voice startles me. It's the boy. He has lifted himself on his good arm and he is staring at me with pure wonder.

'You're awake,' I say.

'You're one of them, aren't you?' he says, as if he hasn't heard me. Like he has woken up in his own dream. 'You're marked. Got the Ladder on you.'

'Who are you?'

He ignores this too.

'Can you see them?' he says.

'See who?'

'Them. You know, Thule people. My brother says mostly it's ice up there. Ice caves, big as Esperanza, all shinin' in this weird light. And they got these kind of fish, that they eat, only they got no scales. They got hair all down 'em. Says the marked ones can see just about anything they got up there, cludin' four big moons that are just fillin' the sky, day and night. Like you can't see nothin' but them.'

'Where's your brother?' I say, trying to make him properly notice me. When he blinks his eyes it's long and slow.

'I wouldn't want to go,' he says. 'Don't like livin' underground. Been in a cave once, not hardly twenty feet down it was. Cold and dark as shit though. Don't know what's gonna come crawlin' over ye.'

'You shouldn't talk so much,' I say.

'That's what my brother says. My Dad too. Keeps saying for me to shut up but it don't make no difference. I just keep talkin', he looks at the logs underneath him and then up at the sky. 'They'll be here any day now. Word is Pioneers got the Third Message. Folks noticed things going on round Esperanza. People on the move. Some stories goin' round about sightings. You know: Salvatores. Sure would be somethin', I mean just to see 'em. I wouldn't want to talk to them or nothin'.'

'Do you know the way? How far is it?' I say, unable to hide my impatience, now that I know how valuable he actually is, this boy we rescued from certain death. And yet his moment of clarity is fading fast. His eyes, which up to now were darting around like windblown sparks, finally settle on a point about a foot over my head.

'Yeah,' he says. 'Exactly.' And then his face slackens and he slowly lies himself back down on the logs.

'Boy,' I say. 'What are you doing?'

He's gone in a second. Slipped away into unconsciousness again with his eyes still open.

I have no time to even think about what he said because I hear a call from far off to the South that is not a wolf or a forest dog or anything familiar. It is followed by another, answering call, much closer. I stand erect in the middle of our boat and watch. The calls are soft as cloud smoke. Distant but piercing somehow. When I look back down at the boy his mouth has dropped open. I check the pulse at his wrist and neck. He is alive, strong even.

The calls sound again. The night shivers with them. I leave the boy and stand ready.

Everything on the river is vivid, silvered by the moon, sharply cut out of the night. The more I watch the hotter my blood gets. It feels like one more hour here and I will have to leave this boat, walk down into the water and let it wash right over my head. If I drown I drown, at least the heat in my blood is gone.

Ulya wakes before dawn and finds me sitting plank-like at the front of the boat.

'Leon,' she says.

'What?'

'Your eyes.'

'What about my eyes?'

'They're shining.'

'What do you mean?'

'Your eyes are all silver. They're Thule eyes.'

'I don't know what you're talking about.'

'Leon, you need rest.' She scrambles up onto her feet. The moonlight shows the bones in her face and the sharp curve of her eye sockets. 'I will take the boat.'

'You can't. You're weak.'

'It's okay. I can take it.'

I ought to resist but I don't. I let her scoop the oar out of my hands.

'Sleep, Leon.'

'I can't. There are things out there.'

'There's nothing out there. Sleep.'

'I'm going to take you to Thule with me, when I go. I'm going to talk to them. I'm sure they'll listen.' I'm thinking about what the boy said: the underground, ice caves. The moons that fill the sky.

'You need sleep. The eyes will make you hot. Give you fever. It's all too much for your head.'

'I'm sure they'll listen. Why wouldn't they?'

'In the morning,' she says. 'Everything will be different.'

28

'Look,' says Ulya. 'On the shore.'

I'm only half awake. Blinking at the folds or aurora above me. The silvering effect in my eyes has lessened but it has not gone. The sharpness. I turn on to my knees, trying to find my balance on the wobbling logs. The water is shallow here. The stony bed only a hand's length below the surface.

On the north shore, pitched up against a tree, is the frame of some wooden contraption, straps hanging loose from its shafts. The soggy ground between it and the river is riddled with hoof prints. I look at Ulya.

'It's them,' I say. 'The men with the guns.'

She shrugs. I look across to the opposite bank of the river, where the hoof prints start again, climbing a steep ridge along the shoreline before turning out of sight. We have come back into forested country. The only stretch of land not buried in trees are the sheer granite and limestone ridges of the distant mountains.

I reach for Stella and draw her quietly out of her sheath.

'Stay quiet,' I say. 'Not a word.'

I step down into the water and carefully make my way to the contraption on the shore, balancing on smooth, slick stones. My eyes make me cautious and slow. Hard to judge distance. I take a moment to scout the shoreline before I climb up to where the object is sitting. It's a frame, maybe a cot, altered to haul something heavy. The slats cut away at both ends to make shafts to walk a horse into.

I've seen the drag marks left by this thing before, on the old road when I first discovered my water drinking skin. When I knew the men who attacked us would never be caught. The ropes they used to hold their cargo in place are now slit open and hanging loose.

They were in a hurry. This device was too awkward to drag through the water and stones of the ford. They must have run into the same creatures we did on the island and they had to get off this shore. What was left of them? How many now? Frightened and on the run. Injured perhaps. Carrying wounded. Surely we could catch up with them? But then we are carrying wounded as well. I look over at the boy. Ulya has lifted him and is trying to feed him some water. He seems to be awake.

I wade back to the boat and hold it steady so I can look at the boy.

'Can you talk?' I say.

'Leon,' whispers Ulya. 'Leave him.'

'No time for that.'

The boy doesn't look up. He sips the water Ulya gives him, his bandaged hand hanging at his side.

'Did you meet those men upriver? Men with rifles? Are you one of them? What were those men hauling with them? '

'Leave him,' says Ulya. 'He's still in shock.'

The boy quietly turns his head towards the north shore.

'A body,' he says.

'A body?'

'All wrapped up in cloth,' his voice is raw and horse with pain. 'Maybe a sunburst.'

I dart a glance at Ulya.

'It was a woman?' I say. 'A Satz?'

He holds his bandaged hand up in front of him and flexes his remaining fingers and thumb.

'Worm huntin' you always lose fingers,' he says. 'Always. Got three uncles been losin' digits since they were my age. Have to put all their hands together to get a full set o' ten.'

'You were worm hunting?'

The boy raps the knuckles of his good hand on a leather tube hanging from his belt.

'A good hunt too, till those men rode right through the traps. All went to shit.'

'Who were they?'

'Who knows? Not from here. From the South somewhere.'

There is no sign of them on the far shore. The hoof prints go straight into the forest, at the only point wide enough for the horses. It is an old road. Shards of broken concrete show through the leaves and branches. In my eyes the concrete glistens with tiny silver points. The boy stares at me and blinks hard.

'Got the eyes,' he says. 'I ain't never seen that before. Little specks of silver.'

'Can you walk?' I say.

He nods.

'What do we call you?'

He blinks at me.

'What's your name?'

'Peter.'

'Alright, Peter. I hope you can keep up.'

I look across at Ulya. Her jaw is set. She is about to protest.

'They have her,' I say. 'It's Vanesa.'

'Not your Bind anymore. Let her go.'

'And let them live? After what they did?' I turn to the boy. 'Where would that road take us?' I say.

'South west. To the coast.'

'Would we find that beacon there? You know about that? The Colina?'

He looks at me. 'That where you headed?' he says.

'Yes.'

'On foot?'

'How far is it?'

'Far.'

'Is that the way?'

He nods. 'One of 'em,' he says.

Ulya jumps off the boat and drags me by the arm until we are out of the boy's hearing. 'They have guns,' she hisses. 'You'll die like Theo and the others. You haven't eaten properly for days. You have no strength.'

'You want to stay on this river?' I say.

She looks around her, probably for any sign of the things that attacked us yesterday.

'Ulya, they want her for what she knows,' I say. 'You heard in that bunker: 'Come to the West. We have good news'. What if there is a message there? Do you want them to get it?'

'So now it's true. Now you believe everything.'

'No – yes. I don't know. The General said she knew something. Whatever it is, those men should not be allowed to get it.'

'We can't stop them.'

'We have to try.'

'Leon, you have to learn this now. You're not the hunter. You're the one who has to stay safe. Stay hidden.'

'Who's going to speak for Sully then? Or Con? Are they just going to lie in that hole and nobody pays for what happened?'

'Still a boy soldier.'

'Still good for something, I hope.'

She is about to respond but thinks better of it. Instead she sighs and nods and takes one last look at the shore and river that brought dogs and near drownings and monsters out of the tall grasses. It is hard to believe that there is anything worse ahead than what we leave behind us.

Ulya takes Peter to the shore while I push our boat downstream and watch it bob on the river's steady flow until it swings through a bend and disappears. No more drifting through tall grasses watching the shadows.

I want to go quickly, make use of the daylight, but Peter is still dazed and can't be moved at any speed. Though he can't be much more than twelve or thirteen, his skin is worn and leathery with a lighter patch, an old scar, running at angle across his forehead. His brown eyes are dull, as if he couldn't see that well or what he could see didn't much interest him. His hair is packed down with dried river mud.

He tests his damaged fingers and winces.

'Worm juice wearin' off,' he says. 'You hadn't made that cut I'd be stiff as a board right now. Could float me down the river.'

'I hope I didn't make a mistake taking you along,' I say.

'You didn't.' He pulls up all of a sudden and looks about him as if he has only just realised that he is in a forest with strangers. 'You really goin' south, huh?' he says.

'Is that so crazy?' I say.

He half smiles. 'There ain't no way in to the Colina. No door. Just smooth glass. They been comin' from all over, hundreds of miles, since October, since she lit up. We got a ferry can take them across the Louis River. Been a good year for us. Sometimes five, six ferries a day.'

'They're coming for the message?'

'Yep, only they won't get it. Message is for sechniks. Pioneers been picking through the land lookin' for 'em. Nobody else goin' in or out of the Colina.'

He looks dimly into the corridors between the trees. All the sharpness has gone from my vision. Getting muddy now, as if it needs to be buffed clean. I am happy Ulya is in front.

'The Colina, this beacon, it's in Esperanza?'

'Close by. A real wonder to see, even when it was quiet and dark.'

Could you get us there?'

'Mister, I'd love to,' he says, backing up. 'I could show the route all right but folks are gonna start to wonder where I am. We lost five men, includin' my cousin.'

He shakes his head and falls silent, gaping down at the bloodied stumps under the bandage.

'What happened back there?' I say. 'How did you end up on that beach?'

He looks at my tattoos again, studying the words inked on my neck.

Not everyone can be saved ...

'We were up in those hills out east, near Cobb's Gorge,' he says, his voice is oddly neutral, as if he was trying to remember all the details from a story he was told. 'We had maybe a dozen traps laid out. Those crazies just arrived out of nowhere. Rode their horses right through the middle.

Shoulda seen 'em when the worms came out of the ground. They screamed. I ain't ever heard anything' like it. Shootin' and screamin' only told the worms where they were. A few of them followed me into the river. That's all I remember.'

A few days ago I might have rejoiced at hearing this news. Taken pleasure in every detail of how these men died. The terror and the shaming panic. And yet I feel nothing. Even the memory of my anger is gone.

'When did all this happen?'

The boy looks up at the sky.

'Don't know,' he says. 'A day? Two days, maybe.'

'You think they could be going the same way we are?'

'Could be. A lot of folks are.'

'For the message?'

'Could be. Though if the Pioneers got the message in there they got it locked up and safe. Ain't no way in.'

'Which is why they took the Satz woman. She might have a way in.'

'Could be. If she's a Pioneer.'

Just then, a fresh call, like the eerie noises I heard last night, travels softly out of the distance. It is followed by answers on this shore but well to the east.

'Worm brood,' says the boy. 'They hunt in packs.'

'The things that bit you?'

'Newborns. Drones. Gone crazy with the change. They settle down when they're older.'

We press on, more watchful now, hoping every time they stop that we will not hear them again, but we always do. My eyesight gets gradually worse until all I can make out are the outlines and shadows of things in front of me. I have to stop, even in the midst of those chilling halloos and whoops.

'What is it?' says Ulya, coming close.

'I can't see. It will go, right?'

She doesn't try to calm me. She just takes my arm and starts to lead me forward.

'This way,' she says.

'It'll go. You said that.'

'Yes, it will go.'

'She's right,' says the boy, now just a glob of shivering colour.

We walk a little this way, listening to the calls from all around us, some close, others miles off in the valleys and hills upriver.

'I'll get you to my village,' says the boy. 'You'll be safe there. Folks there will look after you.'

'We're not going to any village,' I say.

We walk in silence after that, a dread chill settling over us. At first it is dead slow, as I adjust to being led blindly along, but gradually I learn to trust Ulya as a guide and follow her breathing and the light thump of her feet on the forest floor.

'We're out in the open now,' she says, when I stop to feel a steady breeze on my face. All tree shadows are gone and I have only a featureless sheet of brightness ahead of me. I feel exposed now. Less safe. The vague shapes of the trees gave me some sense of protection, of left and right.

'Look,' says Ulya, as we go down a hill.

'What is it?' I say.

'A building. It's old, but we can shelter there.'

'We should keep going.'

'No,' she says. 'Not while you're like this.'

Ulya tightens her grip and drags me along into the building. The air whistles above us. The two of them are whispering together. Peter raises his voice in shock: 'He don't know what he is?' before he realises I can hear him and quietens down. His voice carries and echoes into the space above us. I get the feeling the roof is a long way up, if there is a roof at all.

'It's a tower,' says Peter. 'Goes way up. Folks used it long ago to look out for danger. Didn't matter if they could see what was comin' or not,' he says. 'Came anyway.'

Ulya goes out to find firewood and food, leaving me sitting in my blindness on the floor of packed earth with the boy. She has no snares and no cup for water, only my knife. The tinder box is gone along with everything else on the river and now she has two invalids to care for.

'She your wife?' says the boy. He is sitting closer to me than I expected. Right beside me in fact. It makes me jump a little. He did not start there. He has sidled up quietly since Ulya left.

I shiver against the deep, lake water cold of the tower.

'No,' I say. 'Of course not.'

'Nothin' to me,' he says. 'Didn't mean to upset ye.'

'You didn't upset me.'

'I've got a girl picked out for me, only I ain't never seen her. She's eight years old. My uncle's got four wives. I asked him about it. He says it's nothin' but trouble.'

'We don't have wives. She's my – 'I hesitate, listen out for any sign of her. 'She *was* my divvy.'

'Like some kind of slave, is that it?'

'No, not a slave. A divvy. A servant to a warrior. It's like, long ago, knights had squires.'

He grunts at this. 'What she doin' stickin' round then? She could just run off.'

'She's loyal,' I say. Really I can't answer the question. Could she be standing out there right now, like I did back at that marsh, looking out at the wilderness and thinking she could just walk on? Keep going. No wounded boy, no blind Initiate to worry about. A few strides and then some more…

'She got people in New Brazil?'

'Where did you hear that?'

'I heard her last night. Heard a few things. Couldn't make sense of them then but now it's comin' back to me.'

'Her people were taken by slavers,' I say. 'She wants to go and find them.'

'Thought you wanted to go to Esperanza,' he says.

'I do.'

The boy considers this. A long silence follows broken finally by a click of his tongue.

'She told ye how to control the Ladder? There's ways see, of hiding it, so no one knows you have it and there's ways of bringing' it on, the spikes and all, whenever you want to. You come back to my village they'll show you. Sounds like she hasn't told you everything you need to know.'

I sit in the absolute blindness, listening. Helpless. He lets the dark and the cold chew on me a bit.

Joel would get to the real truth, if he was here. He wouldn't be this blind pet led on a string through the forest. I want to be his Leon again, the one he trained until he was hard and fierce and single-minded, but that Leon is out of reach now, like some stranger brushing past me in the dark.

The boy goes on. Had I ever seen the sea? I should see the sea. He'd been once, and had eaten crab claws.

'They got this hard shell, see, and you have to crack it, to get the meat, only there ain't a whole lot. Pretty much everything you eat there is full of salt. Tastes pretty good though.'

He goes on like this and I get the feeling that if I wasn't here or was just a rock set down in front of him, he'd continue talking just the same, even provide answers to his own questions.

'I'm not going to your village,' I say, when I've finally had enough.

He doesn't say anything to that, not for a while, and when he does, his voice has hardened.

'What's she planning to do when she gets to New Brazil?' he says.

'What do you mean?'

'I mean, she got folks there, right? Slaves. So what's she gonna trade, to get them back?'

'She hasn't got anything to trade. I suppose she'll figure something out.'

'She ain't empty handed. Not completely. She's got a sechnik. Might give her a whole barnful of slaves for one of them. Depends, I spose, on whether or not they've got enough of them already. Sechniks been coming out of the woodwork all year long.'

29

The next morning I open my eyes to a circle of blue sky high above me. The damp, cold, stone walls narrowing to a point seventy or eighty feet up. I can see all of it, everything, clear as I ever could but with none of that silvery light.

I lie there quietly, letting the relief wash over me, but also reluctant to get up and discover my skin has changed again or I have some other nasty surprise waiting for me.

Eventually I lift my head to look at Ulya. She is examining the boy's wound. She has nothing to prevent infection.

'It's okay,' she says, in amazement. 'There's no smell.'

'Worm juice,' he says. 'Good at keepin' wounds clean, long as you only use a little. Too much and you don't wake up for a week, or not at all.'

He notices me, over Ulya's shoulder.

'You're awake,' says Ulya, without turning to look. 'You can see, yes?'

'You let me sleep a whole day and a night,' I say.

'You need it.'

'We lost a whole day,' I pull myself slowly up against the wall. The boy is watching me from behind Ulya. 'Those men will be long gone by now. Could be in Esperanza already,' I say.

Ulya notices me exchanging glances with the boy and sits back, narrowing her eyes.

'You were blind.'

'You don't want us to catch up with them. Do you even want us to get to Esperanza?'

The boy tries to pretend he's not interested. This is an argument between two strangers. He picks at the corners of his bandage.

'I don't know what you mean,' says Ulya.

'South is where we're headed,' I say.

'Yes.'

'The message.'

'Yes.'

I wait for her to say something more. She darts her eyes from face to face. I can see no trick going on there, only genuine confusion.

'Did you find something to eat?' I say.

She shakes her head. 'There's no life here in this place. Maybe because of those things.'

The boy nods at this. 'Worm brood put the shits in everything. Put the shits in me.'

We are two full days now without food. Away from the river and the fresh water, but at least the rain is coming. The first flecks hit us as we creep out of our tower into the daylight. It is cold, carrying an icy bite from the mountains. And right there, bearing down on us from the direction of the Colony, is a dense storm. Black cloud swallowing the peaks. The lighting playing on its surface seems to make it grin.

'Holy shit,' says the boy, from behind me. 'We need shelter.'

'We follow the road,' I say.

'That's the worst way to go. Out in the open like that.'

Just then I hear one of those eerie calls, out to the West. Hard to tell how close. The sounds are drifting, lingering in the air, and seem to darken everything, like the cloud shadow.

Urooooooo

I think of those things crawling out of the reeds: the folds of fat, the black urine, the teeth stained with the boy's blood.

Uroooooo

The answer comes from far away behind us, driven on by the storm. It is these calls they use to draw a net. Somehow, by smell or sound they track us and then move in from all sides. I have begun to recognise the individuals. One of these calls, at least, I heard yesterday.

'We don't get off this road we're worm bait,' says the boy, looking accusingly at me. 'We take shelter, with this storm, they might lose our scent and go right past us. There's a small town a couple of hours out from here.' He points to a hill that rises out of a sea of trees in the distance.

'Why do you want us to go there? You want to bring them a sechnik, is that it?'

'No sir. Ain't got no use for one of them. I just want to stay alive.'

I look at Ulya. 'We have no food,' she says. 'If you don't eat, you don't have a chance. We die here slowly before we get to Esperanza.'

The worm brood call again. A little closer now, or they seem that way.

'If we get surrounded – ' says Peter.

'If we go to this town, they'll feed us?' I say.

'No question. Been there already a few days ago, before we crossed the river.'

I study the weather, trying to judge speed and distance. It's black as anything, sparking over the valley treetops.

'All right then,' I say. 'Take us to the town. What choice have we got?'

The boy suppresses a smile. 'You made the right decision,' he says, looks hard at me, then thinks better of adding anything to that and turns and strides on, in a new direction, downhill.

It is raining properly by the time we reach the hill that Peter pointed out, where the ground is turning quickly to mud. Thunder looms behind us. It is hard to keep up with the boy. The closer he gets to the town, the faster he goes.

When we reach the top, he gets excited and runs up to the edge of the ridge and waves at us to come look but then he stops suddenly. He goes slack, his hand drops to his side, like he was hit by a spell. I catch up with him and stand up with the chill wind at my back and the rain spitting at my head to witness the remains of an inferno: concrete buildings, wooden huts, iron roofs scorched and smoking. A wall broken, its rocks tipped into the dirt. In a pile close to the gate, a heap of blackened bodies, sunk into one another like they were chunks cut from one enormous beast.

The boy stands with his mouth open, wiping the rain that runs down from his hair out of his face. Two of the buildings, both tall and strong looking, one with a square tower, are still burning, the freshening wind pulling their black plumes of smoke out and away up towards us on the ridge. The storm, all knuckles and teeth now, rattles through the fallen town.

We go sideways down the scree slope from the ridge to the gap where the iron gate to the town once stood and now lies twisted in a watery ditch. The place has been thoroughly stripped. Everything movable has been taken. The charred remains of two dogs lie at the ends of their blackened chain, their legs flung out in a last despairing effort to break free. Their teeth bared, their ruined flesh reeking. The boy puts his hand down on a blackened hide and then pulls it back quickly.

'Still hot,' he says. His voice is leaden but there is no expression on his face at all.

Smoke rises in the distance, out of the tilled fields. Ulya points at it.

'We should go,' she says.

The boy doesn't acknowledge this. He totters around in a rough circle, his eyes half closed, the wet pulling his tattered trousers down below his waist. He walks over to one of the large concrete buildings and picks his way through its shell, scanning the ground. Ulya and I follow.

'It's not safe,' she hisses.

'I know.'

I take my knife out. There are no living threats here; it's a place of the dead only. A hand pokes out from beneath a slab of concrete. Another body lies head down, blood matted in its hair. The boy passes into a building behind. He puts his hand on a heavy wooden table that mostly survived the burning, and from there, he spots something. He crouches down and levers a wooden box from out of the arms of a scorched body.

'We need to go,' I say.

Ulya takes my arm and squeezes it.

The boy gently pops the latch and opens the box. Inside are a set of tools: a hammer, a scraper of some kind, other steel pieces piled together.

He mumbles something about needing the tools. Why would they leave such useful things behind? As if this was a victory of sorts, a dreadful mistake by the killers, the pillagers.

We wait for the right moment to move him on. He sorts through the contents of the box like there was some clue in there to everything that has happened. I notice a crude image, scrawled in red paint onto a crumbling wall nearby. I go over to examine it while the boy rifles through the box. It is a symbol of some kind. A circle, around three blobs, or dots. The paint is fresh. The rain has already washed a portion of the circle away.

'Esher,' says the boy. He closes the box and tucks it under his arm. 'They don't ever come this far south.'

I look at Ulya, she looks at me. 'What is Esher?' I say.

'Ain't a thing. It's a place. Couple of weeks north. Savages up there. Cover themselves with tattoos same way you do but don't talk all educated like you. Pagans.'

'They did this?'

The boy doesn't answer. He turns his attention to the smoke drifting up over the burned-out roofs of the village. 'Headin' south west,' he says. 'Guess they want the message too.'

A stab of lightening behind us. We need shelter, and soon. I take the boy by the arm and wave Ulya to follow.

Anything wooden in the town has burnt down to the ground, only the stone and cement structures, relics of the lost days, are half way standing. At the end of a long street we find one of these with a tower that tapers to a sharp point. Its brick walls have been scarred by the surrounding flames, but for some reason the vandals did not set it alight.

'It's the church,' says the boy. 'Why did they leave that? They don't care about church.'

There are two doors at the front, one of them half open. I tell the others to stay put and gently squeeze inside.

The place is gloomy and cold. A single giant room, like our mess hall, but with a second floor, a large wooden balcony, hanging over the entrance. The tall narrow windows let in very little light. Rows of wooden benches have been shoved aside or scattered or piled on top of one another in the corner by the door. The remains of a fire smoulder in the cleared space, the last of the smoke hanging below the ceiling.

They have smeared more of those painted symbols on the floor and between them runs a wide stripe of blood, a drag mark. The trail stops at the point where the balcony ends and just below that balcony hang a pair of dangling feet.

Something tells me turn around now and leave this place. But I can't. I have to see. I go beyond the shadow of the balcony and turn and look up.

It is a man of some kind, his skin unnaturally white, his legs glistening, his stomach ripped open and then carefully stitched back together with loops of black string.

I dare myself to look higher, up to the noose that broke his neck. His left hand is wedged under it. He struggled to undo the knot in his dying moments but when it pulled tight it cracked all his fingers above the knuckles, leaving them struck out in all directions, like heaped sticks. Above that, the blanched face at an angle to the gibbet, and set there, looking at nothing all, dead but still shining: the silver eyes.

30

Ulya and the boy creep in behind me, clacking the door shut.

The flesh on the corpse is not white at all, it is painted that way, but roughly, with his pink skin showing at his ankle and wrists.

It is difficult to understand what I'm looking at. It seems like they have placed a fake, patched-up head on the body. His eyes have been filled with strips of some thin flashing metal, his lips reddened. Whoever did this has taken a ghoulish pride in the thing, working red dirt into the cheeks, charcoal around the gouged sockets. The hair has been carefully arranged into braids.

'It's a bride,' says Peter. 'For Thule.'

'Who could do this?' says Ulya. Her voice as dismal and weary as the boy's had been when we first walked into this town.

'Up in their country they got some weird ideas,' he says. 'That there's a sechnik.'

They have tied a shiny tunic around the man's waist with coloured beads dangling from tassels at its hem. His fingernails are long and painted red.

'We'll cut it down,' I say.

'What's the use of that?' says the boy.

'We cut it. I'm not leaving it like this.'

The boy stares at me like I've gone clean out of my mind. He looks to Ulya for help but she shakes her head and goes back to the door, where the wooden benches have been thrown. She lifts one upright and sits down and puts her head in her hands.

Together, the boy and I make quick work of the body. I find the staircase that leads up onto the balcony and from there grab a hold of the rope, pull it close and cut it. The boy catches the body as it falls. He curses at his useless hand as he takes the weight.

'They won't like us cuttin' it down,' he says.

'I want to see it,' I say. 'Anyway, they're gone now.'

Here and there the arms are daubed with grey dots. The boy says these are meant to be the spikes with the poison tips that the sechniks release.

When I take a strand of the braided hair in my hand it actually comes away a little from the scalp. It is not *his* hair. Some gentle tugging is enough to peel the whole thing away down to the tightly shaved pate. Removing the hair reveals a neat circular cut that goes all the way around his head. The boy gently squeezes the edges apart with his fingertips. They, whoever they are, the people from Esher, have sliced right through the skull.

'Jesus,' he says.

I take the skull in my hands and softly as I can, draw the sliced top section away from the body with a faint sound of tissue peeling, ungluing, exposing a couple of inches of grey, coiled brain. The boy looks around suddenly, as though he has heard something.

'They took it,' he says.

'Took what?'

'The Ladder. Look -'

There is a gap at the back of the brain, a hole, about half an inch wide. When I look down into it I see more coils below, but they are blue instead of grey, with a rough, spidered surface like scales.

'We should go. They could be near,' says the boy in a hiss.

'What is this?'

He sighs. 'You don't know much, do you? That there's the Ladder. If we cut you open right now we'd see the same thing. It's what makes your eyes turn silver, makes your skin drink. You didn't have the Ladder you wouldn't live a second on Thule. You'd shrivel up or somethin'.'

'What are you talking about?' I say, touching my own head.

'The second message. Don't you know that? They gave us this, the Saviours. Sent it right down from up there. So as we could live on Thule. So we could breathe the air and such.'

I grip his arm, hard and look directly into his eyes as I speak, 'First, the strong must separate themselves from the others.'

'Come again?'

'The Second Message. There was nothing about any Ladder.'

'I ain't tryin' to upset ye. I'm just tellin' ye what I know.'

I peer down into the gap, at the blue flesh, neatly stitched into the brain. As I look I could swear it moves. The slightest contraction, withdrawing down into the cavity, flinching even.

'They took a chunk of it out,' says Peter, seeming not to notice. 'Cut it real neat. They knew what they were doin'. Done it before, more than once. You can use the Ladder for things, cures and such. People use it for sunburn. Here, help me turn him.'

Together we roll the body so that we can see the back of the neck. There is no Ladder or mark there, but there is a triangular hole cut with some instrument made specially for the job. The boy pinches the skin and it colours, as if he had pressed a living vein.

'What's left of the mark,' he says. 'Fades when you're dead. I only ever seen dead ones, until you showed up. They took out the devil's purse.

It's where a sechnik makes its poison for the spikes. They tip their arrows with it. One of them arrows breaks your skin you know all about it or maybe you don't, because you're dead before you hit the ground.'

'Why did they do this to him?'

'He's a sechnik.'

'What difference does that make?'

He peers over in Ulya's direction.

'She never told you, did she?'

'Told me what?'

'To some folk, sechniks are aliens, walkin' around on earth. They kill 'em, they hang em up, hell they even eat 'em in some places. Hardest thing a sechnik can do is stay alive.'

We shroud the body as best we can with a torn cloth we find in the building, throwing the ashes from the fire on the painted flesh as if somehow to remove the stain, the mutilation. I take the metal pieces out of his empty eye sockets and toss them away. With the back of my hand, I rub the red from his cheeks and smear those charcoal lines away from around his eyes.

'You ought to be quiet,' says the boy. 'Less you want the same treatment.'

'Stay here,' I say.

He watches me with a shocked face as I march to the front of the church and stand over Ulya, who is still slumped forward on the bench. Still covering her eyes.

'This what you wanted for me?' I say.

She doesn't answer. I wonder, for a second, if she has fallen asleep. I reach down, take her by the arm and haul her up.

'Hey,' she moans.

'You were going to trade me, weren't you? In New Brazil. I see your little plan now. Take me down there with you and offer me up, in return for your family.'

She keeps her eyes away from me, hanging at my grip the way she used to.

'You think I was just going to walk down there with you once you'd softened me up? Made me forget myself.'

Finally she looks up. Spots my raised fist.

'Go ahead,' she says. 'Hit me. If that's what you think.'

'I don't think it. I know it.'

'You don't know anything. Did the boy tell you that?'

'I don't have to listen to your lies anymore.'

'Don't then,' she says, making no attempt to slither away. 'If you think I'm a liar then hit me. Go on. Be Leon. Kick and shout until you feel better.'

'You didn't tell me I could control the spikes. You never said anything about the spikes at all.'

'Why would you control them? What for? Leon, it's more shit. More killing for nothing. Don't listen to it.'

'Did you see what they did to him? That sechnik? Did you see?'

'Yes.'

'Why did they do that? What the hell is going on?'

'I don't know.'

'Is that me? Will they do that to me?'

She reaches out her hand. I bat it away. Her mouth tightens. That muscle twitches at her ear.

'I didn't want to trade you. Not you,' she says, biting the words out.

'Who then?'

'You don't understand. How can you understand?'

'Well I can't if you won't tell me.'

'I owe a debt. I am a bad person, very bad. I don't deserve to be alive but I am and now I have to fix it.'

'Fix what?'

'What I did.'

'Was it to me? Did you do something to me?'

'No,' she says, shaking her head vigorously. 'Not you. Never you. It was a long time ago.'

'You wanted me because I'm like that man over there,' I say, pointing at the body. 'You saw what I was, down in that bunker, when my Bind pricked me with that thing, whatever it was. You came after me because of that. You've been with me ever since.'

'It's not what you think.'

'Then what is it? It's something, right? It's not dumb loyalty.'

'You have to get the message and go with the Saviours. That's the right thing. It's all I wanted.'

'Why would you care what happens to me?'

She drops her head and turns away, tugging her arm out of my grip.

'It was just like Alexie said. Thule shlyukha. They should have left me. The boy –'

'What boy? What are you talking about?'

'The sechnik,' she says, slumping down on the seat. 'I didn't want to be his bride. Now he's dead. Like Sophia in the song. I killed him.'

What is Thule Shlyukha? What sechnik? She won't say.

We leave the town by mid-morning the next day, when the storm has finally blown itself out. The boy finds a stash of potatoes in a pot the pillagers missed, gone hard now but still edible. Enough to give us a good meal and a small travelling supply.

The worm calls shadow us still, drifting out of the distance from all directions, puddling in the damp morning air. The boy looks up when he hears them.

'Ain't goin' near my village now,' he says. 'Can't.'

'Why not?' I say.

'Not gonna lead those things there.'

He takes us on an improvised route over hilly, broken terrain, keeping well away from the *pagans* who hung the sechnik, though it means wasted time backtracking, cutting detours around hills and streams. Most of the morning is gone before we rejoin the road we abandoned when we went to the tower, several miles west of where we left it.

We stick to the road from then on, feeling loose limbed and strong again with our meal and the fresh, cool air cleaned out by the storm. All along the route we find evidence of the men who murdered my Initiates. It seems there are three horses, certainly no more than four. They build their campfires close to the road, either because they are confident they won't be attacked or too weary or injured to venture deeper into the wilderness.

We use a sheltered spot below a rocky escarpment for our first camp, out of sight of any travellers on the road. We need it. The wind that drove the storm is still strong. Ulya goes on a brief hunt and catches two small flightless birds the boy calls 'pidgins', more feather than meat. She plucks the feathers briskly out of the skin with her fingertips as though the end of the job would be the end of all the hurt in the world.

The boy, it turns out, has his own tinder box and gets a flame going in a frame of bark. I have stripped a fallen dogwood of its branches and a tangle of twigs. It is fresh, green. When the fire gets going the smoke is pungent with resin and flows upwards in a straight, neat tower, but low cloud, the tail end of the storm ensures there is little chance anyone will spot us. The feathers Ulya has plucked are drawn to the pillar of smoke, sucked into its orbit and travel on its spiral into the night sky.

'Why do they call it Jacob's Ladder?' I say, making a point of talking to the boy and not to Ulya, the drip feeder.

'That's from the bible,' he says, examining a branch I have collected, turning it in his hand as if it had some hidden merit only I can appreciate.

'What's that?'

The boy blinks into the smoke and then looks at me.

'Christ all mighty,' he says.

'What?'

'Be quicker if you just told me what you *do* know.'

I steal a glance at Ulya, just in time to see her tighten her mouth to hide a grin.

'Bible's a holy book. The word of God. You don't know the Bible you don't know shit. Might as well not even be alive.'

'So Thule and the Ladder are in the holy book?'

'Not those words exactly, but if you read it close. Jacob's this holy man, a saint or somethin' from long ago. He had a dream and in the dream was this ladder went straight up to heaven and there were angels coming down the ladder and goin' up too. So that was how you got to heaven see and how the holy people in heaven came down here. Now you've got a ladder in you that will take you all the way up to Thule. You're goin' to the promised land.

Sechniks are like the chosen people. The Israelites. Not everyone calls it the Ladder though. Folks out there in the mountains, Jamestown and beyond, they call it The Winding Stair. Same difference I guess.'

'The Winding Stair?'

'Yep.'

I touch my necklace. Still with me, through all that has happened.

'Why would anyone want to kill someone just because they've got this mark?'

The boy shakes his head and stands up, casting a gaze over the furze of tree tops going grey now and shapeless in the dusk.

'They want to go too, some of 'em. They forget you can't take the Ladder out of someone and use it for yourself. You try to take the Ladder out of a sechnik, you kill them and that's that. Some are just jealous, I guess. Mostly it's because they're aliens. They don't trust 'em with their weird eyes and skin.'

'Because of the spikes.'

'That and other things. There's a way of butchering a sechnik, to get the bits you can use,' he says. 'I've seen it done in a place down south, near the lakes. They had this sechnik girl they kept in a box. They were waitin' for a travellin' workman to come by with special tools. Queer lookin' knives and a kind of a scooping thing, with a hook. Got maybe a quart of spiker juice out of that girl. Enough for a hundred kills at least.'

'They cut her up?'

'Worth more to them that way than alive.'

'And you? You think these sechniks are going to Thule?'

'It's in the Bible,' he says. 'The day of salvation will come with fire, and rivers of blood. 'Behold, a pale horse,' it says.'

'What does that mean?'

'The sechniks with their white skin. They're the horse you see and they're tellin' us that our deaths are coming but salvation too.'

Ulya's plucking is slow and absent minded now. She peeps at Peter when she thinks I'm not watching.

'And the worms?' I say. 'Are they in your Bible?'

'No sir. Satz made those worms a ways back when the wars were goin' on between them and the NAA. That was a mistake. Worms don't care if you're Satz or Rus or Turk or anything else. They'll take you just the same.'

He takes hold of the leather tube at his belt and carefully loosens the knot. I have wondered all these days what he has been keeping in there. I assumed it was water but then he has never drunk from it. He is just about to release the straps when he spots something, his eyes widen and he stands up.

'What the –'

There is a small, hooded figure standing on the opposite side of the fire. A girl. She has sneaked right up to us, unnoticed, and now stands just a couple of feet from Ulya, perfectly still and unafraid. Before anyone has time to react or say anything she takes a step towards our fire and holds out her hands to warm them. She smiles. She is young, maybe seven or eight years old. Her face almost hidden inside her hood. A blonde curl dangling over her forehead.

'Insanlar,' she says. Her voice is surprisingly deep and rough. 'Bakalim'. She nods in the direction she must have come from. The words remind me of the language those men spoke when they had me at gunpoint.

To the south I can just about see a dark stain that might be woodsmoke rising out of the trees. None of us had noticed it, or it has only just appeared. A faint reverberation too, that I had mistaken for the wake of the storm.

'Insanlar,' she says again, and looks at me and then points down the hill into the trees.

'She wants us to follow,' says Peter.

I'm too surprised to answer. The way she silently appeared, without fear or caution.

'By the look, I'd say she's a leggie,' he says. 'Ain't no harm in them. Travellers. Traders. Might be a Kervan nearby. They might have food.'

'You think we should go?' I exchange a look with Ulya. She is as unsure as I am.

The girl smiles again and flexes her fingers in the warmth. 'Hadi,' she says, and turns and hops swiftly into the tree shadow and vanishes. We look at each other.

'Up to you,' says Peter.

I can see the risk, but I don't feel much safer sitting here at our fire and waiting for an ambush. If this is a trap, I'd rather we met it head on and standing. So we follow the girl before we lose her, staying just close enough to keep her in sight. She skips along with a dancing, twisting gait, springing over undergrowth and fallen branches in her way.

As we get deeper into the forest, the low rumble becomes a steady beat, drifting across to us from somewhere up ahead. The girl continues as if she could see as clear as day, swivelling from side to side on her hips. She comes to a halt at a point where a path crosses the hill. The moment she arrives, a man steps out from behind a tree, rubbing his eyes. He sees her, reaches into the folds of his cloak and then thinks better of it and takes his hand out again. I catch the glint of something metal in his belt.

I slow down, show my knife.

'You leggies?' says Peter.

The man does a quick assessment of the danger, studying each one of us in turn. He nods.

'You gonna rob us?'

The man shakes his head. Peter nods at the girl.

'What she want?'

The man goes back to his hiding place and brings out a glass lantern, throwing a dim, wavering light from a stub of candle, and holds it over a spot on the road, which he pokes with his foot. We approach it slowly. The girl grins. There, in the packed earth is a set of footprints, marked out with a ring of stones. They are deep, not human, something heavy with three parts to it. One large oval, one smaller round indentation and then two long scratches, toes or claws. I crouch down to study it. Some kind of bear with a strange foot and only two claws. Then I think of those worm brood, the *drones* as the boy called them, and their strange, mangled body parts.

'You know this thing, kardashim?' says the man to me. His voice is soft, accented. He lifts his lantern to illuminate my ink, lingering over the Saviours on my neck.

'No,' I say.

'Is Insan. Salvatore.'

I shake my head and grin at his ignorance. 'That's impossible,' I say.

A flash of anger passes over his face.

'This girl saw him. She speak with him. He said to her to come east.'

The girl nods her head and frowns as if he had made an accusation that she couldn't deny.

'See,' he says.

He goes back to where he was hiding and returns with a wooden cup, which he uses to carefully scoop the mud and water out of the footprints. When I step closer to look he waves me back.

'Don't hurt it,' he says. 'It's holy.'

'Are you saying the Salvatores are here?' I say.

He looks surprised and gazes in the direction we came from. The girl speaks to him rapidly in their language.

'He gave his name,' says the man.

'Who?'

'Salvatore.'

He asks the girl a question and she answers with a flick of her chin in the air.

'Yok,' she says.

The man nods. 'She can't say the name,' he says. 'It is not Turk, not Ingeliz.'

Ulya crouches before the girl, straightening the cloak on her shoulders and pushing her hair out of her face.

'What did you see?' she says.

The girl smiles at Ulya and reaches out to touch her stubbled scalp.

'We make a party,' says the man. 'For the Salvatores. Come, I show you.'

32

We follow the path and emerge a little while later at a stretch of land that has been cleared and planted in small plots. At the far side of those plots is a concrete building, broken and full of holes, but with a patched-up wooden roof. The large doors stand open and the room inside is bathed in a warm orange glow, swarming with vast, criss-crossing shadows.

This place is the source of the rumbling, a drum beat, and now we are close enough to hear other instruments, throbbing with powerful, urgent sounds, course and gentle all at once. The figures making the shadow play on the walls and roof are dancers.

Colourful wagons are pulled up in a long row, behind the building. Horses stand close by, tethered to the wagons, their heads down against the wind, plucking stoically at what little grass there is.

'I told you,' says the boy. 'Leggies.'

As soon as we step through the door the music slows and then subsides, one instrument at a time until it stops altogether. There are at least fifty people here, perhaps more. Tables are laid out in rows on one side an immense hearth where the blazing fire feeds smoke through a hole roughly cut out of the roof. I spot a few hands going to weapons. Knives, clubs, maybe a gun or two.

The only one still dancing is an enormous woman with her back to us, a head taller than anyone else here. She has a live chicken held tightly by the feet and she nods her head in the firelight as if the music had not stopped at all, her hips swaying under the burr of sputtering wings.

'Is okay,' says the man who brought us here. He speaks again in his language. The only word that makes sense to me is 'Salvatore.'

Some of the people nod. A few smile at us. The music begins again. Sweet and vibrant under wavering light and shadow, the wind stepping on the rafters. The crowd fall back to what they were doing before we came in: stamping their feet, rocking their heads, some falling into wild, thoughtless dancing, alone or in groups. The tall, heavy woman hands her chicken to another and approaches us.

'Who is this now?' she says, in clear, resonant English. She directs us towards the door where we can talk without being drowned out by the music.

'Tell us who you are first,' I say.

She ignores the remark and takes my hand and draws my sleeve up to look at my tattoos.

'From the north east?' she says, jerking her head towards the fire. 'Up that way?' When I don't answer, she frowns. 'There are Esher Kindred nearby. We spotted their fires on the way down. You're not one of them are you?'

'No mam,' says Peter. 'They smoked Marlton. Every living soul. Hung a sechnik too, in the church.'

'Is that so?' she says, continuing to examine my ink. 'What are these things written on you?' she says to me, tracing the letters of the second message with her finger.

'The messages,' I say.

'The messages?' She seems confused, and then something comes to her.

234

'You're one of those forest men, that keep to themselves. Not kindred, something else … in English, what is it? The True Way?'

'The True Path.'

'Ah, yes.' She grins and nods and then yells something in another language to those not too caught up into their dancing to hear.

'Those footprints,' says Ulya. 'Are they real?'

'A being from Thule was seen here last night,' says the woman. 'There were three witnesses who claim to have spotted him crossing the path through those trees out there. He was at least seven feet tall. White as the moon. Arms and legs and a head, just like you and me but no mouth and no nose.'

'A trick,' says Ulya. 'Someone making a joke?'

The woman looks at her as she hadn't noticed her until now. 'Come here child,' she says.

Ulya does not step forward but she does not back away either, when the woman approaches her. She takes Ulya's hands in her own large and densely scored ones, stroking the bones with her fingers.

'This hand has been broken,' she says.

'Yes,' says Ulya.

'When you were small?'

'Yes.'

'Did the boy break it?' she says, looking at me.

'No.'

'He looks like he would break bones, even though he's only a bag of bones himself. What are you doing with a boy like that?'

'We are together.'

'Husband and wife?'

235

'No.'

'Lovers?'

'No, we are helping each other.'

'Are you now?'

The woman draws Ulya's arms out to their full length. She is trying to steady them.

'How long since you last ate?'

'A day and a night.'

'But you didn't eat much then, not enough.'

'No.'

'You walk with a limp.'

'A cut.'

'Let me see it.'

Ulya obediently lifts her wounded foot and the woman lowers herself to a crouch and tells Ulya to balance on her shoulders. She puts the foot in her lap and removes the shoe and peers at the wound there. She traces the edge of the tear with her fingers. Her face gives nothing away.

'You're strong,' she says. 'How do the Rus breed them like that? Girl's that bend and bend but never break, like reed grass.'

The woman's eyes travel along Ulya's arm and stop and at a tear left by one of the forest dogs. She tut tuts and shakes her head, then she tries to read the picture story inked from Ulya's shoulder to her elbow. The story of mankind: the first men naked in amongst the trees, the cities of the old times, the hand that reaches down from the heavens to take us to Thule, to safety. The words strung between tangles of foliage:

We have heard your call.

'My name is Damla,' she says. She calls out and within a few seconds a boy comes running 'Get these three something to drink,' she says. 'Whatever we have left of the beer.' He dashes off and returns quickly with a cup for each of us, froth spilling over the sides.

'Drink,' says Damla, 'for the coming of the last message, and the salvation of man,' she winks at Ulya. 'And woman, of course.'

Ulya, the boy and I stand there with these strange bubbling, dark drinks in our hands that remind me of poison that came from my own flesh and burned that dog down to nothing.

'This is what we drink,' says Damla. 'It's cleaner than the water in these parts.'

I take a sip, just letting it touch my lips through the foam. It is faintly bitter. The man at our side laughs.

'Don't be afraid of it,' says Damla. 'It will soothe the hurt. Trust me.'

Ulya drinks and appears to like it. The boy throws it back as if it was water, so I follow suit and take a series of long gulps. It sends a sweet rush through my body, out to distant nerves. I feel my cheeks getting hot.

When I empty the cup they clap and cheer and the entire room, especially the ceiling and the fire, tilt weirdly and I nearly lose my balance. When everything settles back down again it is all solid but fuzzy, as if the edges of things have been brushed out.

Ulya sips at her drink.

'Leon,' she says. 'Go slowly.'

'Don't waste your breath,' says Damla, 'Boys never listen.'

She calls for another beer. This one I have to swallow in one go while Damla and Peter and the man beside us count down from ten. No sooner does it hit my stomach then it shoots back up to my mouth in a single hot bolt. I double over and cough up a string of saliva. Damla puts her warm hand on my back.

'Rejoice,' she says. 'Today we are saved.'

Time gets kind of elastic after our drinks. My head is full of a great warm fug, as pleasant as I have ever known. The Leggies are very far away until they come right up to me, when they seem far too large and too close. Ulya's face floats there behind the others, smiling sometimes, mildly disapproving at others. She appears to be in on some joke and I think *I am* that joke and I tell them that humour is forbidden, except during harvest.

'Is that right?' says somebody that may be Damla.

I hear the words Doghru Yol a lot. What is that? What does it mean? It means *you*, they say. I tell them about the messages. About Esperanza. I think I tell them something about returning a hero to the Colony, with the last message. They agree with me. It will be a glorious thing. They give me some of the meat. More of the beer.

We are invited into a circle around the fire where we dance in step, going clockwise. I see joy in Ulya's face. She is alive again. Risen. I wish I had done this before, felt this joy. There is no harm with these people. I tell them we, the True Path, always respected the villagers, the simple people, even with the Risings and the Bind.

There is a face I catch now and again, away from the dancers, at a table near the back of the room. He is staring at me. Something familiar about him. But it is impossible to think. So many women here. Their warm hands slip into mine as the circle changes and flows. They touch my arm. Bump up against me. Their scents fill the air around me. They speak to me, laugh, show me the steps. I am happy. Happy Leon.

Peter is with us, but several bodies away, his head like a dropped noose, but he is dancing too. My mind is numbed, everything comes to me through a wall, muddy and muted. Damla is grinning, twisting her body, stamping her feet. Peter is on the other side of the hearth now and I want to tell him that he is too close to the fire. They are pushing him that way, yanking him forward, drawing him back.

Don't let them do that. You'll get hurt.

Forward, back. Forward, back.

Some game they are playing. I yell to him. The room and the music take my voice and soften it and then pinch it out before it can reach him. They have the canister off his belt and pass it around between them. It's a game. He tries to snatch it back. They pull it just out of his reach.

A huge cheer goes up. The dancers haul him backwards like they are drawing a bowstring and then sling him into the flames. His hands don't stop his fall. He goes right down on his stomach on the logs. Ulya is shouting but I can't hear a word she says. Peter stumbles up to his feet, his clothes burning off his skin, his hands palm up as if to press the heat away from him. He steps out from the logs, trips and the circle surges forward and pushes him back again.

This time he comes down on his back, the logs clatter around him and his body twists this way and that, unable to rise. He grabs at the air but not desperately, it is almost graceful. In tandem with the stepping shadows. He gets to his feet once again, much of his skin on his face sprung adrift and sliding off him. The dancers continue the circle. I realise I am doing it too: circling, dancing. He turns to follow the passage of the faces in the firelight around hm, looking into each one, before he finally collapses, another piece of kindling, into the hearth.

I watch from a place far away, like something seen in the landscape in the distance, unable to summon the horror, the outrage that is alive in my brain but unreachable. They have Ulya. They pull her to her knees and tug her shirt down until her right shoulder is exposed. Then they draw a metal thing from the fire and drive it into that shoulder.

'Ulya,' I say.

Strong arms wrap around my torso and lift me up, to a loud cheer from the room. I try to tear my arms from the grip of the men around me, but I have no strength. They stand me in front of the fire, uncomfortably close, my skin tightening in the heat.

There is a man leering at me. He has something in his hand: an iron with a twist at the end, a shape, a symbol. Have to close one eye to see it properly. It is glowing fiercely. A six pointed star in a circle.

He leans in. Puts his lips to my ear.

'The stars wait for you, Doghru Yol.'

The arms that have me tighten their grip. The six pointed star is deep orange, molten, wheezing sparks. On the wood ceiling behind the man's head, the shadow dancers circle the shadow fire. When he drives the burning star home my scream sounds funny in my own ears, loose and fragile at first but gathering force and shape, like something come striding out of a dream.

33

I have no hands, feet, eyes or even teeth. No face, no ears, just an inch square of flesh that burns without heat, like ice. My eyes won't open. I try to call out to Ulya but though I can form the words in my mind there seems to be no way to get them to my mouth. Where is my mouth?

The same image repeats and repeats and repeats like someone is pulling it out of my head and ramming back in again: the six pointed star glowing a vivid orange in front of me, the red face of the man holding it, his forehead a sheen of heat and reflected sparks.

Impossible to know how long I lie in the dark. Sounds creep into my consciousness. Laughter, talk. The rumble and thunk of wheels on the dirt. At some stage the ground beneath me starts to move which tells me I am in a wagon. The wood floor tilts upwards and thumps down underneath me as we navigate the lumpy ground.

I know I must do something. Something must be done. When I get my strength back, when this drug wears off, I will find a weapon, find Ulya, break out. I listen for her breathing, so familiar now, and there are living people around me all right, I am not alone, but the breathing is raspy and male, and disembodied, everywhere and nowhere at once.

I feel my lips for the first time when the rim of a metal cup or bowl is pressed against them and water tipped into my mouth. I cannot swallow. I panic, thinking I'm going to drown.

'Easy,' a voice says.

He lifts my head off the ground. I force my eyes open getting only a fuzzy view: a bare wooden room, men here and there slumped against the walls. A body strewn in the corner, legs spread apart, face turned away from me, one arm slung across the floor.

Who is that? Whose body is that? I try to say but can't.

'What they give ye, it takes days to wear off. Give it time. '

The wagon rumbles and jolts and shakes. I slide around like a tool in a box. I roll into a leg and a foot kicks me away, finally knocking the words out of me.

'Who is it?'

'Who is what?'

'The ... the ... the ...'

A voice mimics me. 'De ... de ... de ... dedede what, soldier boy?'

I manage to turn a little, onto my arm. Now I can see the legs of the body clearly, the feet pointing up. Shoeless. A dark scar – a rind of crusted flesh – running through the left foot.

'Ul-a,' I say. Spittle dribbles out of the corner of my mouth and slowly down my cheek. 'Ul-a.'

I try to keep an eye on that foot, see if it moves. So hard in the jostling wagon.

'Ul-ya.'

'Ula. Ula,' says the mimic again, but adding a lot of wild screeching to his version of my voice, which is actually just a croak.

The first piece of my body to return to action is my bladder, informing me with a sharp pinch that it needs to empty. I lie for an age with the throbbing ache. Then sometime during the night, when the wagon has stopped, my bowels gently unload down my leg. The smell of my own urine gathers thickly around me. The others shuffle away, as far as they can.

'Ulya,' I whisper.

A mouth appears at the window slot.

'Ula. Ula.' It squawks and is answered with sharp, vicious laughter out beyond the wagon.

There is a horse close to the window, thumping its hoof into the ground. I imagine the sharp hooves hammering and scraping at my skull until a voice wavers out of the miasma of urine and excrement and filthy bodies.

'It's me, Leon.'

'Ulya.'

'It's me.'

The strain in her voice. As if I had fallen from a cliff and she was clinging on to me with her fingertips. Her whole body and mind absorbed by the effort, fraying, unspooling.

'They marked you, didn't they? I wasn't imagining that,' I say, my tongue no longer a lead weight hanging at the bottom of my mouth.

'Yes.'

'We're slaves.'

'Yes.'

'Peter –'

'Don't talk about it.'

'They won't make me a slave,' I say, spittle beading on my lips. 'I'll kill them first.'

243

Nobody laughs at this. They are asleep. Daylight is starting to brighten the square of sky at the window from black to grey. The horse is eating, grinding hay in its teeth.

I talk some more to Ulya. Tell her how I'm going to fix this for us and how those Leggies will pay, each and every one of them, for what they have done to us. She has no answer for all of this or if she does, then she does not want to share it or perhaps most likely of all, she has simply fallen asleep.

It's another day before I manage to get to my feet and hold my balance against the wall of the wagon. We have been stopped for a while, perhaps a day and a night. There are four others here, apart from Ulya and me. They watch us from out of grimy, underfed skulls.

In the morning a hatch is opened in the floor and dry bread and a cup of water pushed in. The men swiftly divide the meal and retreat into their corners and devour their portions. When they're done with their meal, someone comes to the door and leads the men out one by one. Ulya and I are left alone.

Ulya doesn't talk. Doesn't look at me. She tears off the tiniest chunks of her bread and rolls them around on her tongue. She is out in that place her mind travels to in times of trouble and violence, where she is safe, with no slavers, no Leon, no True Path, no boys hurled into fires.

I spot her sliding her sleeve off her shoulder to look at the brand, the six pointed star. She runs her finger in circles around it. Already the multi-coloured halo at the edges is fading, turning black. It sits on top of the dog slash, slicing through the True Path ink.

'Ulya,' I say, into the silence. She turns away or looks vacantly out the window. There is nothing to say about what has happened to us. We travelled only a few days beyond the borders of the valley and already here we are, tricked and captured. Survivors indeed. I was going to come back out of the South, out of Esperanza, with the Last Message, triumphant. Redeemed.

When the men come back to the wagon they are worn out, their shoulders slumped, the reek of sweat from their clothes. I ask them what they were doing outside. They go past me to their corners and sit down. Only one of them meets my eye.

'Working,' he says. 'Soon as you're fit enough. You'll work too.'

It is several nights, many long days before they come for me. They take the other men as usual and then they come back and take me by the arm.

'It's time. You're up to it now.'

Ulya is left. Still too weak perhaps.

We are camped in a forest. There are now more wagons in the Kervan. Our wagon, the slave wagon, is painted dull green with loops of gold foliage surrounding the windows and the door as if there was some treat inside. The air is hot and still. They haul me to another wagon where the man who branded me sits on a stool carving a stick into a sharp point. I notice Peter's tube hanging from his belt. Even turned away like this I know this face, somehow. It has plagued me since my branding at the fire. He doesn't look up from his work, but Damla is there, standing to one side and she examines me a while before she speaks.

'Doghru Yol,' she says. 'Your name is now Gul. It means flower. We have given you this name because of the wonderful colours on your skin. You now belong to us and Mr Ertughral here will be your master. I hope you don't turn out to be a useless or unwanted thing, Gul.'

They press me down to my knees. Then I see it: a man standing a few yards off, the same one that watched me that night from the back of the room. It's his nose. It has broken recently and it has healed badly, bulbous and red with the line of the break neatly marked over the bridge. How could I not have seen this? The swinging belly on the man who branded me. The smashed nose on this one.

'You,' I say, trying to rise, but someone behind me shoves me down again.

'You got away from me last time you little shit,' says Broken Nose.

The reckless arrogance he showed the night he had me on my knees, with a gun to my head has vanished. Something weary and slow in his eyes now. A slur in the voice.

'My men –' I say.

'Mine too,' he says. 'Your little friend and his worm hunting. There is one law and one law only in the West and no one but the likes of him would dare cross it. Leave the worms alone. Don't hunt them. Don't spread them. That little –' His voice catches. Eyes wet and glistening. 'A bit of fucking justice.'

This time I am too quick. I'm up before anyone can react, my knuckles aimed for his nose again. I dive forward but he is ready and steps aside. As I fly past him he seizes my neck in his large right hand drives me, like some errant Initiate, flailing over the steps of the wagon and into the dirt with his boot in my back.

'You want to try that again? You ain't got that little beast to help you now.'

I'm breathing hard. Even this little struggle has winded me.

'Enough,' says Damla. She comes and leans down to my ear, while I squirm under the boot. 'You need to learn to behave. Now, I want you to kiss Mr Ertughral's hand. He is your master.'

Broken Nose removes his foot. I try to turn and look up.

'Keep your eyes down.'

At first I do, but then, feeling a sudden rush of defiance, I rise on my elbow and look him directly in the eye. His grin is like the slit an axe makes in a block of wood.

'Where is she? Where is Vanesa?'

'The Satz?' he says. He casts around him as if he has missed something that would explain this madness. 'You still after that poor bitch? Mother of Christ. Woman's burned up, half-dead. What the hell do you want her for?'

'What did you do to her?'

'Relax Doghru Yol. The bitch lives and she told us a few things too, when she couldn't take the pain anymore.'

'Okay,' says Damla. 'Umut, enough talking.'

Umut steps away a moment and returns with an iron rod.

'You will learn some respect, janum,' he says and then sets to work with the bar. On the back mostly, steering clear of vital organs. He grunts softly while he works as if he was taking a beating himself. When he is finished and steps back, Damla bends into a crouch and speaks quietly to me.

'You are not Doghru Yol anymore. Your *True Path*, as you call them, will not come for you. The sooner you learn this lesson the sooner you will fit in.'

I keep my eyes on him, Umut, with his fat nose. Try to stay mute and stare him out.

'Okay,' he says. 'I understand.'

No one gets a ration that night. The other slaves don't attack me, beat me or show me any resentment, not even an angry look, but for an hour at least during the darkest stretch of the night I can hear one of them crying. Tiny, breathless sobs. And then a long stretch of nothing. He doesn't even breathe.

The next day, when they bring me out to the light I notice unfamiliar birds circling the trees around the camp. They send out loud, bitter cries. White birds turning against the sky, looking down at me, the boy who shivers and stumbles along. What kind of bird is he?

I catch a faint, unfamiliar scent on the breeze. Salt air. I have no time to savour it.

Before the men push my head down towards the dirt I spot the little girl who led us to the footprints, lured us in. She doesn't see me, or she is pretending not to. She holds a cloth figure, with button eyes, in her hands and she is absent-mindedly chewing on its ear.

'What is your name, Doghru Yol?' says Mr Ertughral, stroking Peter's canister again. 'I want you to say your new name to me.'

Blood leaks from my mouth. My ribs throb steadily.

Umut is examining the surface of his iron bar and rubs some flaw away with his licked thumb.

'Boy,' says Ertughral. 'What is your name, flower? Tell me. Say it.'

I crane my head up to him, lock onto the small eyes and bore into them. 'Lenechka,' I say, trying to form a grin of my own though even in my current mental state I know it is badly lopsided. 'My name is Lenechka.'

34

They feed us this time. They are not upset at my resistance.

The next day Damla is there again, looking tired. We are waiting for Mr Erthughral, and when he arrives he and Umut and two others are carrying a bulky, elaborately carved chair on their shoulders. Slumped in the chair, her grey hair pooled on a purple cushion, is an ancient woman, with dark, reddish skin, as if she and her seat were made of the same wood. She is asleep.

The men set the chair down on the grass.

'You are to be honoured today, Gul,' says Damla. 'This is the bashbakan. She asked especially to meet you.'

Damla shoos the other men away while she takes the bowl of water over to the chair and squeezes out a sponge. She starts to wash the old woman's bare arms. They are furred with wiry black hairs, like something you would see on a spider.

'She wanted to meet the Doghru Yol who broke Umut's nose and ran away,' says Damla.

'What is a Doghru Yol?' I say

'It is Turkish for True Path.'

'What is Turkish?'

'Ah,' she says. 'I bet you wish you hadn't strayed out of your hole in the woods now. The world must seem very big and strange.'

She takes the old woman's other arm and lovingly presses the sponge into the wrinkled skin until the clear water leaks out over the red flesh and falls in fat drops onto the cushion. 'Like you, I was taken from my mother at a young age. I have been a slave in the Kervan since I was a little girl, when I was sold by my uncle. Esra Hanum here was also a slave, sold in some market when she was just three years old. But she married the bashbakan and her son was also bashbakan, and that is why she is the most powerful woman amongst all the Leggies, here and in the North.'

She plonks the sponge back into the water and then she leans in to the old woman's ear and whispers. The eyelids flick open. The mouth tightens.

The old lady's harsh voice emits a stream of foreign words as Damla helps her rise up against her cushion. One eye is blind or almost blind, the pupil whited over, a scar making a jagged gulch through the soft tissue and deep into the eyebrow. The other eye roams the camp until it falls on me.

'Is that him?' she says.

Her voice reminds me of Old Sally rasping in the damp ashes of our camp fire. The one clear eye looks right into me.

'Hadi, gel janum' she says. When I don't react, she becomes impatient. 'Come, boy.'

Damla nods to me. Very slowly, I approach the chair. The closer I get, the more I can smell her. It's a sweet, tangy fragrance that only partially hides those traces of ageing: the mouldering lungs, rotten teeth. She collapses into a coughing fit and when she does, Damla leans over and wipes her mouth with a cloth.

'You've come a long way,' says Esra Hanum.

'We were lost.'

'Hear that, Damla? He was lost.'

'Yalanji,' says Damla.

'Maybe,' says Esra Hanum. 'Now you are mine. A repayment for all my troubles. I sent nine men into that valley to bring me the Satz woman. Three returned. I will have something for that, to pay that debt. Let me tell you something Doghru Yol –'

She succumbs again to the hacking coughs. Damla tries to help her and gets swatted away. When the old lady gains control of her body once more, her good eye swings around again until it locks on to me.

'My great grandfather was alive when Grove founded his colonies. The True Path. Back then everybody knew they were dangerous hypocrites. Taking those boys in. Brainwashing them. Oh yes. You think you haven't been brainwashed? Did they tell you about us, janum? About the towns and people that surround your valley? Your Grove was an important man in his time, but he was fond of secrets and codes and a little too fond of small boys.'

'Not true,' I say.

The old woman's face darkens, but whatever she wants to say right now she keeps to herself. She reaches out to Damla.

'Sopa,' she says.

Damla shakes her head and tries to ease Esra Hanum back into the chair, but she's having none of it.

'Sopa.'

Ertughral hands Damla a stick which she then puts it in the old woman's hand. There follows the slow, painful process of getting the weak body out of the deep chair. There are red blotches in her cheeks.

She screws up her face as some agony passes through her, flickering in the good eye.

Once she has her feet on the ground she taps Damla with the stick once and then again, until she backs away, the huge, lumbering Damla brushed aside by the tiny, spider-haired woman who controls her.

'You are mine now,' she says, making her laboured way towards me.

'Show me your mark,' she says.

I just look at her.

'The Ladder. Show it to me.'

I turn and bend my head forward to give her a better view of my neck. No point in trying to hide it now.

'Look, Damla,' she says, bringing the point of her stick up to my mark. 'Jacob's Ladder. There is nothing more precious on earth now, given the times.'

As I turn back, the stick goes into my cheek, just under the cheek-bone, where she rolls the point in my skin as if she was trying to raise sparks in my flesh.

'Do you think, maybe, that you were trained, day after day, to fight and to kill, for life up there? On Thule? Is that what they told you? They made you strong for your new life on a harsh world? Well, let me tell you something, your True Path were breeding boys with Jacob's Ladder and they weren't training them to survive on another planet, they were training them to survive on this one. Once there were many like you, now you are rarer than diamonds. They wanted you to get off this rock in one piece. That was their plan. It still is.'

I feel a pulse running under my skull, a slow, persistent throb. I shout at her. I tell her about the five messages. About the Palladium and how it brings them. About the final test, on the appointed day when the best of the True Path will go to Thule. She listens quietly; not amused, not angry, just listening.

'Is that it?' she says, after its all out of me and I've fallen silent. 'Well, I'm just an old woman. What do I know? My people were free once, a long time ago. The Rus came with bio bombs. They took our lands. They enslaved us. They brought us here. All that time we fought, like everybody else, over Jacob's Ladder. We fought and died in our thousands for it.'

She looks at me. She's about to tell me more but thinks better of it.

'Ah,' she says, swatting something invisible out of the air. 'Recite a message for me.'

'What?'

'Grove's messages. Say them for me.'

One by one she makes me go through all of the messages just like I did on the day of my Rising ceremony in front of the council. I try to speak in the strong, proud voice I learned to say those words in, but I can't find that voice. Not here, now, branded and humiliated. A slave in the power of an old woman.

'And the last?' she says.

'The Last Message hasn't arrived yet,' I say.

She puts her stick under my chin and lifts it.

'Look into my eyes when I'm talking to you. The last message came to Esperanza several months ago. It is deep inside that glowing ball with no doors. They have been bringing sechniks there for months, ready to set out and meet the Saviours. Of course, none of us can go with them, to Thule. Only you can.'

'It's true,' I say.

'Not true in the way you think,' she says. 'I'm not talking about a test. These are the messages,' she says, prodding my neck again. 'There was the first one: *You no longer need to fear,* and then there was this – The Ladder.' She prods at my mark again. 'And now there is the last. Just three in all, Doghru Yol. The Thuleans were men of fewer words than Grove led you to believe.' She gives a short, cynical laugh. 'They used to ask, in the old days, if these Thuleans are so clever, why don't they save us all, and be done with it? But it is not an easy thing, what they have attempted here. Both bodies have to learn to live together, human and alien. It takes time to make the Ladder.'

They are grinning at me. Ertughral, Damla, the other men assembled here. Look at the ignorant boy from the woods. Peter must have seen the same thing in his last moments, surrounded by silent mockery as the flames ate him. I was there. I was one of them.

She laughs that dry laugh again and taps my head with the stick. 'Strong boy. Fattened up with lies. Thin as a rake now on a diet of hard truth. I have heard reports, though I can't say they are entirely reliable, that the Salvatores have arrived already. People claim to have seen them.'

The old woman, lurches back towards her chair, looking feebler now, from behind. 'You have seen the footprints my people found, I suppose?' she says, smiling at Damla. 'We have our own name for the Saviours, in our own tongue: we call them 'Insanlar'. It means *the people.* I'm not sure that they didn't make a huge mistake inviting us to live amongst them. After all, would you?' As she turns to her chair, she winks at Damla, who smiles back at her. 'You no longer need to fear,' she says, brushing a hand lovingly over the plump, softly gleaming cushion. 'I intend to meet them and stand before them, just once. I have some questions I wish to ask them. Oh I won't be going with them, but just the same. We have all paid in blood and hurt for their messages.' The bashbakan taps her ruined eye. 'A rusty carpenter's nail,' she says. 'So that I would lie still for my rapist. We will go into the cloud hill and hear that message for ourselves.'

She slumps into the chair and cranes her head weakly towards Damla. 'Cut away your bonds – isn't that what he said?'

'Yes Esra Hanum.'

'Which one was that?'

'The fourth, I think.'

'Ah yes. The fourth. Cut away your bonds. Have you cut your bonds, Doghru Yol? All of them?' The good eye seeks me out again. It prowls and springs like a cat hunting in the grass.

A sharp cry comes from the direction of the slave wagon – Ulya!

The old lady brightens. Rises in her seat. 'Let's see just how committed you are to your messages,' she says.

35

FIRE

I spin around, giving Esra exactly the reaction she wants. Umut, along with another man and a woman have Ulya by the arms and heave her – her feet dragging in the dirt – to the camp fire that is already piled high this morning. She twists in their arms, trying to grip them with her free legs. No living thing moves quite like Ulya. The drug has worn off, she can fight and twist and flex. It takes all three to manage her. The woman takes the legs, but drops the right one. A mistake that earns her a kick on the chin. She yells and grabs both legs and spits in Ulya's face. We all watch as they grapple her into position, on the windward side of the fire.

She is a wild animal. All the time, since the underground room, this beast has nursed me and guided me along, bound my wounds, spoken encouraging words. A boy raised by a wolf.

'What was it you said?' says Esra. 'After cut away your bonds? Something about history and then a fire. What was it? Those things will be killed in a fire?'

'Those things will die in the fire,' says Damla.

'Beautiful,' she says. 'I like your messages. So will we burn them then?

Will we throw your bonds into the fire and set you free?'

'No,' I say.

'What's that?'

'No.'

'Are you saying that she matters to you? Would you rather disobey the Saviours and let her live?'

They press Ulya closer to the fire. She twists her head away from the heat, her mouth tight, her chest heaving frantic breaths. Umut gives Ulya a shove. She stumbles forward, gets caught by the flames and falls back, screaming. I take a swing at the man behind me, ploughing into his chest. Someone from behind, perhaps it's Mr Ertughral, smashes me on the back of my head, and I fall straight down, hard enough to feel a loud thump when my skull meets the packed earth.

When they drag me out again the next day, and I kiss his hand, Ertughral smiles down benevolently. I am not thinking of defeat and slavery, but about the thickness of his neck and how many slices it might take, with my long lost knife, to open an artery.

During my beatings, when Mr Ertughral stands by and watches Umut indulge himself with the bar, or his boots, I watch that throat and think about gliding my knife through the flesh, the Rising boy. I would hunt him first, let him run as fast as those stumpy legs will carry him and then, when he has collapsed onto the ground and is struggling for breath I'd lift him by his head and finish him. He would have enough blood, I reckon, to fill a wooden cask or two. He's heavy with it, it gorges his cheeks, the swinging belly.

Until that moment, when I have strength and opportunity, I play by the rules they have set. A slave doesn't speak unless asked a direct question. A slave doesn't meet his master's eye. A slave keeps his head down. Slaves don't talk to each other. There should be silence in the 'green wagon'. They rap on the bars with a switch if there is too much noise.

'Don't make me come in there,' they say.

If your fingers happen to be on the bars, then all the worse for you. Ulya has welts under her knuckles from the night she learned that lesson.

The next day she held them up in the light as if admiring them. She has angry red spots on her face, arms and legs, from her split second contact with the fire, some have blistered and the blisters have opened.

'How do you do it, Ulya?' I ask her, while she turns her damaged hand in the light. 'How do you go on, when everything is hopeless?'

She answers the question only on the third time of asking, and then with her head down so I can only see the darkened crown where the ink has vanished under a crop of new hair.

'You have to lock yourself away, Leon. Go into a place where you're safe and shut the windows and all the doors and then put boards on them and then climb down into the basement and pull the door there shut and lock it and get into a box, if you have to and hide there. As deep down as you can go, and then deeper. So you can only hear the sound they make when they beat you like it was at top of the water and you were under water.'

'Is that what you did when you were in the Colony?'

'Yes.'

'With me?'

'Yes.'

'You did that with me? You hid away, down in a box in a basement?'

'I just had to see it out. I was just waiting for that, for the end of it.'

I think of the boy in the Four Walls, looking up at me from the bottom of the ramp, the sand bag at his feet. We must be crushed before we can rise.

36

Over the following days, weeks, I watch Ertughral closely, listen to his barked orders and wait to spot weaknesses, openings. I follow Ulya's direction. I'm a good slave. I bide my time.

The Kervan lurches south west, toward the sea on old roads now heavily used again. Rutted with cartwheels, the prints and dung heaps of horses and mules. The landscape changes. Everywhere are patches of bald, blackened land, the ash remains of forest fires. A hill we pass beneath is still smoking after it was ravaged by fire, heat shivering in the air around it. A stipple of blackened shoots all that remains of its foliage.

Young boys are posted on the wagon roofs to watch the sky for any signs of heat haze or changes in the aurora that might signal a sunburst. On an afternoon when we are descending carefully out of hilly country one of those boys runs ahead, around a bend and yells back to us. 'I can see the sea. Sea ahead.'

When the Kervan rounds the bend, I follow Ertughral and Umut out to a vantage point, a ledge of rock. There it is: a plain stretched out below us, greenish yellow in the sun and beyond that a vast expanse of blue, like a promise of freedom. I almost gasp.

'My uncle told me he saw this place, back when it was still alive. A city,' says Ertughral. 'Had trains, Umut, and electric lights. Only forty years ago.'

He points to a stretch of land further down the coast, where a river comes creeping out of the mountains and splits and sinks in silver threads into marshes and sand. There is a vast, dusty, rusted thing clinging to the water's edge, like a rim of backwash on the tideline of a lake. Even from here I can see it is miles wide. A place. A city. Tall ruins, many times the size of the tower we slept in, stand against the backdrop of the sea.

The forest to the south has swallowed many of the ancient structures and in the midst of the dense canopy, like a gentle reflection of the sun, is a softly glowing light.

'The Colina Nube,' says Ertughral. 'See that Gul? Perfect and smooth, like a baby's ass. That's where you and I are going. The message is waiting there for us.'

We take a winding road out of the mountains. As we get closer to the city we start to see people. Not soldiers, not the inked men from Esher, these are families. Quiet and anxious, crouched around damp, smoky fires or pressed close to each other with no fires at all. Hungry looking men and women, ravaged by the road. Faces like spent seed heads. Dark scraggly children with round bellies and bony arms and legs. So many. They have left their homes and villages to hear the message, or to witness the last days.

The Leggies ignore the thickening crowds and their camps and find a quiet spot in the foothills to set up their own base close to the city. After several days wait, they carry the Bashbakan, in her chair, out of her wagon again. They place her down at a high point with a view over the treetops from where she sits watching the city, occasionally tapping her stick on the ground as if she could hear a secret rhythm there.

Parts of Esperanza are on fire. Smoke gutters from rooftops. Underneath that smoke lives a fierce orange glow.

'The worm brood that attacked us upriver,' says Ertughal. 'In the city now. They're trying to burn them out.'

I listen closely and I think I can hear faint worm calls, their hollow echoes in the empty buildings.

All day we wait for some sign or order from the Bashbakan. She sleeps in her chair through the afternoon, despite the danger of a sunburst. When she eventually wakes, just before sundown, she calls for me.

Mr Ertughral brings me to her and puts me standing beside her chair.

'Do you have that creature with you?' she says to him.

'Always, Esra Hanum,' says Mr Ertughral.

'Let me see it,' she says.

Ertughral unbuckles Peter's leather case from his belt and extracts a glass bottle half full of clay and hands it to his Basbakan. She takes it in her long, misshapen fingers and as she draws it close, the dirt inside stirs, a lump rises, something grey emerges. I take half a step back but Ertughral puts a hand against my spine to stop me. A creature hauls itself half way up the wall of the jar, tiny claws emerging from its belly and popping on the glass. It is at least six inches long. A triangular mouth folds back in layers around two rows of hard disks, like beaks. Above the mouth, the antenna or tongue rises and forks just like it did when I saw the same organ slip of that man's body on the island in the river. So this is what Peter carried with him on his belt all the time we were with him. Why the Leggies threw him in the fire.

It stops moving. A single claw twitches. The segmented outer carapace pulses in a steady rhythm over a tangled black core like dense, matted hair. It reminds me of the dark layer under my own skin when it drank.

Esra observes it quietly. It is attentive, following her eye somehow. What does it look out of?

'You know, of course,' Esra says to me, 'that the worm is not from here, it is a gift, from Thule.'

I look at Ertughral and he nods in agreement.

'They were sent to us in a message,' she says. 'Like the word of God. *In the beginning was the word and the word became flesh and made it's dwelling amongst us.* Have you a religion, Doghru Yol? Have you read the Bible?'

'No, mam.'

'No. You don't even know what that is, do you? What a nice innocent mind you have. We were not supposed to grow the worm, but when you put a power into the hands of *men...*' she glares at me. 'The Colina is not empty. A group of renegades, former NAA soldiers, have found a way in. They are charging fees for access to the message. We know of an entrance the Satz pioneer told us about, but it seems it will not be so straightforward. We may need to fight.'

'Hojam, this plan is –,' says Ertughral.

Ezra swings her stick at him. It is a weak gesture but his flinching reaction suggests she has done it often enough in the past, and with more force.

'The sechnik will go. The message is for him.'

'If you release Ulya,' I say.

Esra makes a funny sound in her throat, as if she was trying to swallow what I just told her and couldn't quite get it down. 'Bring it back to me, or she will be consigned to the flames, like that boy you brought with you. How about that?'

'You don't need her –'

Ertughral strikes me hard on the back of my head and then he grabs me by the collar and presses the glass jar against my cheek. At the edge of my strained vision the elastic tongue springs out of the dirt and hits the glass, a finger-width from my eye.

'You want to meet him Gul? You want to say hello? Because he wants to say hello to you.'

The old lady either has not or pretends not to notice any of this. She settles back into her seat and gazes at the view.

'We are in the last days,' she says, and directs her stick at the city and the black smoke in the streets. 'I've seen books, with pictures: 'Visions of the Sechniks'. There is no dry land anywhere. They are things of the water and the dark. That's what they say. Their cities are underground. On Thule, they breathe through water bubbles, sucked in through their skin, like a fish. Imagine, Gul? It would not be life as we know it. Safe, yes, but alien and lonesome, don't you think? What you wouldn't give for a bit of clean air, a patch of grass.

I've heard they have built a city for us, up on the surface, in the moonlight. A half-way house, all shiny and new and waiting for the first arrivals,' she looks again at me, her face softened. 'Thule might be Heaven, Doghru Yol, or some drab and hopeless tundra. What does it matter? There is a future there. There is none here. This is the roof of Hell.'

When the chosen day comes, a group is assembled to bring me down to the city. The party from the Kervan is led by Umut. It's the first time I've seen him without the iron bar. I try to keep well away from him, he never seems quite in control of himself. He has a glass oil lamp swinging from his belt. 'Goin' to dark places,' he says, when he sees me looking at it. Ertughral walks behind me, his eyes on my back.

We leave before dawn and by mid-morning we arrive at the out-skirts of the city, on a stretch of rough ground that was once a road and is now a torn and shredded weed bed. Flash floods have made it a water course in the wet season, leaving clumps of mud and scatter-ings of torn brush and stones like the path of an avalanche. Rusted metal frames cling to the mud banks. One of them is surrounded by shattered glass.

How many people lived here? How was it possible that the world was so full? So noisy?

Deeper in, there are signs of recent habitation. Sections of the roads have been repaired over the years. Tin roofs arranged roughly on top of mud and concrete, with the vast towers above them, swallowing them in their shadow. Outside one of these dwellings is a dog, tied to a stake. He stands when we approach and he watches us quietly. He's skin and bone. No sign of any owner. He follows our progress like it was some-thing that interested him only a little. Smoke leaks out of a pipe in the stonework behind him.

Beyond the ruins of the city, rising over the forest canopy, is the Colina Nube. Perfectly round and evenly lit. A completely man made thing. I want to reach out and touch it, run my hand over its smooth surface. Feel the warmth of the light on my skin.

The road takes us to a steep gorge, manmade, concrete. Giant buildings stand clustered around a rusted iron bridge. On the bridge's skeleton hangs a new, rickety frame of pliable wood. We cross in single file, going carefully. The wooden platform bends and wobbles underneath us.

We hear the worm calls as the last of our party reaches the end of the bridge. We stop and stand and listen.

I feel a squeeze in my heart. An answering call wavers out of the distance, followed immediately by a single ringing percussion: a gunshot. Worm brood answer that too, with more calls. The shooter has just alerted them to his position.

We push on, more anxious now. Down a flight of steps and under a massive structure standing on pillars. Patches of black on the concrete mark the remains of old campfires. Everywhere are signs of new life, flimsy wooden homes set up against the old walls or climbing through the sheer vertical spaces like creepers.

'Where is this tunnel?' says Umut. He is anxiously pawing the side of his leather coat.

'Relax,' says Ertughral. 'We're close.'

Even down here the worm chatter reaches us and it seems nearer, swelling against the hard surfaces. By the sound of the calls I reckon there are two or more waiting in the direction we are headed and at least one directly behind us. They are drawing the edges of the net in. They know we're here.

The Leggies realise it just as I do. They stop. Look at one another. A call from up ahead that has the faint burr of a growl in it. Close. Perhaps around the next corner.

'This isn't right,' says one of the men. 'It's a trap.'

From the floor above us comes a series of low scampering noises. Someone, something trying the cross the space quietly.

One of the men mutters in Turkish. Umut hisses at him to shut up.

'We could come back in the evening. Worm brood might've moved on by then,' says the first man, who has his knife out, his eyes searching out every corner of the building.

'You think they're not behind us?' says Ertughral, giving the man a withering look.

It is hard to keep quiet on the broken concrete, strewn with shattered glass. When we get to the far side of the building Umut and two others go to check the way ahead while we wait. After a while we hear the grinding and scraping of wood and steel. Some whispered words in Turkish. When they come back Umut looks a lot less grim and frightened.

'Hadi,' he says. 'I think it's here.'

He leads us out of the building into a gulley chocked with debris. Torn strips of barbed wire and a burned wooden enclosure are what remains of some last ditch defence. About fifty yards in, beyond the wire, Umut and the others have uncovered a doorway, set at an angle to the concrete wall of the gulley. They have pulled one of the iron doors open and thrown aside the branches and wooden boards that must have hidden it, exposing the top steps of a metal staircase.

The dark hole below releases a foul breath. The breeze carries dead leaves down into its maw, swirling over the stairs as they disappear. It makes me think of the bunker where I failed my Rising. Where my men died.

Umut peers down into it, baring his teeth.

'The sechnik first,' he says.

37

I feel my way down onto the first step. The cold air touches my ankles. From below comes a damp chill and the smell of rotten wood and stale, recycled air. The little light from the open door reveals a narrow round tunnel lined with pipes and steel drums.

'What do you see?' says Umut.

'Nothing,' I say.

The smell is bad, but mercifully the worm calls are muffled here. I creep down the rest of the steps and splash into several inches of foul water. My arrival sends small things scuttling away with tiny, muted cries. One of them latches onto my foot. A rodent claw prods my skin a moment and then it disappears with a plop into the water.

Umut moves up close behind me, his knife brushing against my shirt. The others follow with less enthusiasm, grumbling about the smell. The air feels damp and stagnant. An oily film has already formed on my skin.

'Bad place, Doghru Yol,' says Umut. 'Lucky it's too dark to see, huh?'

His voice travels through the depths of chill air setting off faint, distant clanks where it makes contact with walls, steel, water – miles of it, by the sound – before it finally goes out of hearing. When everyone is down the Leggies light their two oil lamps. They only seem to emphasise how vast the dark is down here. There is no visible end to the tunnel either in front or behind us, though a gentle movement in the air suggests an opening, or perhaps a vent, some way ahead. A ledge runs along the walls on both sides but it is too narrow for us to climb up out of the swamp we are standing in.

'How is this the way in to the Colina?' says someone near the back of the group.

Ertughral answers him with a long string of foul sounding Turkish.

We are off the street, away from the worm brood. I at least feel safer down here. Umut gives me a shove between my shoulder blades.

'Hadi,' he says, 'Go on.'

The dark licks at our little halos of wavering light. We wade through the knee-high scum in a tense silence. Unseen life scurries and scratches all around. At regular intervals other tunnels connect with this one, and the air from them is no better. Steel tubes and boxes in the ceiling make soft ticks and clangs as if they were coming gently to life. The Leggies debate the way at every junction, but the choice they make is always the same one: straight on.

Umut keeps me in front, using me as some kind of shield though there is nothing ahead of us. We go along at this cautious pace for a long time, our elongated shadows warped against the curved walls. Our lamp light reflects back to us from the greasy surface layer that clings at our shins. At some stage we pass another tunnel and a hollow exhalation comes drifting out, as if something huge slept inside it. It is followed immediately by the slop of disturbed water.

Umut stops and thrusts his lamp into this new passage and peers in. The others pull up behind him. It is quiet now, except for the subdued ripple of the water, but then, as we listen, the sounds start again. Loud enough to be something heavy, man-sized.

'One of those renegades,' offers Ertughral, in a sharp whisper.

'Maybe,' says Umut. 'Maybe not.'

He presses me on but slower now, glued to that noise, as if we had all merged into one consciousness, one single ear. We only get a few yards, I reckon, before new sounds come from up ahead. These are closer, something metal loosely attached and screeching against the concrete walls. We stop again.

The Leggies make noises that aren't quite mutters: Tongue clicks, grunts, soft, quivering complaints. Reacting to the slightest sound.

'Umut,' says Ertughral from the back of the line, in a low voice.

'What?' Umut turns the lamp towards him and traces Ertughral's glance down to his belt and the leather canister hanging there. It is shaking violently, jumping around on its loop.

'Why did you bring – ,' Umut starts to say but Ertughral quiets him with a finger to his lips. With one hand he unlatches the canister and draws it carefully from the leather. The worm is fully out of the soil, pressed up against the glass, its black inner core writhing. It turns on its claws to follow the direction of the light and then stops, shivers and explodes.

The closest man leaps backwards.

The worm's entire body has splattered against the glass with a violent crack, its worm shape all gone. Now a twitching bundle of fibres.

'Solujanlar,' says Ertughral. He nods in the direction of the side tunnel. 'A brood.'

Nobody seems to know what to do. We are stalled in this darkness, crippled. All order and authority is gone. Umut yells but nobody listens. They are all saying, 'Solujan, solujan.' Their word for worm. Each voice

271

carries the germ of panic to the next. The mutterings gets louder, the voices more shrill. Pretty soon everybody is pushing me, using me as a kind of punch bag, while they debate how to handle the situation. Umut eventually loses patience, shoves them aside, takes a corner of my shirt and drags me along behind him, the others complaining, but following nevertheless.

'Come,' he says.

I try to shake him loose. He cuffs me across the back of my head. There is motion in the side tunnel, and then a loud splash. A man screams and his scream is violently cut off.

I can smell it, even in this stinking hole. The worm smell: dense and sweet. Just as Umut turns his lamp to the back again, more slowly and reluctantly this time, we all hear the noise, in the midst of the mayhem: the crack of thick glass against concrete. The tinkle of the broken shards.

Back at the junction of the tunnels, a single Leggie is twisting his torso in a silent struggle while two flabby arms tucked under his chin and shoulder, slide him out beyond the range of Umut's lamp light into the dark. Ertughral is beached on a concrete ledge, his head bloody, his eyes open while he receives attention from another of these creatures, whose face seems to have melted, from the bridge of his nose down to his mouth, hanging in rivulets of flesh over its chin.

Erthughral's hand is empty. The glass is smashed on the ledge beside him. The worm is gone.

Umut makes a low sound, like a muffled scream. The sweat all across his forehead sparkles under his lamp light. He directs the light to the broken glass tube and beside it a dark smear where the worm slid from the ledge.

'Aman tanrim,' mutters the Leggie nearest to Ertughral, who has the other lamp, now dropped to his side. A lump is rising through his trouser leg. He stands there quivering, holding his hands over his torso as if he wants to push the thing away but won't dare touch it. Nobody moves or speaks. We all stand quiet and watch its progress, the lump easing upwards, pausing, moving again. A probing tongue reaches out from under his belt. Another Leggie, standing just behind me, raises his gun to his shoulder.

'Hayir,' says the man with the lamp.

The gunman opens fire. The shots explode into the tunnel, illuminating the whole scene in a series of bright, hot flashes: teeth and worm poison on Erthughral's neck as he slides off the ledge, more drones advancing from the side tunnel in a greedy lope. The shots are wild and aimless, missing the worm completely and sending the Leggie flying backwards. The worm abandons him. A flash of grey as it sinks back into the water.

I break Umut's hold on me and back away. The water churns all around me. Impossible to say where the worm is now. The drones fall on the group. Weapons stab into flesh, making moist thuds, but the screams are ever more desperate, more hopeless. A body goes down in the water, thrashing. I try and boot him away from me, imagining a mouth full of poison, but all I hit is a flailing arm. He makes garbled pleas for help as he swallows water, kicking and thrashing.

Warm fingers brush the skin of my arm. I kick. I run. Stumbling off, reeling into the dark. In just a few strides I am clear of everybody, but I have no plan, nothing in my head except to delay the inevitable.

The drones – there seem to be dozens of them – are calling for others to join them. The responses to those calls come from all around, in front and behind and off in the distance, from whatever is now above us.

I break into a run, all sense of space and distance gone, as the slick walls send the last agonised breaths, the grunts, kicks and screams to me from all sides, clotted echoes, throbbing in my ears.

How tame life in the our Colony seems. The Four Walls, the forced marches, the beatings I got down the years from trainers, Elect, even other Initiates. I would laugh at that now. What I wouldn't give to see the General's grim face on some cold morning, in the rain, on the exercise ground, another predictable day of training in front of me. To hear the grunts of effort, my family all around me. How happy we actually were to get up late at night in our dorms, when the trainers were asleep, and race head lice in a box under the light of a candle. They were good times. We knew nothing about the world.

Up ahead, maybe a hundred yards away, in the ceiling, there's a gray light – an opening, a hole, something. It gives me strength, hope, but I'm not alone. Someone has followed me after all. They are gaining fast. A commotion in the water. Grunts. I lose my balance, trying to run and keep my head together at the same time, and I get a fleeting sense that I am in deep trouble. I gulp down hard on a mouthful of the stale air, before flying out and down, my shoulder crashing against a concrete ledge.

I cry out in alarm but my voice is instantly muffled in the bleary water. A hot tingling travels up my left leg. I cannot tell if I am breathing or not.

Just as suddenly, with a violent lurch, someone hauls me up and out. I vomit a lungful of putrid water and cough and splutter before I can take a breath again.

'You think you're gonna get away, Doghru Yol?' Umut's mouth is close to my ear. I actually want him to kill me. I want him to ram his knife into my back and end this, and if the sound of his voice is anything to go by, he wants that too.

'No way. You gonna go with me, or you gonna die.'

He has dropped or lost his lamp. I can hardly hear him through the water logged ears. His voice might as well be coming from a mile back in the tunnels. My throat is locked shut. Lungs sipping on threads of air. He grabs me around the waist to stop me from swooning.

'Not gonna die yet, Doghru Yol.'

'Leave me alone.'

'What's that?'

'We can't run like this. I'll fight with you.'

'You want me to let you go?'

'Yes.'

The battle behind us has come to an end. The sounds are all low and rhythmic now.

'Let me go.'

Umut hesitates. He is listening to the same thing I am.

'I'll kill you if you run, Doghru Yol,' he says as he presses a blade into the small of my back. 'I don't care if they kill me. I'll kill you first.'

I nod vigorously. He shoves me gently as he releases me. I nearly fall into the water again; my stomach and throat convulsing in empty, dry heaves. It takes precious time to gather myself, fighting the nausea and dizziness. Umut's blade is not at my back anymore. I swing around to him.

He's staring right past me, his mouth forming a question he hasn't asked.

At his right shoulder is a pale figure. Not bloated like the worm brood I've seen, but weirdly, eerily still.

The first thing I think is how strangely brave he is to look so calm in the midst of this chaos. The man is looking at me through hooded eyes, spittle shining on his lips.

Then I see it. A wound on Umut's shoulder, where his shirt has been torn away. It is seething. The man behind him has poisoned it.

In the midst of this frozen scene, the pale man slowly lowers his mouth down to the wound again and blows a frothy spume into it. When he draws his mouth away again, the bubbles silently combine into larger globes. Inside the largest of the globes, tiny larvae glide and dart. Even at that size, they have minuscule claws or mandibles that give them purchase on the edges of Umut's wound, enough to hold steady in the swirling bubble, straighten their tadpole-like bodies and wriggle in.

I want to get out of there, to move, do something but it all happens with the sluggishness of a nightmare.

I take Umut's right hand and he surrenders the knife without resistance. When I finally turn and run towards the light in the ceiling his last shallow breath as a human being pursues me through the tunnel like a curse.

38

The light is coming from a grille in the tunnel roof and below it is a series of iron rungs screwed into the wall. I climb quickly, the dizziness from my near drowning creeping through my head like oil in water, slowing me, forcing me to think everything out.

I'm praying that grille is not nailed down. When I get high enough to push it with the heel of my hand it lifts easily and I drag myself up into a bare corridor.

I am still underground. Lots of dark rooms but no windows. The creature that infected Umut is finally after me, slopping through the water below. I grab the first thing that comes to hand, an iron pipe that has collapsed from the wall, and haul it over the grille. It will hold him for a minute or two maybe, enough time to put some distance between us.

I search for a staircase, another ladder, anything that might take me up. Yearning for clean air.

It feels like the hollow, dampened worm calls have entered my blood and tremble through it.

At the end of another lightless passage, I come up against a wooden door someone has barricaded shut. I push against it, then slam into it with my shoulder. It gives a little. I pile into it again and this time there is a loud creak and whatever was holding it falls away with a clatter. I find a jumble of chairs on the other side.

Beyond the door everything is very different: a long corridor lit by electric lights, warm and yellow in glass cases. A soft covering on the floor. Here and there boxes lie packed or half-packed or open and scattered.

I put my hand on the steel walls and feel a thrum under my fingers. A steady pulse like a heartbeat. This place is alive. The pipes near the floor carry ghostly whispers. Hidden steel and iron clank and whirr and grind.

All around me are dorm rooms with bunks against the walls, recently abandoned. Mattresses and sheets lie strewn on the floors. No blood or bullet holes or damage. It was an evacuation.

So many strange things in glass and steel I have no name for. So perfectly shaped and colourful. I almost stop and look but I have to keep my mind straight. No distractions. From the floor below, through the steel structure, come muffled clanks and the drumming of feet. My barricade has given way.

The soft floor allows me to go quietly. It's a long way. I pass kitchens, latrines, store rooms. A hidden underground city. How many souls here? Is this where my Bind and her Pioneers lived, under Esperanza?

Come to the West. The beacon at Esperanza. You'll find us. Vanesa will show you.

I climb a stair case into another set of corridors that ends in a steel door. From here, the ringing calls of the worm brood are distant and threadbare. Instead, from behind the steel walls come the faint patterns of conversation. One male voice above all the others, shouting and muttering and laughing.

An iron wheel in the centre of the door opens the lock. It is stiff, rusted in place, and takes a huge effort to turn, but when the door finally swings open it reveals a narrow passageway with a floor is thick patterned wool in purple and blue. Elaborate lights in carved iron and glass boxes hang from the ceiling.

To the left the corridor branches off to a small staircase with three steps ending in a metal door. The source of the voices. As I climb the steps I hear the rattle and clink of bottles or glasses.

I test the handle carefully and it turns in my hand. The lock clicks. I press the door open and then I let it swing the rest of the way.

Just about everyone in the room looks up. Some of them have glasses at their lips, all are in some state of undress. At a table in the centre, a woman sits chained to a table leg, the barrel of a gun resting on her bottom lip. The tall, bull-necked man holding the gun to her mouth has his shirt open, a mound of long grey hair spilling over his shoulders.

There are others around the table, a couple of them have fallen asleep with their heads resting on their arms.

The glass wall at the back of the room looks out on a vast open space, a steel wonderland of suspended walkways, ladders, metal drums. Hanging above it all, in a network of cables and stays, is the Colina Nube. The great glowing dome. We are inside it. Only in here it is a gloomy, underwater light, as if we had crawled inside a stomach.

The man with the gun is the last to lift his head and when he does his mouth twists in anger.

'For Chrissake,' he says. He takes the gun out of the woman's mouth and slams it on the table.

'Are we stopping?' says a man to my left, rising on his elbow out of a mound of glossy cushions. All around the walls are machines with winking lights, like the box I destroyed back in the bunker. The thing that talked to me. To one side, close to the door, is a tall object – seven feet at least – covered in a purple cloth.

'Of course we're stopping. Didn't you notice we have a visitor?' says the long haired man, looking down at the woman chained to the table. 'Anyway, it's no fun like this. The life has to matter.' He picks up the gun once again, thoughtfully this time, and gazes down the barrel, before putting it to his own temple.

'What are you doing?' says the same man on the cushions, still sitting upright.

'Never you mind.'

His finger lightly brushes the trigger, a grin forming on his lips. There's something odd about the way his mouth slumps at the edges as if he hadn't the energy to lift it. He turns the gun and points it at one of the men in the room, takes an imagined shot, and then he spins on one foot, jams the barrel into the woman's head and fires. The barrel turns. The gun clicks. Nothing happens.

'Reynolds,' he says. 'Does this ancient thing even work?'

The woman at the table did not even flinch at the click. She is young, with supple, pale skin, dark around the eyes like Ulya, but with no light or strength there.

The man with the grey hair sighs and attempts to button up his shirt but he is clumsy. His co-ordination is not equal to the job. Instead, while he gets his balance, he takes a proper look at me. Something begins to dawn on him while he surveys my ink.

'Well I'll be –' he says. 'You're one of them, aren't you?' He turns to the man on the glossy cushions. 'Mattheus, what do they call them? True something…kind of pompous … True. Truth. Holy Truth – what the hell is it?'

The man he called Mattheus hardly acknowledges the question. He is busy trying to get the stopper out of a bottle.

'True Path,' I say.

The grey-haired man smiles. 'I knew it sounded religious,' he says, jabbing a finger in my general direction. He slips off words, fumbling with them the same way he fumbled with the buttons of his shirt. He comes right up to me, a pungent odour on his breath, earthy and sweet all at once. I have to turn my head away. 'How did you get in?'

'Through a tunnel,' I say.

The grey-haired man stares at me for a moment and then turns and scans the faces in the room. They seem only half interested in what he is doing and follow his display with nods of the head, the occasional weak laugh.

'Alone?' he does a half turn, his eye drawn to the girl at the table and then to the tall object against the wall. The news slowly percolates through him.

'Jesus,' he says. He goes pacing the room again, it seems to be the only way he can assemble his thoughts. 'Well congratulations to you,' he says, and waves at the object under the purple cloth. 'There it is, take a look. The Last Message. The Pioneers left it here. Fled the place a week ago. Can you believe that? I mean there are people here who travelled a long way to meet them,' he points at the woman at the table. 'No dice. Vamoose. Gone into the East with their wagons.'

I stare at the purple cloth. I know now. I understand what I am look-ing at. It makes perfect sense.

'You're the ones who took the Colina. The ones charging for access to the message.'

'The message from another world,' he says. 'The last one.'

'The message is in there?'

He grins at me. 'It's in there. Only you have to have a special gift to get it out. It doesn't speak to you. There's no little paper you can read. I tried it myself. So did Mattheus here. Nothing. She'll tell you,' he says, indicating to the woman. 'She's one of the Pioneers, a Satz bitch. She laughed at me when I tried it, can you imagine? Bitch laughed in my face and told me there was no way I was getting the message. Not now. Not ever. Apparently it will only give its secrets to the Elegidos. As for the rest of us, well –' he looks again at the woman. 'We get to stay here.'

I put Umut's knife carefully on the floor and then I take my shirt in both my hands and drag it over my head and drop it in front of me. I turn my back to them all so they can see it properly. The thing I have never seen.

'Jesus,' he says after a while. 'That's a first for me. First in the West I mean. I ain't never seen one out here. Jackson, you seen one of these out this way before?'

'No sir,' says one of the men seated at the table. He is using his hands to scrape up a pile of white powder that has spilled across the table in front of him.

I take a step towards the object under the cloth. There is one guard here. He raises his rifle and points it at me. He seems to be the only one in the room who is fully awake and engaged.

'Daniels for Chrissake put that down,' says the grey-haired man. 'We are all friends here. Listen True Path, or whatever you are, we have plenty of time for messages and the end of the world and all the shit to come,' he traces some vague pattern in the air with his right hand. 'First things first. I need you to help us with something else.'

282

'What?' I say.

Daniels does not lower his gun, but he takes his eye from the barrel.

'These gentlemen here,' the grey-haired man goes on, 'have never witnessed the sight of a marked man spiking another human being. Never. They're all from the West. Out East, we're used to the sight. Any night in New Brazil, and I mean any night, fifty bucks will get you a dog spiking, a slave spiking, women, men, black, white, you name it. I've seen a guy vomit ten feet into the air when he got clicked. The eyes came out of his head. Of course, these men here think I'm exaggerating.'

He sees me look at the girl chained to the table.

'We were hoping someone like you, an Elegido, would turn up sooner or later. Predictions were made, money changed hands, that kind of thing,' he says. 'So since luck has brought you here, and we have time, perhaps you could give us a demonstration. If you're up to it.'

'A demonstration of what?'

'A spiking,' he says, jerking his head in direction of the woman at the table.

'You want me to kill her?'

'Simple enough transaction. Her life in return for your salvation. Those people up there on the hills, the pilgrims, those poor, big-eyed hungry multitudes, do you think they'd hesitate for even a second to take an offer like that? I doubt it. You do this one simple thing that I ask of you, then Daniels here steps away and you take that message and you walk.'

I look across at the tall, draped object standing like a sentinel on the other side of the room.

I try to think. My skull feels like it's buckled too tight around my brain, stretched to the last latch hole. Things are happening. People are talking. Sooner or later I will have to act.

'What's the matter?' he says, grinning, 'She too young? I've got another one here you could have a crack at. In fact, I've got three or four.'

He indicates with a nod to the armed man he called Daniels. Daniels leans down and unlatches a steel hatch set into the floor, revealing the top rungs of a ladder and the snaking forms of pipes and cables.

'Turns out the pioneers left some folks behind, in case there were any late comers in need of salvation, like yourself. That was a short straw to pull, huh?' his grin fades as he watches my reaction. 'Come on, don't feel bad,' he says. 'It's the last days of the world. All bets are off. There are no more consequences.'

39

The grey-haired man is constantly trying to rouse his drowsy audience. Shaking his head at them. Waving his arms in exaggerated gestures of disbelief, astonishment.

'Take your pick,' he says. 'You can do Maria or whatever her name is at the table here, or you can have your pick from the stock below.'

I take a step back, wondering now how I can manage the situation. One armed man, another unarmed guard, the rest in varying states for consciousness. Will they even put up a fight if I go for the message?

'It's not always easy, so I'm told,' he goes on. 'Some don't have the jissum or whatever. There's got to be a threat, something to get the blood moving. Those creeps up in the mountains show you how to do it?'

I keep my mouth shut. Allow myself another half-step retreat. He takes my measure from head to toe and tightens up his mouth in disappointment or disgust.

'Not to worry,' he says. 'We are prepared for all eventualities.' He grabs a glass tube from the table and holds it up for me to see. The tube is half-full with a clear liquid. At one end is a needle.

'It just so happens,' he says. 'That our recreation and your stimulation can both be achieved by the same means.'

'How can I be sure you're not lying to me? How do I know you really have the message here,' I say, nodding towards the object under the purple cloth.

I am trying to force some confidence into my voice but really I'm coming undone. Like something spooled tight inside me is unravelling and sliding away in rapid loops and soon there will be no holding it.

'You can't,' he says. 'That's the beauty of it. Just like Russian Roulette. You know there's only one bullet, eight chambers in the gun. Beyond that you've just got to trust in your luck.'

'Show me the message.'

'Not until you complete your side of the bargain. But believe me, the time will fly by. You see, my estimate is thirty seconds tops, but I'm surrounded by doubters. Jackson here is close to the mark and says a minute. Mattheus, who has no clue because he's a hillbilly from up in the North or some place, says two minutes. There are various other guesses around this table, most too ludicrous to mention. All I want from you is to settle the matter for once and for all and shut these fuckers up.' His mouth forms one of those gleeful grins that sits so unnaturally in that ravaged face. 'Thirty seconds and you'll be out of here.'

'I don't understand,' I say.

The grey-haired man approaches again, until we are nearly nose-to-nose.

'That's because you are an ignorant cannibal from the forest. But that's okay. You can't help that. What I want is simple enough even for you to understand. We're going to give you a small dose of phenyl-propyl whatever is in the magic wand there, to stimulate your Thule brain into attack mode and then you are going to spike this woman here in the neck, head or body part of your choosing. Daniels, a reliable neutral, who has a fine timepiece about his person, is going to count the seconds until her brain melts. As I said, the likely figure is below thirty.'

'I want to see that timepiece,' says Jackson. He has much of the powder gathered up around him. His shirt cuffs are stained white. He dips his index finger into the pile and then rubs the powder into his top gum. The artery in his neck pulses under the skin.

'Daniels,' says the grey-haired man.

Daniels takes a device from his pocket and brings it over to Jackson to inspect. It is metal, with a round face of glass and regular, tiny markings on the inside. Jackson brings it so close to his left eye he can't possibly be able to see it.

'Satisfied?' says the grey-haired man.

'As always, Carter, you run a tight ship.'

'The tightest, Jackson. You'd do well to remember it.'

He takes the glass tube with the needle and waves it at me.

'So,' he says. 'Are we all set? I jab you. You do the deed. I let you get the Message. Everybody's happy. You've done it before, right? You've spiked someone?'

I don't answer. I'm thinking of the forest dog that had the bad fortune to meet me. The stink from his carcass. The mayhem.

'You have,' he says. 'I can see it. What must it be like to have a gift like that? I mean, eyes boil in their sockets. You know what those 'Let It Go' people used to do with that poison, right? The Leggies. They drank the stuff. Didn't you hear about that? That was their thing, come out west, watch the sunset that might be the last sunset ever and then all holding hands, all smiling, go out together in one massive convulsion.'

'Carter, we've heard this a thousand times already,' says Jackson.

'Then one more time won't hurt, now will it?'

There's a change in this grey-haired man, Carter. Like he's stepped out of watery shadows into the light for the first time. He's younger than I originally thought. Those drooping pieces of flesh on his neck and cheeks give him an old, sickly look, but underneath that layer are fine bones and clear eyes. It is a face you can't stop watching, can't refuse.

'Scaring yourself are you?' he says to me. 'Hankering for some blood? A boy's got needs. We understand that here. That of all things. Ask anyone of these jaded pieces of shit.'

'It's not like that,' I say. My voice hits a high note that makes a few people in the room smile.

'Warrior boy, it can be whatever you say it is. You're the boss here. It's your deal. Why are you even hesitating? Isn't this what you people do for a living? Don't you have some coming of age right? I heard about this. You have to slit a throat to become, what is it? A warrior, one of the inner circle, something like that.'

'Elect,' I say.

'Right. So you're a man, aren't you? You're an Elect. You must be old enough. So didn't you do it? Didn't you take a life? There's no shame about that here. We've all done cracked a skull or two in the name of survival and prosperity. If we didn't, we got somebody to do it for us.'

There's a deep shame rising inside me, tingling in my scalp, but I also feel a weird thrill, like watching lightening approach over open country. This is the day I was waiting for all along. The day of my exposure.

'Haven't you licked blood from your knife? That there is primordial satisfaction. Once you've found the power to end someone you always have it over people. They always fear you. It's nice to see that. See how they look at you. And you an Elegido. A spiker. You can deal out some awesome death.'

'No,' I say, taking a half step back

'No?' says Carter. 'Then it's time you popped your cherry.'

I didn't even see him move. I don't think anybody did because all the faces around me register surprise. With the force of a punch, he plunges the needle into my arm, where a heat like a fire brand flares in my skin and sets my blood racing, bulging through my veins. Even as my bloodstream heats, my body temperature sinks drastically. My head swarms. The barbs bristle along my skin. There is no blackout this time. Instead, my awareness is heightened, all the fug from the tunnels burned away.

Carter yells at me. 'Hit her. Hit her now. Quick. Show us what's in you.'

I try to suppress it. Send the poison-tipped spurs sliding back down to where they came from. It has some effect, a backward pressure, but it is not enough.

He pushes me towards her. He's not afraid to touch me. The woman turns to see the source of all the ruckus, her mind already bled out. What difference to her? A mercy maybe. And yet not dead. A flicker of something –

I take half a step back. Carter presses his knuckles into the small of my back.

'What the –'

I swing a barbed arm, not at her but at Carter. He ducks, wobbles, falls against me and sends me crashing into one of his half-sleeping men at the table.

At first I'm crushed against him, keeping my arms spread out as wide as I can, but as he wakes and rises I slip and my arm goes out automatically for balance and catches him behind the shoulder blade. The spikes latch onto his clothing and the skin beneath. The contact lasts less than a second before I'm rolling back, staggering, trying to stay on my feet.

He's gone rigid. Spots of blood dot his shirt.

'Daniels, please tell me you've –' Carter doesn't have time to finish his sentence. The wounded man arches his back and sends a dark mass of vomit arcing across the table all over the pile of white powder Jackson is still gathering and all over Jackson's shirt and face. The sound I hear first is not the voiding of his throat, but his back breaking. A deep, muted crack, like the snapping of a dry branch under leaf mould.

My skin is already returning to normal, smoothing out, my blood cooling. I doubt if anyone else is even aware of this. All eyes are on my handiwork. A stench of cooked flesh and Thule poison wafts from the body that was still alive on my last blink.

40

Into the deathly hush that follows the spiking comes a slow, sharp clap from Carter who is leaning over the body to admire my work.

'Did you fucking see that? I mean did you?' He looks at me, warm appreciation in his eyes. 'I take my hat off to you sir,' he says. 'In all my years I have never seen a spike like that. Never. I've seen 'em spew their guts out, I've seen brains pretty much dribble out of their eyes – but to see a spine crack like that? I mean, did you hear that, Jackson? You had a front row seat. Tell me you heard that.'

All I can see of Jackson now are the whites of his eyes. He is seated bolt upright in a pose as frozen as his fellow reveller, now dead, on the opposite side of the table. His hands are halted right in the middle of some task they were performing with the powder before he was doused in vomit.

'Jackson, tell me you heard that,' Carter's voice is pleading, childish. 'Mattheus. What the hell? Did I give you a show or not? Did I deliver?'

Just like after the other spikings, I am drained, washed out. I feel like the woman chained to the table must feel.

'What about the Message?' I say.

I can't look at the dead man. That whole area at the edge of my vision presses on my mind like some chronic pain I don't want to acknowledge. Carter's eyes become slits.

'You're kidding me,' he says. 'This can't be happening. What is wrong with you people? I just gave you the show of your pathetic little lives.'

He turns to Daniels, who has retreated to the hatch which still stands open. 'Daniels. You got the time right? I mean that little creep was dead in ten seconds. Fifteen tops.'

Daniels is not listening to Carter. Attention has already shifted to the hatch and the sounds of struggle coming from the tunnel beneath. Daniels drops his gaze to his foot, which is in the grip of pale, two fingered hand, or claw. A fingernail almost the size and thickness of my old knife is embedded in his calf.

He doesn't get a chance to scream. The head that owns the hand pops up on the ladder and sinks its teeth into his leg, just below the knee. The venom foams up through his thin leggings.

Daniels falls, hits the rim of the hatch. His head thumps on the ladder and he goes crashing into the flailing arms of his attacker.

'Shit,' mutters Carter.

My heart, pulse, mind are racing so quickly now, like a coursing wheel, that I register a lot of details in the brief moment it takes me to adjust to the new circumstances.

There is nothing between me and the object against the wall. I have a minute maybe, before someone reacts – Carter or his friends or the worm brood below – but whatever Carter shot into my arm has cleared the last of the murk from my brain.

I skirt around the shocked and silent men at the table and go straight to the platform and yank the cloth to the floor.

There it is. My heart sinks to see it in front of me, after all these years: The Palladium. Smooth, cold and sheer. At its base the two green lights I remember vividly but also one more, larger light, glowing red: The third message.

Not four. Not five. It had always been there, right in front of me. I had seen the truth as a child and never understood. Three messages. The simple fact of this registers in my mind but I cannot make sense of it.

The Thuleans were men of fewer words than Grove led you to believe.

I glance back. Daniels is gone. His foot is the last thing to slip into the darkness with the hand that grabbed him. With him goes the last bit of sense in the room. The open hatch is like an unspoken threat. There is time to get one of the couches over it or even to turn the table upside down and use it to block the hole. Nobody is going to do this. Nobody is going to arm themselves or run either although Carter does, absent-mindedly, take the gun in his hand and check the only bullet is still in its chamber.

Worm brood are already climbing the ladder. He waits for the first to get his shoulders above the rim before he aims and clicks his way through the empty chambers all the way to the one live round.

The shot is a good one. The creature's head flies backwards, hits the hatch door, smashing it off its hinges and then jerks forwards again, as if he's on a spring. When it does, his left eye is gone. His body falls, lopsided against the remains of the hatch door and that's where it stays, like an uprooted shrub.

Carter is as calm as he was before the worm brood appeared, still admiring his kill.

'I shouldn't even let you over there,' he says to me. 'You were supposed to spike the woman, not the customers,' he says.

I ignore him, reach out with my fingertips to the cold surface of the Palladium and hold them just a hair's breadth away from touching it.

I am a cub again, in the secret room behind the council chamber, the old councillor beside me.

What will it do, sir?

It will put something into you.

Carter looks at me. A tired, disappointed, vicious look. 'Hope you like it up there in all that ice,' he says.

I try to ready myself. I am not a coward, not that, though I did run when Theo called out to me and I did leave my men for dead.

Are you frightened?

No, sir.

A little?

A little, sir.

You should be. We are all being watched and judged, every hour of every day. We must pass the test if we are to be saved.

The Palladium will not know me or what I've done. It doesn't read my mind. That was a child's terror. And yet...

The worm brood are up out of the hatch. I don't have to look to know it. That strange, laboured breathing. Some trouble with the air.

Someone is shouting something from the table, but the voice is giddy, not frightened. I close my eyes, press everything down and away, all thoughts, every jibbering instinct, and I reach out and press my hand against the surface of the Palladium.

First comes the shudder, the smooth movement. The ripple against the flesh. It slides beyond my hand and then stops and returns.

I draw a deep breath. Just like I did all those years ago. A good obedient boy. The blood runs in my hand.

An alien thing in my veins, swimming through the vessels, travelling up my body, and then I see it, all of it. The dim red sun over the Thule ice. A voice in my head. I know the name of this voice, though I cannot pronounce it. It has a Thule name. I can feel it in my head as if it had weight, texture.

'Listen Leon,' it says.

One by one it shows me the things I need to know, about Thule and what will wait for me there. Everything is told to me in this voice that appears to have no source and it shows me these things through its own eyes. Images, sensations shooting past.

Dark water. The surface miles away. Bodies entangled. Like clumped bait lowered into the deep. A steady thrum shaking every particle inside me.

'Bind yourself in the knot. The knot is safety,' says the voice.

A hill. A sharp red moon on its shoulder. Grey snaking shapes on the land below. They are plants, or roots but all on the move, crawling out of the water. Spreading thickly over the land.

Too much. Far too much to comprehend: a blur of image and sound, impressions, snatches. I am not to think now, just receive, accept in a paralysed state. The worm brood running amok in the room, but the noise of them so dimmed and washed out under the stream of images and that voice.

Listen Leon.

The voice stops. Everything goes blank, white. I wait, poised for something. There is no time for this. The silence lengthens. Into the blank void comes a loud metallic click, followed by another a second later, and then another and another. They echo like they have gone clacking down the walls of a deep well.

And then just as suddenly it releases me. My mind pops free and all the sound and smells from the room rush back in. Someone is struggling, moaning through gritted teeth, and something else: a change in the room. I can't at first tell what it is.

I finally open my eyes and look at my hand. It's bone white. Three clumped fingers. As I pull away, gently, I spot my own shadow on the step up to the platform.

The shock balls in my throat. The men at the table have fallen silent, staring. Carter waivers, his gun dropped to his side and then, very slowly, despite the danger from the worm brood advancing on him, he falls to his knees.

He mouths a word. I think it is *Salvatore*. Jackson makes a sign with his hands, down over his face and then across his shoulders. My shadow almost reaches them at the table. My new shape stretched out across the floor in front of me.

Listen, Leon.

I am listening, but I am no longer Leon. In the dead still of the room, the worm brood haul a semi-conscious man from his chair by the table. They are slick and glistening from the watery tunnels. The largest of them is pockmarked with sores leaking the white strands I saw back on the river, stretched like gut across his shoulders and from his torso to his chin.

Carter and his men only have eyes for me. Carter himself is blubbing, tears flowing unchecked along the side of his nose, over his mouth. They watch me intently as I pass them, on my unfamiliar legs. My boots shredded and kicked aside. My splayed, clawed feet snapping on the hard floor.

What am I? I say in my own head, into this new world that has opened inside it.

I get no answer.

At the door I turn to see, through the glass, the grey light of the massive dome silvered, the dust motes glinting like bobbling stars.

The worm brood have descended on the table.

41

So there is a test after all.

Maybe not the one we prepared for, but a test all the same and I must pass it now. Stamp the fear down, the worm of doubt. Hilles, the Council, Joel, they all got me ready for this moment, when I finally become a man, or at least, the man I am going to be.

I go to the place that always steadies me: I recite the messages.

We have heard your call ...

I am still here, Leon, in this body. The voice that spoke to me is locked away in my mind, but it is quiet now and I am alone in here, suspended.

My new skin tingles. My new body and limbs are heavy, cumbersome. I go slowly back the way I came, through the silent corridors and abandoned dorms and kitchens, down the rungs in the wall into the stinking tunnel, but I see it all differently now: A series of sharp, silvered impressions. The greasy water sparkles between the curved walls.

The brood themselves are nowhere to be seen. Must all be in the room with Carter and his people. I get back, without a fight, to the junction where we were ambushed. My Thule eyes can trace the contours of the blood pools on the ledge, the body of one Leggie face down in the water. Must have drowned in the struggle.

I climb the steps up to the hatch and the gulley. My legs are so heavy. At first I welcome the fresh air but then my lungs, if I have lungs, start to struggle. The silvering makes things hard to make out in daylight.

Fine details seem to spring out at me: the spidering cracks in a wall, the briars choking a doorway.

Have to steady my breathing, understand it, get used to it.

First, the strong must separate themselves from the others.

In the distance, from out of doorways and alleys come the curious to look at me. They are afraid of what they see. Hands go to mouths. Children point and yell, but I see no weapons raised. Just fear and wonder.

Saviour. Salvatore.

A small following gathers behind me, keeping a distance. They stay with me all along the broken road downhill to the sea.

Esperanza is on fire. The scream of burning tin. Iron roofs popping. Worm calls. I don't know where I'm going except that it is away from that terrible heat.

The tight streets shadowed by the giant buildings gradually widen and give way to open ground and the shore and the sea. Here it is cooler, clearer, the drifts of smoke from the fires fray as they cross the water. There are patches of blue sky ahead. I stride all the way out, straining for the clean air, over the stoney beach to a platform that stands on wooden legs in the ocean.

I clamber on to it, struggling to lift my own bulk and balance. Once up, I thump across to the platform's edge and breathe and breathe – this is my test, the moment that cancels all the others – and look down. My reflection is too bright, unsettled and wavering in the rolling, choppy waters, but even still I feel a tear in myself.

Listen, Leon.

I hear the voice that spoke to me still as if it just came on the same wind that drives the smoke out to sea. Nothing again will ever be the same.

This is the price of safety. They know it, because Thule is not their home, it is their second home, their refuge. Their original home is gone. Lost forever. They have had to change, to adapt. This is a lesson about losing.

Those things will die in the fire.

I force myself to watch the quivering shape that is my shape and think am I equal to this? How many have gone mad at this moment and drowned themselves? How many have slashed their wrists? Shot their own brains out? Those footprints on the path the Leggie girl showed me the night we were enslaved, were they real after all? Some sechnik boy or girl, unrecognisable to themselves, fleeing in terror and despair.

I gaze across at the buildings. The fires to the south have crossed the river and pump smoke over the high towers around me, dark and quaking in their muddy coronas. Even still, the bravest onlookers have come as far as the edge of this open ground to look at me and point and mutter.

Even if the messages we learned in our yard every morning never came from Thule but were dreamt up in Grove's head two hundred years ago they still make sense. They still go to the heart of the thing. They wanted us to cut our bonds. To be capable of self-destruction. To be crushed before we can Rise.

That is what the True Path wanted. It is what our Saviours wanted. I understand it now.

The life ahead of you will be different from everything you know.

Out there on the wooden platform, it is not long before the collapse begins. My strength is all gone. I start to swoon.

I squint at the people gathered at the edge of the open ground, just blurred shapes now, and make an effort to properly see them, to separate bodies and faces, but instead they become this shapeless stain of colour against the fires and the quivering walls of the buildings.

I reach out. Try to speak. But the boards of the platform are racing towards me and the impact is a hot black rush into nothing at all.

The sun climbs above me and then sinks beyond my view. The sea comes rolling in and lifts the platform, drops it again, seethes in the pebbles as it retreats. I wait for each wave, arriving like some broody thought. Wait for it. Wait for it.

Could be hours and hours like this, helpless.

Gunfire in the streets. Cries and shouts. A single shot that could be the final defence of a cornered man or a cry for help.

Still I can't move. Which wave will bring nightfall? I count the time with each thunk on wood. The clanking and jangling of steel.

It is dark when I try to move once more and drag my hand towards my chest, twisting to look at it. It is not the claw I expected, but a hand: four fingers and a thumb. I flex those human fingers. Test them. Probe my arms and face with them, afraid of what I might find, but no alien traces remain.

With that thought, a vague relief, I black out again.

I wake with a start. It is not yet morning but there is plenty of warm orange light. The fires. Even here, part way out on the water my scalp is hot, the hair on my arms prickling. Masonry is moving nearby, scratching and scraping, working itself loose. I have to get up, while I still can.

It is much later, maybe, before I finally manage to sit up and then roll and vomit into the sea. I am all human, all Leon, down to the scars and rips and tears, the ink, the slave brand. All around me sparks flutter under a canopy of black smoke.

I watch them. My mind is in shards. It's like some invisible hand is taking a hammer to every thought before it can form.

Fire – worms – Ulya.

She is in the Kervan. I must get back to the Kervan.

There are no more cries for help in the city. No more gunfire. The people might have abandoned the place. I might be the only one left. The light is changing, dawn is creeping in. How long have I been lying here?

Hard to get to my feet. Harder still to stay there. A gust of wind nearly knocks me flat again. This is how I go. Fifty, maybe a hundred yards and stop, hand on knees heaving breaths, or stagger around, gulp the air and then start again. Trying to skirt the buildings and keep to the shore.

As the smoke drifts it reveals the moving shapes of worm brood hidden inside it like fish shadows, elastic in the heat, shimmering. They cannot see or hear any better than I can. I pass close to several bodies, even brush up against one of them but nothing grabs a hold of me. The smell and the noise of the wind scrambles all senses.

I find an iron bar in the rubble, one end sharpened to a point, and grip it tightly – it is hot, but I can just about hold it – using it to test for obstacles ahead. Where is the sea? I need to keep it to my right.

Away from the buildings the smoke thins. When I dare to look up, I find I am at the edge of an open stretch of the city, where there is nothing to burn. I nearly stumble over a corpse, lying crumbled in the gutter of a wide road, and take his clothes and boots. They are not my size but close enough.

I follow the road back to the sea and then I use the sea to guide me until there is no more city and the air is cool and then I collapse again and cough up the dust and ash of the fires and retch until my ribs ache.

42

I see no one on my loop around the burning city. I cross a road out to the South where horses and carts have recently ploughed up the packed dirt but they are long gone now, not even a distant sound from them.

With an iron bar in my fist, half naked, half-roasted and all fear abandoned long ago in that filthy tunnel, I feel as though I have just Risen after all. A man fresh from his first kill. I imagine Hilles and Joel looking on in satisfaction. Their boy, unbroken and pared down until he is just this blackened instrument of violence. Thin and wasted but screwed tight enough to thrum, like a length of gut.

I touch the slave brand on my shoulder, run my finger around its rim.

They weren't training them to survive on another planet, they were training them to survive this one.

As soon as I see the Kervan I go striding in, only it's not a bunch of Leggies turning to meet me. The Leggies are mostly dead.

Their bodies are all around the camp fire, one slumped in the dying embers, some twitching in the first spasms of worm infestation. Worm brood lurch between the wagons looking for any fresh bodies left cowering in their homes. It is all too quiet. The occasional bang or shout. The silence after battle.

One of them notices me and, ungainly with folds of new fat, makes his way in my direction. Someone has set him on fire. The last bits of his humanity, the clothes he was taken in, burning off him while he walks on, oblivious. His face and neck are streaked with soot. Flesh open and blistering on his arms. His worm-ridden eyes sit livid white in the blackened skull.

I don't let him touch me or get too close. Instead I use the bar from a distance, finding I'm surprisingly quick on my own feet. Maybe it's the fresh oxygen up here on the hill, out of the smoke.

A blow to the back of his skull puts him down. A few more and he stops moving. The other brood have no fear, do not back away, but they are not fighters. Their awkward bodies are new to them. In just a few minutes I have the area around the fire cleared and I go looking for the green wagon.

'Ulya,' I scream. 'Where the hell are you? Ulya.'

The green wagon is empty, as are all the wagons in that part of the camp. I run frantically from one to the next, calling out her name, taking out my fury on any worm brood that cross my path. Smashing with the bar. Stamping on their heads. Calling. Running now. In full panic. Have they all been infected? Should I be looking for her in the faces of these creatures? Have I killed her already?

I cast around in all directions and I spot a stumbling figure trying to climb the hill into the trees. He has something in his arms, a person.

I run to catch up, calling to them, but as I do, two infected creatures emerge from the forest and close in. Much too fast for me. They fall on the man. He screams.

I raise my bar and go yelling into the fray. I recognise the man, he is the one who first showed me the footprints and brought me to the Leggies that fateful night. In his arms is the Bashbakan, Esra Hanum.

As the brood attack, he puts her gently to the ground and raises a bent strip of steel, his only weapon.

My arrival distracts him and the creature closest to him takes the opportunity to dive, getting both arms around his left leg. He beats at the its head, which comes apart in bits of shattered bone like kindling. But the creature has a surprise for him, a mouth with a full set of teeth in a mound of folded flesh above its left breast. The teeth come down on his arm. The man howls, a mass of white foam already seething over the bite.

Meanwhile the other creature has arrived, takes his head in its lone, two fingered hand and sinks its incisors into his ear until the blood flows. Once the wound is open it pulls back and dribbles a string of saliva onto the exposed flesh. The victim's feet kick and slide around in the dirt in a brief, futile effort to hold on to his consciousness. The worm brood don't even wait for their poison to take full effect before they deposit their bubbles of larvae into his wounds.

Though it's already too late to help him, I charge in behind the first creature and hit it with the blunt end of the bar. When it goes down, I drive the sharp end into the belly of the second one. The newly infected man – who is making to crawl into the trees – I finish with one blow to the head.

I haul Esra up into my arms. She is so light, no weight at all. I carry her until we are a safe distance away from the worms and I place the fragile body against a grassy stump. She is torn at the neck, worm poison hissing in the wound. She looks at me blankly.

'Where did she go?' I say. 'Ulya. The Rus girl. Tell me where she went.'

There is a little light still in Esra's good eye. She turns that eye to the south, the treeline, avoiding the wagons of her dead tribe. All around us, the silky ash from the city floats and settles in fat flakes.

'She went south?' I say. 'On the road? Is that where she went?'

Her lips move. At first I think she is trying to speak but actually she pulls the sides of her mouth slowly into a faint grin. With great effort, as if it weighed several stone, she lifts her arm, puts out her index finger and presses it into my breast bone.

'You,' she says. 'Janum. Did you –'

'Yes,' I say.

She nods and grins again. 'Kill me,' she says.

With a shaking hand she reaches into the folds of her shirt to a bulge at her hip. She has no strength to take hold of what she has hidden there, so I help her and take the familiar shape and draw it out until I have my own knife in my hand – Stella. Lost on the day of my slaving. My loyal blade. I study the length of steel. Still sharp.

No sooner do I have it out than I spot the worm that has made a home inside the Bashbakan. It ripples just under her skin, sinking and rising. Under the rib cage, into the neck.

I jump back. For the first time there is something like fear in the old lady's eye. The ridges of the creature's body show at her throat. They wriggle, dig and sink away.

Spittle bubbles and winks at Esra's lips. She cannot speak anymore. She tries to raise her hand again but it won't lift.

This would be fair justice now, to leave her here. Worm brood are climbing the hill. Four at least.

I consider what I will do, look down at the burning city, now sunk entirely under its fires and I take her hands and pull her up into my arms once again and carry her into the forest.

She looks up into my face, her hands looped around my neck, as I take her over the broken ground to the river that runs down from here through the centre of the city. I point her feet forwards to push through the canes to the river bank and sink down into the mud and water and wade out until it is up to my hips.

The brood are following. I can hear their footsteps snapping twigs. I lay the old woman into the water and I think I see in that old face some shadow of the girl that must once have lived in that skin long before she was ever Bashbakan.

There is only gratitude in that one good eye now, as I press her head under the water.

She does not fight or resist at all. Bubbles stream to the surface. Esra's body goes taut, she struggles to breathe, and yet she doesn't try to rise against my firm grip. The worm inside her senses the danger, comes sliding over her skull and slips into her neck, under my hand, between my fingers. A hard segmented lump.

It takes only seconds for Esra to die. Her muscles suddenly release like she has let out a last deep breath, only I sense it is not the water, but the break from the worm that has killed her.

The worm's probing tongue comes twitching out of her mouth. I'm ready. One of the brood has reached the water. It makes an eerie sound: a hollow, breathless moan, before it goes sloshing in, unbalanced in the river mud, confused by the unfamiliar surface.

Esra's worm pushes out from the slack body, a sliver of white in the murk. I catch it the moment it clears her mouth. My skin has already changed, the Thule spikes rising out of my flesh helping me to grip the tough, greasy body.

The worm flexes in my balled fist. I can feel the violence of the poison in its blood. Its skin pulses with each exploding vessel. It does not vomit or scream. Instead, when its struggle is done, it goes limp in my hand and when I let it go, it sinks quickly, a pale glow and then a grey shadow and then nothing.

The current eases Esra's body downstream towards the city. I give the worm brood the slip through the canes and head back to the Kervan, where I pick through wagons looking for Ulya. So many dead. My mind can do the inventory, but there is no where to put it, no stored rage or sadness, a numbness has spread under my skin, right down to the marrow.

I leave the camp and go in search of the road I crossed on my way from the city. I don't get far from the Kervan before I spot a figure ahead, someone small hauling a heavy weight on their back, wobbling in a weaving pattern across the road.

'Ulya.'

She turns with great difficulty. Her face is just a smudge on the road in the trailing smoke and the drifts of ash.

'Ulya.'

She has found Vanesa, and Vanesa's unconscious body, still wrapped in our True Path bandages, is slung over her left shoulder. Where did she think she was going?

43

STORIES

Vanesa is barely alive. When I take her from Ulya and put her on my shoulders she rests her head against my neck as if I was some old friend and not the boy that once taunted her with his knife.

We need to get away from the city and the Kervan, but I need water. My throat is nailed shut. After several fruitless searches we stumble upon a stream, running through a concrete gulley, furred with lichen. We drink through cupped hands and then we wash our faces as best we can. Ulya looks at my wounds and gash on my shoulder where I hit the ledge in the tunnel. She puts the palm of her hand over my slave brand.

'What happened in the town?' she says.

'Do you want to know?'

'Not really.'

'It was the worm brood, from the river.'

'I suppose they deserved it, those Leggies,' she says. 'But I don't know who deserves what any more.'

'Nobody deserves the worm. Not that.'

Ulya looks down at Vanesa.

'She is weak,' she says. 'I don't know what I can do for her.'

'Can she talk?'

'A little. She said to me that we must get down to the city, when the fire is dead and the worms have gone and get the message. It will be there.'

'I have the Message,' I say, not meeting her eye.

'Leon –'

'I have it. I was there. I touched the Palladium and I received the Last Message. It was all true, what you said. Everything.'

She sits back. Her mouth drops open.

'I can't explain it to you. It's not a message that I can put in a sentence, even two sentences. I'm not sure I can ever describe it. It's like someone is in here with me,' I say, pressing my hand against my forehead.

'So you know then,' she says, slowly, 'where to go, and when … when they –'

'No,' I say. 'There were things shown to me, pictures, but I didn't know what they meant. Maybe Vanesa can help me understand.'

'It needs time, maybe.'

'It's inside me,' I say, tapping on my skull. 'Right here.'

'Give it time.'

Ulya lifts Vanesa's head to feed her some water from her cupped hands. For the first time I see what Old Sally has done to her head and face. Not as bad as I had feared. She is scarred. Patches of her hair are missing. Two runnels of burned flesh run from her left eye through her cheek. Her right eye is hooded, the skin fused over a corner of pupil. I had half expected her face to be destroyed, burned away. She was quick in the meadow. My worthy adversary. My Bind.

Ulya whispers something into her ear and points at me. Vanesa lifts her head and peers in my direction. It's hard to tell if she sees me at all but she nods and takes the water and then leans back with her head against the tree. Eventually she speaks in a thin voice into Ulya's ear.

'She says she is sorry,' says Ulya when Vanesa slumps back again, her mouth dropping open as if in sleep.

'Sorry for what?'

'That you couldn't have your prize, for your Colony. It was important to you.'

'So she understands who I am.'

'Yes.'

'Does she want me dead?'

'No, she doesn't. I have told her about you and what we have done together. She says that you are a gift to her, because you are an Elegido, a chosen boy, and she helped bring you to Esperanza. It will be good for her family. A blessing. Her soul will go to Heaven.'

Vanesa leans forward and speaks again. Ulya gives me a worried look.

'Her son,' she says. 'She has a boy.'

'They are all gone,' I say. 'The Pioneers. Gone into the East. I'm sure he is safe.'

Vanesa listens to this with her eyes wide open and then she nods vigorously and tears well in her eyes until they are pouring out of her and she starts to shake. Ulya tries to hold her and comfort her, whispering soft words in Rus, but the Satz woman continues to shake and when she lifts her head again I see she is smiling. These are tears of joy.

'James,' she says. 'Él se llama James.'

We make camp where we are, with no strength to go further. We clean ourselves as best we can, our hides emerging from beneath the soot like pale roots turned out of the soil. Ulya dips her hand into the stream and watches the water run over it just like she did on our boat a lifetime ago.

I go over to where she is sitting, take a handful of water and raise it above her head and let it run between my fingers through Ulya's new blonde hair. She does not look up. She let's the water run over her nose and mouth and down her neck.

'What is it for?' she says.

'You are free,' I say. 'Whatever you did, or you think you did in the past, it doesn't matter. You are now a new Ulya. Just like me. Nothing before matters.'

'You are not new, or free. Not yet.'

'I am.'

'No. You still want to please them. Those men in the Colony. You still want to be a soldier.'

'They don't matter to me anymore.'

'Yes they do.'

'Maybe,' I say, wondering what it is she sees in me and if she is right.

'You are not the lion. It's not something you win, to go to Thule. It's a gift.'

'Maybe.'

'There's no maybe. It's true.'

'And you? Can't you be free?'

'You can't wash my sin away. Even if you poured the sea on my head.'

'What is sin?'

'What I did.'

'And what did you do?'

She gives the sky an agonised look, as if she was pleading with it for mercy.

'Come,' she says. 'There is something we can do.'

Ulya reaches into her tunic and takes out a glass bottle half full with a cloudy white liquid.

'From the devil's purse,' she says. 'A sechnik. I stole it from Damla.'

I reach out and grab her wrist.

'What are you doing? That could kill you in an instant.'

'Just a little,' she says

'For what?'

Ulya draws her tunic down to expose the brand under her collar bone.

'Nobody owns me anymore. And nobody owns you. We do this for each other.'

'It will hurt.'

'I want the hurt. I want to feel it burn.'

She lies down on her back and waits for me. 'Me first,' she says. 'Then you.'

She takes a stick and bites down on it.

'It's dangerous,' I say. 'I don't know how much to use.'

'It's not so strong. She mixed it with something,' says Ulya. 'It's safe.'

I twist the stopper out of the bottle and let a drop fall on the ground and watch it sizzle like Old Sally.

'Ulya -,'

'Do it.'

I look at her. Her body is tense, the muscles standing out on her forearms. If I don't do this, she will do it herself and her hand won't be so steady.

I slowly bring the rim of the open bottle to her brand and tip the tiniest drop onto her skin. She bites down on the stick. Her eyes shoot open. Her body stiffens.

The liquid trickles through the furrows in the brand, releasing a little smoke. The only sound that escapes Ulya through her gagged mouth is a low moan.

Another drop. Her spine flexes. She arcs her whole body. For a terrible second I think her back is going to snap, just like my victim at the table in Esperanza, but gradually she eases, sinks down again and as the last of the poison bubbles wink out I see the brand has become an indecipherable stain. A simple burn, like something she might have gotten from a sun burst.

It takes her a while before she removes the stick from her mouth. I hold her hand tightly. She returns the grip. Her eyes are full of tears again.

'They don't own me,' she says.

'No.'

'You don't own me either.'

Ulya Moiseyev. Stronger than any living thing I have ever known. She stares at me, breathless, and she takes me by the wrist and pulls me close.

'I was never going to trade you,' she says. 'It was me. I was the thing. The slave. Their freedom for mine.'

I nod.

'I know,' I say.

She breathes hard. Squeezes those last tears out before she takes the bottle from me.

'Now you,' she says.

I get a stick of my own and lie down.

The next morning, we move out as soon as we are up. I load Vanesa on my shoulders and we pick our way carefully down to the road again, hugging the coast.

On higher ground, to our left, a more ancient route mirrors this one. It was solid and straight, cutting through the mountainside where the mountain got in the way. Now it is strewn with the skeletons of metal machines the forest creatures have made their homes in.

Our ragged party, charred and exhausted and coughing up smoke and dust makes its slow way across the shadows cast by these fossilised shapes. Once we reach the hills to the south of the city we push through the undergrowth to a high point where we get a view of the destruction below us. A carpet of smoke now and little more. The furnace that glows underneath it is hot enough to warm us up on this hill, a few miles away at least. The fire has reached the clearing where the Kervan is camped. It may yet burn to nothing, leaving no evidence of Esra's people and their wagons.

This is an old story. I know that now. It has played out in other worlds far from this one and there are dead there too and ash and dust where there were once cities. They would not call themselves Saviours. If they could, they would have taken more, taken everybody.

We turn our backs on the destruction and return to the road. We rest only when we are out of sight of Esperanza and the smell of burning is gone, replaced by murky tidal odours on a westerly wind and pine resin and things that bring me right back to the closeness of the forest where Ulya and I once lived in a different life long ago.

I lay Vanesa down once more. Her chin rests on her breast. Her breathing is thin and feeble, a bare rattle, as if a tiny insect was trapped in there and each breath sent it skittering through her windpipe.

Ulya stares at Stella, and then at Vanesa. She takes my knife hand in both of hers and gently prises the knife from my grip and as I watch, lifts it by the blade and hurls it, spinning into the trees. I'm going to protest. We need that knife, but there is something resolute in Ulya's expression that keeps me quiet. She takes my hand again, examines the cuts there, and then she seizes it and tugs me along behind her into the trees and there she throws her arms around my neck and grips me tightly to her. There is strength in those arms. I don't dare move. Don't dare breathe. There is nothing to be said or done but to absorb it. Everything.

When she finally pulls away there are tears in her eyes and Ulya, the girl I first met when I was wounded in the forest, is finally here completely with me, unguarded.

'Lenechka,' she says, allowing herself a sly grin through the tears. 'We are free.'

ACKNOWLEDGEMENTS

Jacob's Ladder was many years and many hands in the making. My agent Faith O'Grady was there through the whole process from the first pitch to the final draft, and her early observations helped to shape the novel. I have to say thank you to the wonderful Arvon Foundation in the UK, who provided accommodation, warmth and company in their beautiful houses in Yorkshire and Shropshire. Among all those at Arvon who read drafts and provided guidance were Jim Crace, who helped me get to the heart of the story; Liz Jensen, with essential advice about genre and plot; and Joanna Kavenna, who showed me how to edit like a pro.

Betsy Cornwell, at Inkwell, read two complete manuscripts and was, effectively, the first editor of the book. Without her detailed and insightful critique, *Jacob's Ladder* would never have made it to publication. Finally, when O'Brien Press got behind the book, Eoin O'Brien patiently guided it home. I can't imagine a more sensitive editor. I feel very welcome in the O'Brien family. They care about books.

My wife, Birgit, put up with obsession, distraction and countless hours of clacking keyboards. She listened to pitches and read drafts while I pretended not to look. This has been going on since we first met, in Bursa, all those years ago. I can only say thank you and brace yourself: there's more to come.